MW01042587

My Highlander Husband

Nancy Pennick

Published by
Satin Romance
An Imprint of Melange Books, LLC
White Bear Lake, MN 55110
www.satinromance.com

My Highlander Husband ~ Copyright © 2017 by Nancy Pennnick

ISBN: 978-1-68046-415-3

Names, characters, and incidents depicted in this book are products of the author's imagination or are used fictitiously. Any resemblance to actual events, locales, organizations, or persons, living or dead, is entirely coincidental and beyond the intent of the author or the publisher. No part of this book may be reproduced or transmitted in any form or by any means, electronic or mechanical, including photocopying, recording, or by any information storage and retrieval system, without permission in writing from the publisher.
Published in the United States of America.

Cover Design by Caroline Andrus

To my husband
Ron
This one's for you

Acknowledgments

Thank you to Caroline Andrus, book cover designer extraordinaire, for the awesome cover for *My Highlander Husband.* I love when you sent the message with the first draft pointing out what would change, then said, "But look! His kilt is the right colors!" You knew that was important to me.

I want to give a big thanks to my editor, Chris Hall, for her patient work to get the best story from me. Not only is she a great editor with a sense of humor but a knowledgeable historian. Getting it right was essential to me, but also to her. A huge shout out to her.

And thanks to Melange Books and Satin Romance for adding my book to their collection.

Although I've written many young adult books, this is my first historical romance. I love to read that genre and historical shows on TV draw me in so when an idea came to me, I took a chance.

When I began to write the story, I saw it from only Juliet's point of view. Then I realized there was much more to tell. The MacLaren Clan consisted of five children, and I began to develop their personalities one by one. Their story, Clan MacLaren, grew out of Ross and Juliet's love story.

As always, I have to thank my family for their love and support. I couldn't do it without you.

Also thanks to the 3-R's book club who swooned when I first revealed the cover to them before the release, and they can't wait to put the book on their list. These women have supported me from the beginning of my writing career, and I appreciate each and every one of them.

I want to thank my husband Ron, *my* Ross, who would do anything to help, protect and even save me.

Chapter One

"Scotsmen are greedy and stingy, Juliet, so always watch what you say and what you do. You cannot trust them. They will lie to your face and stab you in the back. They are power hungry bastards, and that is why I send you away with a heavy heart. But for the good of God and country, I must let you go. Your life," her mother said as she wiped tears from her eyes, "will never be the same."

Those words lay heavy in her heart as Juliet sat astride her horse, overlooking the small village that led to Glenhaven Castle. King George had given orders that she come to Scotland and marry the laird's son. The Scots and English had a tentative relationship, and the marriage would help bond the countries, hopefully preventing war. But she was not sure why she was chosen out of all the noble families in England. Juliet shook her head. *It does not matter. I am here now.*

Lady Juliet Anna Marie Kingston, daughter of the Duke of Norchester, sighed then blinked to fight back tears. She knew her mother's words were true. On this day in May 1715, her life would change forever and never be the same again.

Gray stone cottages with dark brown thatched roofs filled the valley below. Juliet's father told her the English called the Scottish homes smoking dunghills. She thought they looked quite pleasant but hadn't ridden through the village yet to capture the smell. Animal pens, attached to the sides of houses, held pigs, goats, sheep, and a few horses. Crops grew in a huge field beyond the last row of homes. Her eyes followed the dusty brown path through the center of the village and continued up the hill. *The road to the castle*. She scanned the elevated landscape, searching for the place she would call home.

Castle Glenhaven was nestled among ash and elder trees. Spring flowers had bloomed on the crab apples, making the scene appear magical in the noonday sun. The pale gray stone and rounded corner turrets of the three-story building reminded Juliet of home.

She wiped a tear that escaped her eye. More of her mother's words flooded her mind. "It's your duty, Juliet. Donnach MacLaren is a powerful chieftain. He keeps the peace. The laird wants his son to marry an English lady, one of nobility. You have been chosen by the king. Hold your head proud."

Juliet shuddered at the thought. She left her happiness back in England, and nothing could fill that void. She loved Lord John Alder, the son of the Duke of Essex, and no Scottish Highlander would change her mind. John had fought for her, begged her father, and offered money to no avail. No one could contest the king's orders, not even John.

She pictured John's dancing gray eyes full of mischief, as she stared up at the cloudless blue sky. They sparkled every time he laughed. He kept his blond locks clean and pulled back in a tail except for formal attire. Then he wore a powdered wig, making him look quite regal. He had a slender build yet was well-muscled and strong. Juliet loved that he was just the right height to place her head on his shoulder when they went for walks.

"I'll come for you," he promised. But Juliet knew he wouldn't. Her fate had been sealed. John would be arrested before he stepped on Scottish soil.

"Lady Juliet?"

The male voice startled her. "Yes?"

"I am sorry to interrupt your peace. We have to continue on. As you can see, we are close to the castle. We should arrive within the hour."

"Yes." Juliet shook her head and returned to the moment. "Carry on, Edward. I will follow behind you." Her mother wanted her to ride in a carriage, but being an expert horsewoman, Juliet insisted on her own horse.

A small entourage of soldiers and servants escorted Juliet to her new home, but only her maid would stay on. The rest would return to England. Juliet kept her eyes on Edward's back then decided to make a daring move. She guided her horse alongside him. "Edward," she said so no one else could hear, "please tell John I still love him."

His eyes made brief contact with hers. "I think it best not. The man is suffering. I cannot do that to my friend."

"Then how shall I live if you do not?" Juliet tossed her chestnut brown hair over her shoulder, and the sun bounced off the locks giving it an auburn glow. She knitted her brows together in a worrisome look. "Please, Edward, if you were ever a friend." She'd known him for many years, even before she met John. He had been the one to introduce them.

"If you insist, my lady. I will have to oblige."

"I insist." Juliet hoped her eyes held the look of determination.

Edward galloped ahead, shouting directions to his men. Juliet dropped back and searched for her maid, Eva, who had difficulty staying on her horse most days. More than once they had to stop and wait for her to be retrieved from the ground, brushed off, and returned to the saddle.

"Eva? How are you faring?" Juliet called over her shoulder and pulled up her reins to wait for her.

"I am fine. We are almost there so I doubt I will drop from the saddle many more times." Eva giggled as she batted her lashes to stay focused. She was seventeen, two years younger than Juliet. They had grown up together, and Juliet thought of her more as a friend than her maid.

"You have held up well. I am sorry for your troubles. We will practice riding once we are settled and have established a routine."

"That may be a while, milady. You are to marry this Saturday."

"Yes, about that." Juliet looked into her friend's blue-gray eyes. "You will have to help me get through the festivities."

Eva twirled her sandy brown braid around her finger. "I do not know how much I can help. I am just a tiny thing." She laughed, and Juliet joined her.

Eva came to the tip of Juliet's nose. She had a lovely, heart-shaped face, small nose, and rosebud lips. Her petite size never held her back. She would stand up to anyone who dared to cross them.

"Your size has nothing to do with your strength, Eva. Remember I have seen you take on many people you thought wronged you or I."

Eva lifted her shoulder. "Yes. I guess you are right." She looked ahead and pointed. "We are at the village. Hold your breath!"

Juliet assumed Eva heard the talk about the smell of peat and dung. The Scots burned peat in their fireplaces, and she wasn't sure about the dung. Juliet shook her head as if to get the phantom smell from her nose. She had no idea what to expect. London had its own peculiar smells, and yet Englishmen thought this odor was worse

The party emerged from the forest and headed down the wide dirt path through the village. People came out from their homes to gawk at the parade as it passed. Juliet raised her hand in greeting, hoping they would like her. They must have heard the news that Laird Donnach MacLaren's son, Ross, would marry an English girl the end of the week.

"Och, no! The English." An old man spat at the ground. "Sassenachs. Get home where ye belong. We dinna want yer feet touching Scottish soil."

Juliet raised her brows. "We are not that bad," she whispered to Eva, "for him to speak of us in a rude way."

She noticed Edward had pulled up his horse and returned to her side. "Who said that?" His face had turned to stone.

"No one," Juliet said then whispered to him, "It is quite all right."

"No, it is not," he answered back. "I have been sent to protect you. You know there has been talk of a Jacobite uprising. The Scots have never been fond of the English. They want their own king back in power."

"I am aware. That is why I am here, is it not?" Juliet glared at him.

"My apologies." Edward tipped his hat and tapped his heels into his horse.

"Men!" Juliet glanced over at Eva. "And their wars!"

They reached the base of the hill and started the upward climb to the castle.

"What do you think he will look like?" Eva edged her horse closer to Juliet.

"The laird?"

"No, silly! Your husband."

"Oh. I had not thought of that." Juliet's stomach clenched into a tight ball. She would never tell Eva, but she *had* put much thought into what her new husband might look like, and hoped he would be decent enough. She might have to live with him for a very long time, and her stomach rolled at the thought.

"I hope he has good teeth and a nice smell. I was told most Scots are ragged and do not care about their appearance." Eva wrinkled her nose. She looked back at the village. "But that was not too bad, do you think?"

"I had not noticed." Juliet grinned. "I am sure there are more smells to come." She took in the spring scenery to pass the time as they rode along the edge of a wooded area.

The grass had turned a pale shade of green with pink and white wildflowers sprinkled among the blades. Patches of shade came and went as the group traveled through canopies of trees. The smell of dried leaves and fresh grass filled Juliet's nose as she rode along. The entourage came out into a sunny field, the final leg of the journey. Castle Glenhaven loomed before them.

The castle, made of light gray stone, stood three stories high, and looked more majestic than it had from a distance. Arch-shaped windows ran along the first two floors. Square windows with triangular peaks sat above each arched one on the third floor. A dark gray roof offset the lighter gray, as did the turrets on top of each corner tower. *A prison or a home?* Juliet had yet to decide.

~ * ~

"His lordship will be with ye shortly," a servant said with a bow as she backed away then disappeared down the hall. The entourage had been escorted into a small room. No one had greeted them in the castle courtyard except the girl and the men who tended their horses.

Juliet locked eyes with Eva as a strange feeling crept over her. This was not the welcome she expected. No formal greeting. No beverages had been offered. The room barely had enough seats for them. *Do they even want me here?* Her hands shook with fear, and she buried them in the folds of her gown.

Donnach MacLaren finally made his entrance, sweeping into the room without a word. His gray hair stuck out wildly in different directions as if he had just woken from a deep sleep. Juliet took notice of his kilt and stockings, something she'd never see a man wear in England. He stood in silence, studying the people around him. His hazel eyes landed on Juliet, and he lifted his brow.

"Laird MacLaren, I am your most humble servant," Edward said. He stepped forward and dipped at the waist. "I am pleased to meet you. May I introduce—"

"Och," Laird MacLaren said with a wave of the hand. He walked toward Juliet, took her hand, and planted a light kiss on top. His eyes traveled up to hers. "Save it for tonight, lad. We have a feast planned in the lass' honor. I have business to attend but didna want ye to feel unwelcomed." He smirked.

Unwelcomed? Juliet sank her teeth into her bottom lip trying to erase that exact feeling.

"The servants will show ye to yer rooms," the laird said. With that, he turned and walked through the door, leaving them in stunned silence by the welcome they received.

~ * ~

Eva helped Juliet dress for the evening. She would be presented to the family and important members of the MacLaren clan before dinner. "Your mother instructed that you wear the blue dress to bring out the color of your eyes." Eva held up the silk dress with a white ruffled inlay. She tightened Juliet's corset and slipped the outfit over her head. "There you go," she said as she tugged at the waistline.

Juliet had grown used to Eva's hands on her body, poking and primping to make her look her best. She didn't flinch as Eva adjusted the material around her breasts, which were quite prominently displayed.

"Laird Donnach did not act as if he was happy to see us." Eva took in a breath of air as she tugged on the skirt. "There goes my mouth again."

"No, Eva, you are right. He seemed reserved." Juliet recalled staring into his cool hazel eyes, unable to tell what he thought. "He *was* kind." She pictured him towering over her, his bow and the kiss to her hand.

But when he looked up at her, his smile did not reach his eyes. Her stomach twisted in a knot. “He is the one who requested an English bride for his son. Mother said it would be a union that helps both countries.”

“If you wish to think he is kind then let it be so. Sit.” Eva pointed to the chair in front of a mirror. “I will fix your hair.” She worked without speaking, brushing out Juliet’s long locks.

“What are you thinking?” Juliet sat without moving to make Eva’s job easier. “I know you have an opinion.”

“I am not supposed to have one. My job is to serve you.”

“When we are in private, you are my friend. I need to hear your thoughts.”

Eva stepped in front of Juliet, comb in hand. “I think it odd we were not given a royal greeting. The laird had to be summoned when we arrived. He greeted you and sent you to this suite.”

“We may have arrived earlier than expected. The laird said a feast has been planned in my honor tonight.” When she was shown her room, Juliet thought the accommodations were much smaller and sparse by English standards. The suite had two rooms, a bedroom and boudoir, but having time to study the décor, she deemed it tastefully done. The four-poster bed had a red velvet canopy with matching bed cover and beautiful tapestries hung on the paneled walls.

“Well then,” Eva said as she walked over to a table, “all is settled.” She returned with a bouquet of flowers in her hand. “I picked some wildflowers in the field. When I am done with your curls I will place them here.” She touched the back of Juliet’s head. Her hand brushed the side of Juliet’s neck as she reached for a lock of hair.

The contact made Juliet think of her future husband. How would he touch her? Did he want to touch her even if he did not know her? Of course, that was what all men wanted. Her mother told her so. She had pulled Juliet aside before she left and said, “Oh, my sweet daughter, I only have time to tell you this. Strange things happen to men when they take a woman to bed. Be prepared to accept what happens.”

Juliet had no idea what her mother meant. She had kissed John many times and nothing odd happened. They held hands, and sometimes he wrapped his arms around her making her feel loved and safe. She liked it all. "Mother?" She wrinkled her brow and squinted. "You do not make sense."

"It will make sense all too soon, my dear." Her mother kissed her cheek. "Now go. Do your country proud. Remember we love you."

Juliet did feel loved by her parents and brother. So why had they seemed eager to send her away?

"It is the way of the world, is it not, Juliet?" In private quarters, Eva called Juliet by her first name but knew better when they were in public.

Juliet blinked. "I have no idea what you said, Eva. I am sorry."

"I was saying how I left England and will live in Scotland for the rest of my life just like you. Women live where their men live. Since I am in this country, I hope to find a husband here."

"Oh, Eva, I hope you do too. You have an adventurous spirit. *I* would have preferred to stay in England."

"With Lord John."

Juliet sighed. "Yes, with John."

A knock came at the door. "'Tis time," a voice said through the wood.

Eva shuffled to the door of the suite and opened it. "Oh! Whoever it was, they are gone. They did not wait to escort us." She looked at Juliet and shrugged. "Do you know the way to the grand hall?"

Juliet shook her head and took one last look in the mirror. The red tones in her brown hair shimmered in the candlelight. Eva had pulled back the sides of her hair and curled the locks into long tendrils down her back. The tiny, white wildflowers were expertly placed within the curls. Her skin looked creamy white against the blue dress. Long, dark lashes framed her sparkling dark blue eyes. She pinched her cheeks to give them a flush of color.

Juliet tied a dark blue ribbon with a small cameo around her neck, a gift from her parents. "There, I am ready." She stood and took Eva's hand. "If we get lost, it is their fault." She tossed her head back and stood straight. If they wanted an English lady, then a lady they would get.

Chapter Two

The girls headed for the staircase. When they reached the bottom of the stone steps, a hand reached out and took Juliet by the arm.

"There you are. I was afraid you would be late." Edward's gaze went to the neckline of her dress and back up to her eyes. "I am to escort you into the hall for your introductions. Eva, you will walk behind us." He extended his arm and Juliet placed her hand on top of his. "I leave tomorrow," Edward said as they walked toward the hall.

"You are not staying for the wedding?" Juliet lifted a brow. "You have someone waiting back home. You cannot wait to return." John had told her Edward fancied someone at court.

"Perhaps." He stared straight ahead. "There are many entrances to the hall. We will use the far doors so I can walk you up the aisle to the front of the room. The laird and his family will receive you there."

After walking through the day in a foggy haze, Juliet suddenly became aware of her surroundings. Voices and the sound of laughter spilled from the hall. The hallways throughout the castle were made of stone, but the rooms had walls of solid timber panels. A spring breeze drifted through the outer castle, cooling her skin as they walked to the grand hall's entrance. They stepped through the doorway then paused. When the musicians spotted them, a bagpipe began to play. Torches, stuck into holders embedded in the walls, gave an eerie glow to the entire room.

Juliet looked at the long rows of tables filled with people on either side of the aisle. The clan MacLaren, faces she did not know, stared up at her.The hand she had placed on top of Edward's began to tremble. Her knees grew weak. She bit the inside of her lip to remain composed when she noticed all eyes were on her.

As they headed down the aisle, Juliet felt faint. The smell of many people in the warm enclosed space overpowered her. Smoke from pipes and the torches wafted through the air. The peat fire blazed in the huge fireplace behind the head table. She blinked as her eyes began to water. Juliet did not want the crowd to think she cried. *Concentrate! Eyes straight ahead.*

Laird Donnach MacLaren sat at the huge head table that stretched across the front of the hall. He looked regal in his tartan green and blue plaid. The blue was dark as midnight, and the green reminded Juliet of a plush lawn on a summer's day. He'd changed from the simple white shirt she had seen him in this afternoon to a ruffled shirt beneath a five-button black waistcoat. A huge golden brooch with an intricate design and one green emerald was pinned at one shoulder and held the plaid in place across his chest. His gray hair had been combed and pulled back in a tail. In his younger years, she thought he'd probably stolen women's hearts.

His wife sat next to him. Her face, lined with age, still held an air of beauty. She had dark black hair with streaks of gray. Their eyes met. Juliet gazed into the most dazzling emerald green eyes she'd ever seen.

The MacLaren children stood behind them, three girls and a boy. Juliet had time to study them as she slowly approached the table. She smiled as she thought of her mother. She said the Scots bred like rabbits and to expect nine or ten children. The family appeared small on that account.

Juliet's eyes shifted to the son, the one she was to marry. She blinked once, then again. Juliet heard a slight gasp behind her. Eva must have spotted him at the same time. Ross MacLaren might be a half head taller than she, if that. His body shape could only be described as rotund. He had the cheeks of a baby, the kind people loved to pinch. His dark hair had been pulled back in a tail, matching his father's. He, too, wore the green and blue plaid and looked quite uncomfortable in the fancy shirt and jacket. Juliet thought his face had turned from pink to red as she walked up the aisle.

Edward stopped in front of the table. He bowed, and she curtsied. "My laird, may I present Lady Juliet Anna Marie Kingston, daughter of the Duke of Norchester, William Roderick Alexander Kingston. King George the first blesses the union of your son, Ross Alec Landon MacLaren, and this woman."

Laird Donnach stood and raised his glass. "Mìle Fàilte!"

His wife stood to join him. Juliet could see where Ross got his short stature as she sized up his mother. She barely came to her husband's shoulder. "Mìle Fàilte!" She touched her husband's cup with hers as the crowd roared the same sentiment.

Edward leaned over and whispered, "A thousand welcomes. I know a little Gaelic."

"Oh." Juliet glanced over to catch one more glimpse of him as he retreated. *Goodbye, Edward. Please remember my request.*

The laird held up a hand. "My dearest daughter-in-law, I would like to introduce ye to me wife, Lady Fiona MacLaren. We welcome ye to the family." He swept his arm toward the children. "May I introduce my oldest daughter, Greer. She has returned with her husband, Ewan Kincaid from the most prestigious Clan Kincaid, and son Alec for the weekend festivities."

Greer gave Juliet a cool smile. Her dark locks hung loosely around her shoulders. She wore a forest green silk dress with the family plaid draped across her chest. She resembled her mother—straight nose, wide mouth, and the famous green eyes. Juliet had been told that Ross was twenty so she guessed Greer to be five and twenty.

The girl standing next to Greer had a similar look but appeared bored and struggled to stand still. Juliet sympathized.

"And next in line is my daughter, Glynis." Laird Donnach gestured to the girl who gave Juliet a half-hearted smile then smirked. "Dinna turn yer back on this lassie." He took a long drink from his mug as the room filled with roars of laughter.

"Still trying to marry her off?" someone yelled.

Donnach turned to the crowd. "Any takers?"

"Aye! Ye have one here, Donnach." A silver mug went up in the air, then another, and one more. Juliet knew those mugs had been filled many times, and the night could grow more raucous.

The laird turned to Juliet and winked. "A double ceremony may be in order this weekend."

"Da!" A loud whisper came from Glynis. Juliet swore she saw a blade in the hand stuck inside her plaid.

"Now to my sons!" Donnach called to the crowd.

Juliet crossed her brows. *Sons?*

"My oldest insisted on hunting. He came home smelling like the deer he bagged. I sent him for a bath before dinner." Donnach's eyes met hers. "I am sorry, my dear. Ye will have to wait a little longer to meet yer husband. He is late as usual."

Juliet let out the breath she held. The chubby boy next to Glynis was not Ross. She had come to terms that the heavyset person would become her husband. She tried to conjure up an image of the missing son. *Tall or short?* His father towered over his mother so there was a chance of either. *Thin or fat?* Hopefully he might not be thick around the middle if he ran through the woods chasing deer. If the new man liked hunting, would he smell bad as Eva suggested? *Short, scrawny and a bad smell?* Did she dare pray for a decent husband? Her stomach twisted in a knot. The night took a turn for the worse.

A clash of swords, loud bumps, and bangs interrupted her thoughts. Two young men engaged in battle burst through a side door.

"Oh, my good man, if only ye knew how much I am up for a good fight," the man with his back to her yelled as his black hair loosened from its leather wrap and fell around his shoulders.

"I will fight ye to the finish, my swine-loving friend," the man facing her shouted. Juliet thought his hair color leaned toward a pale orange, hard to tell in the candlelight. When the light hit it, she saw streaks of blonde. He had a stocky build—wide chest, broad shoulders. His ruddy complexion turned a deeper red from the heat of the fight, but he was still quite handsome.

The crowd began to cheer in Gaelic. Juliet had no idea who they wanted to win and wished the two would stop. The introductions had been interrupted by this upsetting display of swordsmanship, and she wanted to know which man would be her husband.

"Enough!" The laird held up his hand, and the room fell silent. He turned to the two men. "Do ye have no manners? We have a guest," he said in a sarcastic tone as he waved his hand through the air. It came to rest in the direction of Juliet. "Lady Juliet Anna Marie Kingston, may I introduce my oldest son, Ross?"

The dark-haired man swung his head her way. The bright emerald green eyes of his mother met hers. He, too, had the wide mouth and straight nose. His strong jaw tightened. She did not know if he suppressed a laugh or a groan. He shook the hair back from his face and grinned. White teeth showed through the small opening.

Juliet's heart raced. The blood surged through her body at a rapid pace. Something warm and pleasant filled her inside. Ross MacLaren was the most beautiful man she'd ever seen. She swallowed then curtsied. "Good evening to you. sir. It is my pleasure to meet you."

"Och, no, the pleasure is all mine." He bowed and came up with a smile, one side raised higher than the other. His one eyebrow lifted as if to ask if she liked what she saw.

Juliet realized he wore his dress plaid during the fight. She looked him over from head to toe then raised an eyebrow back at him. That got a full smile from him.

~ * ~

Ross MacLaren couldn't take his eyes off the beautiful girl that just gave him the same look his mother would to keep him in line. The firelight cast a glow upon her. It took all he had not to reach out and touch her creamy skin and press his mouth against her rosy lips. His heart pounded against his chest, but Ross hoped he looked the part of the laird's son instead of a lovesick lad. *Ye are taken by her beauty. Ye dinna ken her. And remember, she is a Sassenach.* He shook his head to focus.

When Ross' father told him he would wed an English noblewoman, he had argued against it. He reminded Donnach that he had given Ross his word long ago that he could choose his bride.

"That was before we received this rare opportunity," his father had said with a sly smile. "Marry the lass. Ye may grow to love her."

Ross put up a fight right to the last minute, when he decided to go hunting instead of greet his soon-to-be bride. A part of him now regretted the decision.

~ * ~

"Juliet," Donnach said. "Now that ye have met Ross, I would like ye to meet his younger brother, Duncan."

Duncan had broken out into a full sweat. Small beads of water dotted his forehead and upper lip. He nodded, and Juliet noticed his kind green eyes. He, too, had a handsome face hidden under those cheeks. She gave him her best smile.

"And finally," Donnach said with a swell of pride, "my youngest—the only one that gave a horse's arse to look like her da." He bowed to his daughter. "Heather."

Heather stood tall over her brother, Duncan, and two sisters. She had a smooth complexion with skin lightly browned from the sun. Juliet had a hard time telling her eye color. It wasn't a striking green like the rest of the family. Hazel perhaps? Her nose resembled her father's—straight at the top, wider at the bottom. She didn't have the wide mouth of her mother, but rather a smaller, fuller lip. The hair caught Juliet's attention, red with flashes of gold when hit by the light. So different from the rest, she commanded attention. Juliet guessed she had many suitors.

"May I escort ye to the table?" Ross offered Juliet his arm.

"Thank you." She gazed at the floor then up into his eyes. She saw he had questions, but ones that could wait. He appeared calm on the outside but felt a slight quiver in his muscle as she took his arm.

Servers began to bring food from the kitchen. Plate after plate of venison, haggis, and boar were placed on tables along with pitchers of ale. One of the musicians played a folk tune on his fiddle as people dug into the steaming meats. Loaves of bread had been stacked in the center of tables.

Ross handed Juliet a glass of wine sweetened with honey after she settled into her seat. His mother sat on one side, and Ross slipped into the chair on her other. He leaned toward her and said, "Have ye been treated well while I was away?"

The smell of the fresh outdoors, grass and pine, mixed with a manly scent of musk overcame her. She fought to find her voice. "Yes."

"'Tis verra good to hear." He tipped his chair on its two back legs, holding a mug of ale between his hands. "Will ye do me the honor of escorting ye to yer room later?" He lifted the brow again. "No dastardly intentions implied."

"Of course." Juliet longed for her fan she left in the suite. She could cover her face and gain composure. She felt a tap on her arm, turned toward the woman on her other side, and said, "Greetings, Lady MacLaren," Juliet bowed her head.

"Please, call me Fiona." She gave Juliet a closed-mouth smile.

"Fiona." Juliet tried it out. "A lovely name. You have handsome children. You must be quite proud."

"Aye, proud as a mum can be. Happier if I can get that Glynis married off!" She laughed, and Juliet saw her teeth were yellowed with age and two were missing near the back. She felt a little uneasy around the woman and hoped their relationship would grow.

Fiona stared at her. "Ye need to ken that Ross and Glynis are my two rule breakers. They always had their heads together when they were wee ones. I never knew what to expect by the end of the day. Broken limbs or dead creatures." She chuckled.

"And Greer and Duncan followed the rules?" Juliet asked.

"Oh, aye, they were good bairns. My poor Duncan looks as if he will pop from his plaid soon, does he not?" Fiona nodded down the table.

Juliet smiled at the thought as she glanced his way. "Oh, I hope not." She looked back at Fiona. "And Heather?"

"She is a bonnie lass. Sixteen and ready for marriage. I told her da it should be soon. Do ye not agree?" She lifted her eyebrow just as Ross had done.

Juliet spotted Heather walking through the tables, talking and laughing. She stopped and bent over one young man. Her cleavage almost touched his nose. "You may be right," Juliet mumbled. She would marry into this feisty, proud MacLaren family, having learned that much in the short time spent in the grand hall. Juliet could feel the positive energy run through the room but knew it was not because of her. Every time she made eye contact with someone, she got a look of distrust.

After dinner, Juliet scanned the room for Eva. She sat at a back table with the English soldiers who had escorted them to the castle. Eva seemed to be enjoying the evening. Every once in a while, Juliet noticed Eva searched the room with her eyes. *Looking for a husband?*

"Juliet?" His breath felt warm on her neck. "Would ye care to go for a walk before returning to yer room?"

She looked up into Ross' face. Kindness filled his eyes. She saw no ulterior motives. Juliet took the hand he offered. "Yes, that would be lovely."

They walked along the outer hall, passing the staircase to her room. Ross gave directions to places she may need to go and told stories of how and where his brother and sisters played when they were young. He stopped at the far corner of the castle and guided her into the rounded turret to look at the night sky.

"In two days, we will be wed." He took her hand. "Do ye think ye may come to love me?"

Love? No one had ever spoken so directly to her. "Um." She sank her teeth into her bottom lip. "I just met you."

"Aye, I ken." He placed his hand around the back of her neck. "And so, I ask permission to kiss ye."

"Kiss me?" Juliet's mouth went dry. She wished she still had the glass of sweet wine in her hand. *You are going to marry him. You have kissed John. You know what it is like.* "Yes, you may."

He leaned in closer. The other hand went around her waist, bringing her to him. She felt his breath on her cheek, and the scent of ale was pleasant. His lips touched her face so lightly she jumped.

"I willna hurt ye," he whispered.

Juliet's heart fluttered as she looked into his eyes. Green pools of summer, ones she could dive into and never come out. She nodded and placed her hand on his chest, feeling the hard muscle beneath the coat. She opened her mouth slightly to tell him she was all right, but instead found his lips on hers.

Ross tightened his grip on her, pulling her so close she fought for breath, yet she did not want him to stop. His lips felt soft against hers as he pushed her mouth open wider. She felt the tip of his tongue on hers.

John had never kissed her like that. *John!*

Juliet pulled back, head spinning. Ross did not let go, still holding her close. He rested his chin on the top of her head, nuzzling her hair. "Ye taste of summer and honey."

"I think you should give credit to the wine." Juliet tried to laugh but could only think of the kiss. She wanted another.

"I will take ye to yer room." Ross offered his arm. "Because if I dinna, we may have to marry tonight."

Chapter Three

Ross paced back and forth in his room then stopped to gaze out the window. He could not get Juliet out of his mind. The taste of her kiss lingered on his lips, and he touched them as if he could still feel her mouth on his. "By God's bones! What am I thinking?" He pounded the windowsill. "And yet…" Ross looked off into the distance. "I can see us married and living a good life here."

Breakfast would be served shortly, and Ross had promised Juliet a tour of the grounds afterward. *Here I stand in my shirttails. I best get ready.* He shaved carefully, checking to make sure his face felt smooth. Not happy with the results, he lifted his chin and swiped the blade from neck to jaw line once more. Satisfied, he wrapped his plaid around his waist and made the necessary adjustments, wanting to look his finest. His dark hair had been washed earlier, and he checked to see if it was dry before pulling it back to plait it. Ross reached for the leather tie and wrapped it around the end of the tail. He took a deep breath and headed for the stairs.

Juliet already sat at the breakfast table, looking lovely in a green linen dress, and trying her best to talk with Glynis. *Good luck with that, lass.* Ross cleared his throat. "Madainn mhath, Glynis." He nodded at her and turned toward his future bride. "Good morning to ye, Juliet."

Juliet bowed her head, looking at him through long, dark lashes. "Good morning to you, Ross." She appeared more beautiful in the morning light than she did last night in the fire's glow. Ross sucked in a breath, greeted the rest of his family, and took his seat next to her.

The MacLarens were a loud, jovial group. As each member appeared, someone always had a joke or story to share. They teased each other good-naturedly. Ross loved that Greer came home for his wedding along with his best friend, Ewan, and their little boy, Alec.

Ross tried his best to concentrate on breakfast, but it was difficult with Juliet in close proximity. He made sure she had been served all the dishes, being as attentive as possible. Once, their hands brushed when they reached for the platter of bread and jam at the same time. A tingling sensation made him want more of her, and he longed to get her alone. He questioned his sanity, never feeling this way before. *Have I gone mad?* He let out a long breath. *Will she ever love me?* He peeked at her from the corner of his eye, searching for a clue.

After breakfast, Donnach signaled that the family was excused. Little Alec had already knocked over a pitcher of buttermilk and crawled through a sea of legs, giving everyone a start. Ross smiled at his oldest sister, serene and proud, gathering her child into her arms. They had always shared secrets since they were young bairns. He could always trust her to stay quiet and valued her opinion. Perhaps he should speak to her about Juliet. Ross shook his head. *And ask her what, ye daft fool? Do ye think I am in love?*

Greer looked up from Alec and caught his eye. She gave him a knowing smile as if to say it would be all right. Ross returned the look with a wink then turned his attention to his future bride. "Juliet, would ye like to take that walk I promised ye?"

"I would love to go on a walk with you," she said as she looked at him with those beautiful sapphire blue eyes.

Ross pushed his chair back and helped her from her seat. "Ye may need a wrap. The May mornings are still cool."

"I will be fine." Juliet straightened her body, and he decided not to argue.

Ross folded his hands behind his back as they walked along the outer hallway, keeping a small space between them. "Last night we walked through the halls of the castle, but I would like to show ye it during the day. We can leave from the back door that leads out to the field. That is where we will marry." He stopped in the same tower they occupied the night before. If he was lucky, he may get to steal another kiss. "Ye havena said much, lass. Are ye ill?"

Juliet looked at the floor then lifted her eyes to meet his. "No, I am not ill. I am a little overwhelmed. Do not worry about me. I will be fine."

She is trying verra hard to be a proper lady. Ross reached for her waist, emitting a gasp from Juliet. He lifted her up onto the open window ledge and set her down. "Look." He pointed. "The sun is hiding behind that cloud. Do ye think it will come out?"

Juliet gave him a confused look. "I do not really know. It could stay behind the cloud."

"Or come out in its full glory, smile down on us, and warm the day. That is what I wish for. And ye?" Ross hoped to distract her, help her see the beauty of his home as he did.

"I wish the same." She let out a breath.

"This," Ross said as he waved his hand around the turret, "was my favorite place as a lad. Glynis, too. We'd spend hours here fighting battles with our wooden swords, always on watch for English soldiers," he said with a laugh. "Sorry."

"You needn't be. I am not an English soldier."

Ross noticed a spark in her eye, yet her face held no expression. He tried once more. "Glynis and I always challenged each other. Once, when I was six and she was seven, we had a jumping contest to see who could land the farthest..." He pointed past her. "Out there." Ross saw he piqued her interest. "And guess who won?"

"Why, you, of course," Juliet said as she gazed out the window.

"Och, no. I would love to lie and say it was true, but I canna." Ross shook his head. "Wee Glynis almost always beat me back then."

"And now?" Juliet turned to look at him, seeming more relaxed.

Ross laughed. "I can take her now … most of the time." The corners of Juliet's mouth twitched. Would he get a smile? "But winning sometimes come with a price," he said. "She may have won the jumping contest, but she broke her arm."

He could see her biting her lip then a full-blown smile crossed her face. She let out a small laugh.

"I don't mean to laugh, but for some reason, I could picture Glynis flaunting it in your face that she won and did not care she broke her arm."

"Aye," Ross said as he lifted Juliet from the sill. "Yer right about that." He brushed her silky, chestnut hair away from her face. "Yer hair…is so soft." He thought he could hear her heart beating and pulled her close so he could feel it. She lifted her chin, and her lips were a breath away. He melted into them, gently at first to test the waters. She smelled of wildflowers and tasted of honeyed tea. His grip tightened on her, and he kissed her more passionately. *Sassenach or not. Ye will be mine.*

~ * ~

"I feel so guilty, Eva." Juliet looked up with tears in her eyes. "I am betraying him and our love."

"No, you are not. John is in England. You are here, betrothed to another. I understand you love John, but you must forget him." Eva put the finishing touches on Juliet's hair for the wedding ceremony.

"No, you do not understand," Juliet wailed. "I feel guilty that I could betray him so easily. I think I could fall in love with Ross. If that is true, was I ever really in love with John?" She covered her face. "I am a horrible, shallow person."

Eva pulled Juliet's hands away from her face. "You are kind and loving, Juliet. You would not hurt a flea." She patted the hand she held. "Maybe Ross was meant to be. He is quite handsome if I may say so."

"It is not just his looks. He is kind and gentle. He has made sure I have not been alone for the last two days. He spent most of that time with me, showing me the land, introducing me to the people and talking about his life."

"That is an extraordinary man." Eva pulled the wedding dress from the wardrobe. "You are lucky."

"And John? What do I do about him?"

"Be grateful for the time you spent with him. He is part of your past. Ross is your future."

"Eva, you are wise for one so young." Juliet took in a deep breath then let it out. "You are right. What good would it do to pine away for someone I will never see again?"

"It will all work out. Now stand. It is time to dress for your wedding."

The pale blue silk dress dropped over Juliet's head. Eva laced the back of the dress, while Juliet adjusted the bodice in front. The stays pushed her bosom up for display and could be quite uncomfortable if not positioned well. Gold beading ran across the square-cut neckline and down the front to the waist of the dress. An inlay of gold brocade had been cut into the center of the skirt. The sleeves clung to her arms and flared out from the elbows to cover most of her hand. Eva placed a crown of flowers with an attached veil on Juliet's head as the final touch.

"You look so beautiful!" Eva clapped her hands together. "You and the lord make a fine couple."

Juliet shivered, from nerves or delight, she didn't know. "I am going to try to love him, Eva, but I do not know if I can. I will take heed of your advice. John is my past. I will always love him and keep him in my heart."

"Just make sure your Highlander husband does not know." Eva stared into Juliet's eyes. "No need to make trouble before the marriage even begins."

A knock came at the door, and Eva rushed to open it. "Before they get away," she said as she looked back at Juliet with a smile. "Heather!" she said as she pulled the door back. "Come in."

"I have been sent to escort the bride. Och! Ye look beautiful, sister Juliet." She held her hand to her mouth.

"Thank you. And so do you." Juliet admired the dark blue silk dress her attendant wore. The MacLaren green and blue plaid crossed over one shoulder, draping loosely under her exposed breasts. A sparkling emerald lay in her cleavage. "The necklace," Juliet said as she touched her own chest. "I have never seen one like that." She compared the stone in size to her thumbnail. "Exquisite."

"When ye join the family, ye will have one too." She covered her mouth again. "I do not think I was supposed to tell."

Heather seemed to let words tumble from her mouth before thinking. She was adorable, and Juliet loved her exuberance. "You ruined nothing. I will act surprised."

"Thank ye. Da would have my head for that." She stuck out her hand. “Come with me.”

A sunny spring day greeted them when they reached the door that would take them to the outdoor altar. Guests mingled in the yard, some sat on the benches provided, while others took drinks from a table off to the side.

Greer rushed down the hall and stuck a bouquet of heather and crabapple in Juliet’s hand. “For ye.”

Glynis lumbered along behind Greer, pulling at the edge of her dress as if she choked. The scooped neckline could not really bother her. Juliet smiled. “Not your favorite dress?”

Glynis glared at her. “Not fond of dresses. Give me a kilt and plaid, and I would be happy. But what would ye ken about that?”

Juliet glanced out the doorway. The men of the family already stood with the priest. She wondered what could be under those kilts. *I will find out soon enough.*

She looked back at the three sisters, all dressed alike. The two similar dark-haired girls, almost as tall as Juliet, wore the same blue dress as their younger sister. Heather, a half-head taller than the rest, stood straight with her red hair flowing down her back. She looked regal and lovely.

Heather began the procession. When the musicians saw her, they began to play their bagpipes. Tears filled Juliet’s eyes. No one in her family would see her married. The people outside were strangers. She watched in a daze as Greer and Glynis walked through the grass.

They are your family now. Ross will be your husband. You belong to him. Her heart felt a tug, and her stomach dropped. The priest gave her a nod to say it was time. She took a step then another. Her feet kept moving, but she felt as if she watched from above as she walked toward the man she would marry. When she reached the priest, Ross joined her and smiled as he took her hand. In that moment, Juliet knew she had to come to terms with all that happened and accept this new life.

~ * ~

The night air was mild for May, almost summerlike. Juliet stood at the window, staring at the stars in only her shift. The servants had moved her things into a new room, one she and Ross would share. The larger four-poster wooden bed had a dark blue canopy with matching quilt and heavy blue drapes at the small windows. The MacLaren blue and green plaid was spread across a table for two in front of the fireplace. Smaller rooms, a cabinet for Ross, a boudoir for her, had entrances on either side of the fireplace. She waited, staring out the window, as Ross said farewell to the guests. He had sent her ahead when one man after another suggested a toast with the groom. She wondered if he would be able to stay upright when he arrived.

Warm hands wrapped around her waist and pulled her against a strong body. She did not flinch. His familiar scent gave him away. His lips caressed her neck, traveling to her ear. Strange sensations swept through her body, ones she had never felt before, not even with John.

Juliet turned in his arms and let out a gasp. Ross wore no shirt, just his plaid wrapped around his waist. She put her hand on his chest muscles, drawing her finger along each one. She ran both hands up and over to his well-formed shoulders, feeling him quiver at the touch. He lifted her into his arms and brought her to the bed.

"Oh!" She bounced onto the feather mattress. No turning back. Tonight, she would be his. And he would become hers. *My Highlander husband.*

Ross treated her as if she could break, so gentle she never felt afraid. She accepted each kiss as a sign of his growing affection. When he lifted her shift over her head to expose her naked body, she felt ready for whatever would come. Then she found out what Highlanders wore under their kilts. Nothing at all.

~ * ~

The next morning, Juliet woke to find no one lying next to her. Her heart skipped a beat. *Did he not like me?* She felt around the mattress then searched the room. Ross sat in the corner, one leg propped up on the chair arm as he watched her, wearing no clothes. Juliet looked down to see she also wore none and shyly pulled the sheet up in front of her.

"Come to me." Ross waved two fingers.

"I cannot find my shift." Juliet lifted the bedding.

"Ye dinna need it. We are married."

She slipped out of bed and went to him. He pulled her onto his lap and kissed her shoulder. "How are ye this fine morning?"

Juliet took a deep breath and let it out. "I am fine. More than fine." She kissed his lips. "I love the way you kiss me."

Ross lifted one eyebrow. "Have ye been kissed before?"

Juliet smiled. "Yes, but only by one. John was fine, but you are better."

"John?" Ross' face changed from playful to serious. "Ye loved him?"

"Yes," Juliet whispered before she realized. Eva told her to keep John a secret. Now she ruined everything.

Ross stood, placing her on the floor. "Then I am sorry for marrying ye. Ye should have told me. I would have sent ye back to England."

"No! It would not be allowed." Juliet panicked. "Besides, I do not want to go back. That is what I am trying to tell you…ye! I think I could like it here." Juliet surprised herself.

The eyebrow rose as Ross half-smiled. "Aye?"

"Aye." She fell into his arms. "Could we start the day over again?"

"Oh aye, lassie, we could." He guided her back to bed. "And we definitely will."

Chapter Four

Spring gave way to summer. Juliet enjoyed morning walks with Ross as he told her story after story of Scottish history. She came to understand the importance of clans, their name for family. He cared about the people living on their land and talked about ways to make their lives better. She could see in the villagers' faces that they felt the same about him.

One hot August day, Ross took Juliet to a hidden stream in the woods. They stripped their clothes and jumped into the pool of water. Juliet crossed the narrow creek in twenty strides then headed back to the deepest part, which came only to her waist. The water upstream rippled over a three-foot drop, creating a waterfall over a pile of rocks and shale. Surrounded by greenery as the sunlight peeked through the tree leaves, she forgot any worries she had.

After they emerged from the stream, Ross spread his plaid on the grassy bank. The sun beat down through a spot in the trees, drying their naked bodies. He rolled toward her and took her in his arms. "I love ye," he whispered in her hair.

Juliet held back a gasp. To be told he loved her, lying together in a summer forest, was something she would never forget. "Make love to me, Ross." She nuzzled his neck.

His strong arms swept her on top of him. "Ye dinna care ye are outdoors and could be caught?" She shook her head. "Ye have become a feisty lass." He smiled up at her as she lowered onto his body.

"You have made me that way," Juliet whispered in his ear.

"And what about ye? Do ye love me?"

"Ross!" A man's voice called in the distance.

Grateful for the save, the words "I love you" had stuck in her throat. Juliet's feelings for Ross had grown over the months, but she still felt torn between the life she gave up and the one here.

Ross sat up, bringing Juliet with him, and wrapped his plaid around them. "Here, Duncan!" He looked at Juliet and shrugged a shoulder.

She clung to his body, not knowing whether to be embarrassed or not. She could see Duncan's wide figure tromping through the underbrush to get to the stream.

"There is a path," Ross said as Duncan came out of the bushes.

"I…er… I followed yer voice." He stared at the ground when he reached them.

"Duncan? Would you mind?" Juliet gestured to her clothes on a rock. He rushed to the spot and back, adverting his eyes. "Thank you." She slipped her shift down over her body as Ross retied his plaid.

"What is it, brother?" He slapped his hand on Duncan's shoulder. "What is so important ye had to scour the countryside for me?"

"English soldiers," Duncan said out of breath. "They have come to Glenhaven to speak to Da. He wants ye there."

"They have heard the rumors, I take it." Ross said, as he turned to help Juliet fasten her dress.

"Aye." Duncan nodded his head; his cheeks flushed pink.

"What rumors?" Juliet's eyes widened.

"In March, our exiled king in France appealed to the pope, asking for him to support the Jacobite rising," Ross answered. "He was denied. We thought that was the end. But rumors have recently surfaced that they will continue to grow an army without the backing of the church."

"James Stuart is in France under the protection of Louis XIV. Why would he want to return and start a war?" Juliet asked.

"To become king of England, sister," Duncan said as he wiped sweat from his brow. "And overthrow those Protestant pretenders."

"Oh." Juliet looked at Duncan then Ross. "Would you both fight?" Her heart raced as she waited for an answer.

"Aye, we would be at our king's side." Ross nodded. "Da, and all the men in the village too."

"James or George?" Juliet asked as she held her breath. George I was her king. She had sacrificed her old life to come to Scotland in the name of peace. How many other women had forfeited their lives for the cause? And for what? Now, Juliet stood in the middle of an uprising discussion.

"James, of course." Ross stared at her with blazing green eyes as if to say he would leave today to fight. "We are loyal to him."

"Then you need to go to the castle. Find out what those soldiers want." Juliet would not make him choose between her and his loyalty to Scotland. She turned to Duncan. "Did you bring horses?"

"Aye, I did."

"Show us the way." She started for the path.

Ross took Juliet by the shoulders. "'Tis not yer fight, lass. Ye dinna have to come."

"This is my home now, husband. Do you think English soldiers would care if I was English if they came to Glenhaven during a war?" She suddenly realized that was true. She could pledge her allegiance to George I, but she lived in Scotland and was married to a Highlander.

"No." Ross kissed her. "Stay quiet in the background. When I nod, go to our room."

Juliet held her chin up. "I will do as you ask … for now."

They rode through the field at a quick pace and arrived at the castle to find five horses tied to the hitching post in the open courtyard. Juliet hesitated and studied one of the horses, thinking it looked familiar. She shrugged it off and followed Ross and Duncan to the receiving room across from the grand hall.

Four soldiers, wearing the crimson red coat of the English army, were seated in front of a large wooden table. Donnach sat on the other side talking to one man, not in uniform, who stood with his back to them. Juliet recognized him immediately. "John!"

He turned as soon as he heard her voice. His blond hair had partially come undone from its tail and dust covered his clothes. "Juliet! Lovely to see you again." He held his arms out in greeting as his dancing gray eyes locked onto hers.

Juliet tried to hold back, but the joy of seeing a familiar face won out. She slipped into his arms for a hug. He smelled the same, a light lavender scent mixed with sweat from a long ride. "It is so good to see you," she cried.

She pulled back and saw the love in his eyes. Could Ross see it, too? She turned toward her husband and felt a thunderstorm had entered the room. "Ross, this is my dear friend, Lord John Alder, son of the Duke of Essex."

Before Ross could answer, Donnach spoke up. "He brought word from the king, son."

"James?" Ross said without blinking an eye. Juliet flinched, hoping John had not heard the wrong king's name.

"King *George* has sent word with me," John answered.

Had he heard? Suddenly, Juliet felt as if John was a stranger. She had always been able to tell what he thought, but his face wore a blank stare when he answered Ross.

John cleared his throat. "The king needs to know that Clan MacLaren is behind him." He looked at Ross then Donnach. "All you have to do is sign these papers, and we will be on our way."

"Och, no, ye will not be going anywhere, Lord John," Donnach said with a laugh. "Stay for supper and be on yer way tomorrow. It will give me time to read over the papers."

John nodded as he bowed. "If you would be so kind to show my men to their quarters?" He looked at Ross. "May I request a visit with your wife? To catch up with an old friend?"

Ross grunted, and Juliet assumed it meant yes. She touched his arm as she headed for the doorway. "I will not be long."

"Take as long as ye like," he said as he bolted from the room ahead of them.

Juliet looked at Duncan. "Please, go after him."

Ross had asked if she loved him, but Juliet could not give an answer. Her heart was torn between her new love for him and the one standing before her. She wanted to give herself completely to Ross but needed time. He would not understand if she tried to explain, so she had kept silent. Now he ran from her without ever hearing what she had to say.

"Have your say, Lord John, and keep it short," Donnach grunted. "One of my guards will be along in a few minutes."

John gave Juliet his arm. "I will let you lead the way."

Juliet took him toward a path that ran through the field behind the castle and ended at the edge of the woods. "It is a hot day." She smiled.

"You appear cool and collected, Juliet. Beautiful, as always."

"I cooled off in a stream earlier." She blushed at the thought of the early swim, and the lovemaking that almost happened.

As they walked farther from the castle, John relaxed. "I am sure no one can hear us." He removed his tri-cornered hat and wiped his brow. He was fashionably dressed in a dark blue silk morning coat, knee breeches, and white silk stockings. "I received your message from Edward. You still love me."

Juliet had begged Edward to tell John she still loved him. After all these months, she had forgotten she sent the message. "Yes, well, about that—"

"Juliet, I have come to take you home. I will fight for you until the end of my days. We can say I found you beaten and broken and had to rescue you, an English subject, from this dire situation. I know I will lose my title and any claim to Father's land, but I have enough money saved that we can live in the country. I have purchased a small estate with a cottage. The land is good. We can plant crops. It is not much, but I hoped—"

"That sounds lovely, John." Juliet stopped and took his hand. A few months ago, if she had been offered a way home, she would have taken it. "But I am happy here."

"What?" He lifted his brows, and his eyes widened. "I thought we pledged to be together forever."

"That seems like a lifetime ago." Juliet sighed, not wanting to hurt him. "I thought I would never see you again, John. Please understand that."

"Understand?" He threw his hat to the ground and a puff of dust floated up in the air. "I have risked my life coming here. I begged the king to make me his liaison so I could bring the message to the MacLarens. If he realized my true motive…" He hung his head.

"I must keep my family's promise to our king," Juliet said.

"He would not care." John stared into Juliet's eyes. "If only you knew..."

Juliet squinted in the bright sunlight, confused. "Knew what?"

"What does it matter?" John said with a wave of the hand. "I have spoken privately with Donnach MacLaren. He knows my true feelings for you."

Shocked by his boldness, Juliet tried to make him see reason. "I am sorry." She rubbed the side of his arm. "I made a vow, and I have to uphold it. I am married in the eyes of God. And besides," Juliet blushed as she dropped her eyes. "I could be with child."

"What vow?" John yelled. "A vow to that thieving cannibal? It is not a real marriage!" His face changed to a deep shade of red and he lowered his voice as he said, "If I leave tomorrow, you will never see me again. Is that what you want?" He looked away as he waited for her answer.

"I believe it is," a voice answered. Juliet swung her head toward the woods to see Duncan step out of the brush.

"John, this is my brother-in-law—"

"I do not bloody care who he is!" John stormed away in the direction of the castle, grabbing his hat off the ground on the way.

Juliet faced Duncan. "Did you hear us?"

"Most of it, aye. I believe ye may love my brother ... or will some day."

"Did you find him?"

"No. He willna come out until he is ready."

"I wish he heard what I told John."

"Ye need to tell him, sister. But if I find him, I will tell him. Ye can count on that."

Juliet gave him a kiss on the cheek. "For luck."

~ * ~

Juliet searched the grounds for Ross most of the day. "I give up!" She blew a strand of hair from her eyes and wiped the sweat from her forehead. The sun winked at her from the top of the trees, signaling supper. Donnach had ordered a feast for tonight's guests. She started for the castle, giving one more glance toward the woods. The day had begun with love and happiness and now ended in regret. She lifted her shoulders and let them down slowly. "Oh, Ross, I did not mean to cause you pain."

Her mother's prejudices and harsh words came back to her as Juliet walked slowly toward the castle, still hoping Ross would appear. Mother had been wrong about so many things, and Juliet wished she could have the chance to tell her one day. "Well, she was not wrong about some men," Juliet said with a chuckle as she thought of Donnach. She decided to write her mother a letter and let her know she was well. Hopefully, John would agree to deliver it once he came to his senses.

As she approached her room, Juliet heard voices. "Ross?" She rushed through the doorway.

Duncan sat on a bench next to Eva in the bedroom. They snuggled closely together, foreheads touching. When they heard her voice, they jumped to their feet.

"Sister!" Duncan's already pink cheeks transformed to bright red.

She raised an eyebrow at him then looked at Eva. She also had a flushed face but not from embarrassment. Her rosebud mouth trembled. *She's just been kissed.* Juliet glanced back and forth at the couple standing in front of her. How had she missed the signs?

Juliet folded her arms. "Which one of you wants to tell me what is going on?"

Eva stepped in front of Duncan, head held high. "I love him."

Duncan took Eva by the arms and placed her next to him. "We are in love. I want to marry her."

Juliet's mind whirled in every direction. Eva was a lady's maid. Would the MacLarens allow it? She did not think so, protocol always won out in the end. She could see Eva feared the same as tears welled up in her eyes.

"Oh, Juliet, we did not know what you would think," she said. "We met in secret. I fell in love the moment I saw him." She pinched his cheek. "How could you not love him?"

Eva's gasp from that first day took on new meaning. She found Duncan appealing, not the opposite as Juliet had thought. She looked at

Duncan. "What would your parents think of you marrying my maid?"

"They would give their blessing if ye support us. Tell Da we can marry." He stared at the ground shifting from one foot to the other. "And besides … she is—"

They were afraid to tell me? "Did you think *I* would not approve?" She stared at Eva with wide eyes.

"Aye." Eva bowed her head.

Juliet stepped forward and pulled Eva into her arms. "I am so happy for you. Of course, I approve. Why would I not?" She glanced at Duncan. "I can see you love her, but there has to be more to it than love. I need a strong argument as to why I approve. Can you give me one?"

"Yes," Duncan said then grunted when Eva put an elbow into his ribcage. "I mean not for ye to use, my lady, but I do have a very good argument and reason for marry Eva."

"Well then, use it. And if I can be of help? Just ask." Juliet crossed her brows as she studied her friend. Was there something she did not want her to know?

Eva hugged her, squeezing so hard Juliet gasped for breath. "I will still serve you, Juliet. Duncan is fine with it." She released her and took Duncan's hand.

Juliet smiled. They made a find couple. Duncan stood a head taller than Eva. His round size dwarfed her slight body yet somehow they complimented each other. "Duncan, are you certain your parents will approve?"

"Once I tell them everything, they will." He slipped his arm around Eva. "If they dinna want her as me wife? We will run away."

"Oh, please! Do not do that." Juliet prayed all would go well then her thoughts went to her husband. "Duncan, I hope you came here with news."

"Aye, that is why I came. I have no news."

"What?" Juliet's heart began to pound. "You came with no news? Where could he be? He could not just disappear."

"No, magicians have not passed our way in a while so he has to be somewhere." Duncan smiled, and his eyes crinkled with amusement.

"This is no time for jokes!" Juliet stomped her foot. "I am sorry,

Duncan. I am not mad at you. I am angry at what happened. Why did those soldiers have to come here?"

"The king wants my father to sign the decree that he is loyal to King George. It will be read to other clans and hopefully discourage them from joining the Jacobites."

"He has quite a burden to bear." Juliet shook her head. "Ross should be here to help him."

"That is it!" Duncan held up a finger. "I ken where he is!"

Chapter Five

Eva helped Juliet dress for supper. They chose a simple green silk brocade dress, decorated with silver fruit and flowers, one that was not too revealing. Juliet did not want to give John any ideas.

"So he wants you to return to England with him?" Eva asked as Juliet sat on the dressing room chair to have her hair done. "And you told him no." She looked over the top of Juliet's head into the mirror. Their eyes connected through the looking glass as they had many times before. "Did you expect him to get so angry? I always thought he was a kind man."

"You never know what is in a man's soul until he is tested. But he has time to think, and the John I know will accept the situation." Juliet patted the hand that rested on her shoulder. "After we finish, we will get you ready."

"Oh, no! This is not my night."

Juliet continued to stare at the mirror. "What better night to show you off?" She turned and smiled at Eva. "Somehow Donnach agreed to the marriage. Do you know why?"

"I will get my dress," Eva said without answering the question, but Juliet shrugged it off, knowing they were in a hurry.

"And I will help you," Juliet called to her.

Eva stopped at the doorway. "No, you will not."

"That is the only way I will let you continue to serve. You help me, and I will help you." Juliet pressed her lips together, waiting for the answer.

"Fine!" Eva huffed and left the room.

Juliet let out a small laugh. She had been distracted for a while, but her thoughts drifted to Ross. He had been gone less than a day, and she already missed him. "Where are you, Ross? Duncan seems to know. I hope he will tell me soon."

After waiting endless minutes for Eva to return, Juliet made the decision to head downstairs early and seek out Donnach. Ross may have returned and went straight to his father. She found Donnach alone in the receiving room, pouring over the contract. His brows were knitted tightly together, and he rubbed his forehead with his hand as he studied the document. "I am sorry. You are busy. I was hoping Ross might be here." Juliet backed away from the door.

"No, 'tis fine. Come in." Donnach waved his hand at her. "So ye did not find my wayward son?" He lifted his eyes from the paper. His hazel eyes, so like Heather's, showed no emotion and gave nothing away. "He will come around soon. We Scots are stubborn." He smiled as he pointed to a seat in front of the table. "Perhaps ye can help."

"I do not think I can."

"Please."

He said the word like a command. Juliet headed for the chair and took the document he handed her. If he signed, he pledged his loyalty to King George I and could not in good conscience go against him. "You are in a terrible situation. If you sign, you cannot join the Jacobites in their fight." Juliet swallowed, and her mouth went dry. She glanced around the room, hoping Donnach had something to quench her thirst.

He seemed to read her mind. "I only have ale. Will that do?"

She nodded as she waited for him to pour a glass. Drink in hand, she held the cup to her mouth and took a long swallow. Donnach shifted in his seat and cleared his throat.

"Sorry." Juliet set the cup down. "I am finding it hard to believe you want a woman's opinion, and an English one at that."

"Aye, I do want yer opinion, an English one. Tell me what ye think the king would do if I did not sign?"

"You would be branded a traitor to the king. Soldiers would be sent to take you to prison, maybe Duncan and Ross, too. Your money would be confiscated. Nothing would be left for the people who remained behind." Juliet wriggled in her seat, afraid she spoke too freely. She remembered her mother's words to watch what she said and trust no one.

Donnach shook his head, the braid on the back of his neck showing on one side then the other. "As I thought." He lifted the quill and dipped it in ink. "Hand it to me, lass."

"No." She held the paper to her breast. "I want you to be sure."

"I am. Me family must be protected. *I* am signing the paper. Not Duncan or Ross. They can still choose." He lifted one brow. Juliet assumed he had learned that from his wife just as Ross did.

"So if there is a rising, you would stay here? Not join the fight?" she asked as she leaned forward, and the emerald necklace Donnach presented to her at the wedding swung out in front of them. She wrapped her hand around the stone. "I swear my allegiance to you, Father. I will do whatever is asked to protect the family." She may not be on the side of the Jacobites, but the MacLarens were now her family.

Donnach dipped the quill into the dark liquid and signed the paper. "'Tis done." He leaned back and stared at Juliet. "The soldiers *will* come. When they do, ye must be ready. Do what is asked of ye."

"I will." Juliet nodded, wondering what he had in mind. She felt as if he were setting her up, not truly asking her opinion. *Stupid girl! Why would he listen to you?*

Duncan burst into the room. "I was right. I ken where he went. Juliet, I found him!" His emerald eyes shone with pride. "I told him he was a fool too." He winked at her.

"And the fool has come groveling back to his wife for forgiveness." Ross stood in the doorway.

"Ross!" Juliet flew out of her chair into his arms. "There is nothing to forgive!" She did not care who was in the room; she placed her lips against his and kissed him for a long time. "Please do not ever doubt me," she whispered as they pulled apart.

"I told her ye were a stubborn lad," Donnach said as he poured two more glasses of ale.

"Make it three, Da," Duncan said.

Donnach's eyebrows crossed then relaxed, and he smiled. "Ewan!"

Juliet turned to see her brother-in-law standing next to Ross. The first time she saw him, he had been engaged in battle with Ross. His ruddy complexion and pale orange hair made quite the contrast to her husband's dark looks. Slightly shorter, his stocky build made him handsome in a different way. He smiled and nodded at her. "Juliet. Greer sends her greetings. She is home with Alec but would have loved to come for a visit."

Duncan turned to Juliet and said, "That is where my brother went. He wanted Ewan here, representing the Kincaids."

"I know you want to talk," Juliet said as she looked at the men. "I am going to my room." She glanced at Ross as she passed by the men.

"Juliet!" Ross sprinted after her.

She waited for him to catch up. She felt his tall, muscled frame against her back as he wrapped his arms around her, resting his chin on the top of her head. "Duncan told me everything. Are ye all right?"

"Yes. I did not know John had a temper. I tried to explain he was my past. I am grateful for the time we spent together, but my place is here."

"And I with ye." He kissed her hair.

She felt his breath travel through her locks of hair and shivered. "We still have to finish what we started this morning, husband."

"Aye, we do. Too bad we have to get through dinner and entertain guests first."

Juliet turned in his arms and looked up at him. "Do you think Donnach would mind if you were late to the meeting?"

She dashed for the stairs and did not look back. Out of breath, she waited at the top. No one followed. Her feelings crushed, she dragged her feet as she walked to her room. Then she caught a scent of outdoor pine and knew it was him. Juliet felt her feet leave the floor as Ross swept her into his arms.

"Ross, I did not think you were coming."

"Oh, aye, I planned to come. I had to let Da ken I would be late for the meeting."

~ * ~

Juliet approached John in the grand hall, knowing this could be the last time she ever saw him. "Good evening, John. I hope you are enjoying your stay." Juliet stuck out her hand in greeting. He bowed and gave it a light kiss, lingering a little longer than she liked.

"Basic accommodations. I have had better," John said stiffly as he returned to a standing position. He frowned, and his eyes closed to mere slits.

Juliet found it difficult to make eye contact after their last conversation "Then you will be glad to be on your way." She gave her best smile but inwardly wanted to slap him. "Will you stop by my home and tell my parents I am well?"

"Tell them yourself, Juliet," John said, under his breath. "It is not too late to leave with me in the morning."

"There ye are!" Ross' voice was a welcoming sound. "Thank ye, Lord John, for entertaining me wife. If ye dinna mind," he said, and offered Juliet his arm, "I will escort her to our table." He wore his plaid over a plain white shirt, but Juliet noticed he put on his best silk stockings. They came up to the end of his kilt, tied with a strip of blue and green tartan plaid.

Juliet wrapped her arm around her husband's and whispered, "Do not make him any angrier than he is. I never saw him in such a state."

"A wounded dog canna be trusted," Ross said as he gestured to her seat.

"No, it surely cannot." Juliet smiled at Ross then caught John's eyes on them. He stood scowling in a corner. Her smile faded. A chill traveled down her spine, and she folded her hands together to steady her nerves.

Eva slipped in the seat next to her. Juliet turned to her friend. "Does everyone approve?"

"Duncan said he put up the good fight. We announce our engagement tonight." Eva giggled and showed Juliet her hand. She wore an emerald ring surrounded by diamond chips, similar to Juliet's but smaller.

Juliet wondered if John would see Eva's marriage as a betrayal to her old life and country when he heard the news. Or would he care if her maidservant married a Scot? He knew she and Eva were friends. She hoped he'd congratulate her or at least acknowledge the union before he left. She shuddered as she looked around the room. *John, what happened to you? Or was this always you?*

She pictured the gardens in England, strolling down the path with John by her side. She could almost see and hear him, hands folded behind his back, talking and being so attentive. He could make her laugh and tell sensational stories, gossip from the court. Juliet blinked and bit her bottom lip. Polite and handsome. But did she really know him? Her heart broke at the thought.

Ross, on the other hand, gave his soul to her every night. They stripped bare and hid nothing from each other. She had seen his jealous streak today, which only made her care for him more. He had a temper, like all men, but it flared only when he saw injustice. Juliet looked over at him, deep in conversation with Ewan. She grasped his hand, and he squeezed back as he continued to speak with his brother-in-law.

Laird Donnach made his grand entrance into the room, Fiona on his arm, stopping behind their seats. The chatter slowed and finally came to a stop when they saw him.

"Lang may yer lum reek!" Donnach reached for his cup on the table and held it in the air.

Ross leaned over and whispered in Juliet's ear. "May ye live long and stay well."

She leaned her head against his, smiling. "A wonderful sentiment."

"We're a' Jock Tamson's bairns!" Donnach's eyes swept the room.

"We're all God's children, nobody is better than anybody else. We are all equal." Ross looked into her eyes and lifted one corner of his mouth. "I hope John does not know Gaelic."

Juliet shook her head. "He is as clueless as I am." She touched his cheek. "Is your father sending the clan a message?"

"Aye, in his own way. He signed the paper. He has to appear loyal, but is reminding them we are still one."

Juliet bit her bottom lip until she thought she would draw blood. If war came, she had no idea what would happen at Glenhaven. "Does your father have a plan if…" She could not say the words. Her father had told her stories of war. He did not make it sound romantic as some of her silly friends did. They longed for a soldier to go off to battle and come back to sweep them off their feet. Juliet now longed for everything to stay the same. She had found a bit of happiness in this far-off place.

"Dinna worry, my bonnie lass." Ross placed a finger under her chin. She stared into his emerald eyes, hoping he told the truth.

"If I may, Da?" Duncan stood behind Eva's chair waiting for the signal. Donnach nodded, and Duncan said, "Today I have the pleasure to announce that Eva Erin Katherine Powers has agreed to become me wife." He gazed around the room. "And ye are all invited to the wedding!"

The sound of a fiddle filled the room, lightening the mood. People cheered and laughed, making toast after toast. Juliet glanced at the corner to find John still there, arms crossed, leaning against the wall. His face appeared to have a greenish cast with his lips pressed tightly together. She hoped he would not be sick. *For his sake, of course. He would not want to delay his trip.*

Juliet felt her body pulled from her chair. Ross' arm went around her waist. "I guess we are dancing before supper," he said.

He spun her out onto the wooden dance floor, set in front of the head table, and wove between the other dancers. Some people bounced at their seats, and others danced alone in the aisles. She noticed Heather moving from one partner to another. Her red hair had slipped from its pins and hung loose down her back. When her body moved, the curls swayed with her. Juliet giggled as she watched a man try to coax Glynis onto the dance floor.

"Has this become a party?" Juliet questioned Ross.

"When Duncan told Da he wished to marry Eva, he thought it would make a good distraction. That may have helped Duncan's cause. We sing, dance, and drink until the soldiers can no longer stand and go to their rooms. They will be gone in the morning. John will have his document, signed and sealed with the MacLaren crest."

"That is a very good plan," Juliet said.

"How would ye like to slip away after dinner?" Ross looked down at Juliet's bodice. "I would like to get ye out of that dress. That is," he said as he gave her a sly smile, "I ken how much ye hate the tight corset."

"So that is the only reason?" Juliet lifted his chin to meet her eyes.

"I have been raised a gentleman." Ross gave her a mock look of surprise.

"Then let us put him away for the evening." Juliet kissed his lips. "And bring out my Scottish Highlander."

~ * ~

"I dinna want ye near him, Juliet." Ross tugged on her arm. She felt soft and warm to his hand, and suddenly he wanted her again. Twice last night was not enough. He also felt overprotective to the point he could march into Lord John's room, carry him over his shoulder, and throw him on his horse then wish him a good day.

It had been so easy to tell Juliet he loved her yet she held back. His heart felt a gentle stab every time he thought of it. *Will she ever love me? She could go back to England with John but chose to stay.* He smiled, hoping that was a good sign.

"If I do not say goodbye, Ross, he might feel you are keeping me from him. John needs to see I am happy here and willing to stay. I do not want to give him an excuse to come back." Juliet crossed her arms and pulled her lips tight.

"Yer gonna do what yer gonna do. I canna stop ye." Ross held his hands in the air and smiled. "Just dinna stray too far. Keep me in sight." His heart pumped the blood faster through his body as he curled his hands into fists.

Juliet wrapped her arms around his bare waist. Her silky hair tickled his chest. "Then I think you need to get dressed. You cannot go out like this." She looked down at his naked form. Her hands traveled from his waist up the front of his chest. She placed her hand over his heart and stood still for a moment. He felt it beat against her small palm. She ran her fingers to a scar on his left shoulder from a dagger incident, gently running the tips around it, sending chills down his spine.

"Keep that up, and we willna go." Ross placed his hands on her bum and pulled her closer.

"Mmm, you will lock me in the room?"

Ross gave her a sly grin. "That and more." He lifted her up into his arms, their mouths a breath away. “Please be careful.” He gave her a long, soft kiss then set her down.

“Oh.” Juliet put her hand over her heart.

“Ye need more than that shift to wear, lass. Ye best get dressed, too.” Ross nodded at the dress lying on the bed.

“You will have to help me. Eva is late. Too much eating and drinking last night, I guess.” She placed her hand on her forehead as if to remember the evening. “I believe Duncan announced he and Eva would marry the last Wednesday of August. Pitchers of wine and ale seemed to magically appear, filled to the brim, in celebration. One would empty and another took its place.”

“Aye,” Ross answered. “There was a lot of drinking. Dinna be surprised to find a few men sleeping at the tables this morning.” He chuckled.

A knock came at the door and as it opened, they heard a familiar voice. “Juliet?” Eva poked her head in. “Are you here?”

“Yes.”

Ross grabbed his shirt off the floor and threw it over his head. It hung almost to his knees, and he felt properly dressed for the visit.

“I am sorry I am late.” Eva shuffled into the room. “Lady Fiona insisted I be fitted for a wedding gown. I told her I did not need such finery, but she would not be swayed.”

“Do not worry, Eva. You will soon be busy with your own life and will not be my maid.” Juliet hesitated then said, “As it should be.”

Ross noticed the maid’s eyes fill with tears. Juliet had mentioned they grew up together, and now he realized his wife did not see the girl as a servant. He heard that his brother had put up quite the fight to marry her, but something had suddenly changed his father’s mind. He made a mental note to find out exactly what had happened.

“That does not mean we stop being friends,” Juliet said. “We are best of friends. That will not change.”

Eva let out a sob and a laugh at the same time. “I was so worried.” She flung her arms around Juliet’s neck. Juliet had to bend down to accept the hug.

Ross reached for his plaid, draped over a chair. “Eva, my little lass.

Ye will be my sister soon. Juliet is right. Ye are not a maid. We can get someone to take yer place. In fact, ye should have someone to assist ye."

"Oh, no, Mr. Ross. I do not need assistance."

"We will discuss that at a later time. For now, we need to say goodbye to our guests." Ross finished wrapping the cloth around his body and offered Juliet his arm.

"Wait!" Eva called. "I have something to tell ye!" Her blue-gray eyes shone with fear.

Juliet turned toward her friend. "Did something happen?"

"Aye."

Ross smiled as Eva slipped into her Gaelic accent. She embraced his people and the culture with a wholehearted exuberance. He could see why his little brother fell for her. "What is it, wee lass? Ye can tell us."

"Lord John."

Juliet let out a gasp. "Out with it."

"Early in the evening, before the announcement of my engagement, he pulled me aside to ask for my assistance."

"To do what?" Ross asked and stepped between the women.

"To convince Juliet to return to England with him." Eva looked up at him with watery eyes. "He said there was a substantial reward if I did." Her voice shook as she continued. "I told him I was happy here. I wanted to marry Duncan and live in Scotland. I said ye felt the same way, Juliet. He may try to say I agree with him and would return with you. If he does, it is all lies." She let out a breath and relaxed. "I just wanted ye to know."

"Thank you, Eva. I will not believe a word he says." Juliet walked around Ross and patted her friend's arm. "Now come. We must say our goodbyes."

~ * ~

They found John and the soldiers in the courtyard. Ewan, Duncan, and Donnach tended to the horses while making idle conversation with them. Juliet thought they put on a good show. Laughter filled the air as one of the soldiers joked with Ewan. Donnach gave John a friendly slap on the back after they shook hands.

"Och, look who has come to send ye on yer way." Donnach nodded at Juliet. "I am sure the lass has a message to send her family. I will let ye speak."

The men and Eva followed after Donnach, leaving Juliet alone with John. She studied him. His blond hair had been pulled back in a smooth tail. He was clean-shaven and wore a traveling outfit of breeches, boots, and a long woolen coat. He held a black tri-corner hat in his hand.

"Juliet." He bowed. "Have you reconsidered?" His smile did not reach his eyes, and she assumed he knew the answer.

"No, I have not. I would appreciate it if you would deliver this to my mother." She tried to hand him the letter, but he kept his hands on the hat he held. "John, please?"

"Deliver it yourself." He stared at her with cold gray eyes.

"How can you be so cruel? It is just a letter." Tears filled Juliet's eyes. "Will you tell my parents I am well?"

"No." He straightened his back. "This is what I will tell *you*. You will live to regret this, Juliet Kingston. You should have returned to England with me, not live with that savage in this godforsaken land." His face became hard as stone. "Mark my words and do not forget them. You will regret this." He waved at the soldiers and turned his back on her.

The soldiers mounted their horses and headed for the path that led down the hill. It would take them through the village and up into the forest on the other side. In a week, John would be on English soil without Juliet. She stood with her mouth open as she watched the entourage ride away. She prayed his words would not come back to haunt her.

Chapter Six

Joy and sorrow filled her waking thoughts. Juliet went for long walks to clear her head. The more time she lived at Glenhaven, the more she enjoyed it. But deep in her mind, John's words filled her with fear. She did not tell Ross what he said, except that he refused to deliver the letter. Ross called him a few unrepeatable names then apologized for his bad manners. Juliet smiled as she recalled the words in her head—bloody bastard, pile of fecking shite, and a horse's arse.

As she grew closer to the stream, Juliet heard a girl's laughter. She stopped and tilted her head to listen. "Come on, Jamie! I am already in the water. Yer shirt will cover most of yer parts. I willna look." The girl giggled.

Juliet rushed to the end of the path and stepped onto the grassy bank. "Oh!"

Heather stood knee deep in the water, wearing only her shift. The hem of the slip was soaked with water and clung to her legs. If the outfit became wet, she would look as if she wore nothing at all. "Juliet!" Heather's giggling stopped. "What are ye doing here?" She folded her arms and crossed her brow.

Juliet returned her hard stare. "I like to come here. Ross brings me to the stream on our morning walks." She glanced around. "Come out, lad! I know you are in there." She heard a rustling of bushes, the crackling of dry leaves, and a boy pushed his way through the brush.

He looked at her with smoldering brown eyes. Juliet could see why Heather might be attracted to him. His dark auburn hair hung loose past his shoulders. He stood tall, almost a head taller than Heather. Juliet could see muscled arms through his lightweight shirt. His chest heaved up and down as his eyes went to Heather and back to Juliet. She did not know if it was nerves or being caught that made him skittish.

Heather waded out of the water. "Juliet, this is Jamie MacGregor. He came to our village to learn his trade." She held her head up, throwing her hair over her shoulders. "Jamie is a blacksmith apprentice. He lives with Gordon and his family. 'Tis a fine trade."

She is stubborn and defensive. MacLaren traits. I will have to be careful what I say. "A blacksmith is an honorable profession. They are held in high esteem. Without them, we would not have tools for our cooking, hunting, and sewing. Well done, Jamie." Juliet nodded at him.

"And he will learn to work with silver and copper." Heather's eyes widened as she stepped next to the boy.

"This is how he learns his trade?" Juliet pointed from the top of their heads and down to their toes.

"Och, no, Lady MacLaren." Jamie spoke for the first time. "We were gonna cool off, and I would get right back to work."

"I see. It may be a good idea to do that now." Juliet crossed her arms and tapped one foot. She glanced at Heather. "And you need to get dressed."

They scrambled for the bushes, talking to each other in low voices. Heather came out alone. "Jamie has gone back to the village," she said as she sat on a large rock, and her shoulders dropped. "Please dinna tell Da." Her eyes welled with tears. "I love Jamie. I dinna want to be married off to a Kinkaid like Greer."

For some reason, Juliet thought Greer and Ewan had chosen each other. "I did not know," she said as she sat next to Heather on the rock.

"Aye, Da wanted her close by. The Kincaids and MacLarens are loyal friends." She looked into Juliet's eyes. "Have ye met any more of the Kincaid clan?"

"No, I cannot say I know any except for Ewan."

"They were at yer wedding and some of the feasts." She stared hard at Juliet as if that would help her remember.

Juliet shook her head. "I met so many people, I cannot recall."

"They all look like Ewan, except not as attractive! Argh!" She ran her hands through her hair and held it out to the sides. "Most are smaller, squattier versions of him."

Juliet suppressed a laugh. She pictured a row of Ewans, each one shorter and fatter than the next.

"And their hair? The color of carrots or those orange tatties. Ewan's is nice enough though." She shrugged.

"So you judge them on their looks? Do you *know* any of them besides Ewan?"

"Och, aye, I do." She closed one eye. "And dinna be so quick to judge. I saw yer face the first day at the castle. Ye thought Duncan was Ross."

Juliet covered her face with her hand. "You did?" She let out a muffled laugh.

Heather laughed with her. "We lassies are allowed one prideful fault, aye?" She wiped tears of laughter from her eyes. "Juliet, ye are going to help me. I want to marry Jamie, not a Kinkaid."

"What can I do?"

"Talk to Da for me."

Juliet pulled her brows together. "Me?" *She wants me to be the one to get in trouble.*

Heather nodded. "Ye gave him advice when he had to sign that paper and agreed to help when the time comes. He dinna like that the king foisted a Sassenach upon us, but ye might have changed his mind." She covered her mouth. "Och, I did it again."

Sassenach? Not a very nice name for an Englishwoman. I have heard grumblings in the village, but is that how they all refer to me? "What do you mean foisted?" Juliet's eyes blazed. "You have it wrong. Your father wanted his son to marry English nobility. He made the request to King George."

Heather shook her head. "He did not. Think, Juliet. Why would Da want his son to marry an English lass? The king sent word about ye with an offer for marriage, and ye wouldna be here without Da's approval. By the time ye arrived, he had weeks to think about it and decided the marriage might work to his benefit."

Juliet's mind flashed back to the conversation she had in this very spot with Ross and Duncan. The Jacobites were gathering the clans together for war. They would fight for James Stuart so he could become king. The MacLarens supported the Jacobites. From Donnach's perspective, if Ross married an Englishwoman, it might protect the clan and give King George false hopes of an alliance. "No, it cannot be," she mumbled.

"King George acted as if this marriage was a great gift," Heather scoffed, as she twisted a piece of her hair around her finger. "He said it was a symbol of friendship and a way to keep the peace, not a command from the King of England."

"I am like that piece of paper he sent with John, just a treaty or a document." A tear slipped from Juliet's eye.

Heather slid from the rock and stood in front of Juliet. "I am sorry. I thought ye ken." To Juliet, she looked far from sorry.

"Oh, I knew something. But that was not the story I was told." Juliet shook her head then also slid from the rock. She began to doubt her parents and what they had told her. Her mother's words came back to her. *The laird wants his son to marry an English lady, one of nobility. You have been chosen by the king*. Her mother got one thing wrong. The laird did not really want his son to marry her. Yes, the king chose her but why? She may never know.

"Juliet." She felt Heather's hand on her shoulder. "Will ye help me? Ye ken how it feels to be sent off to a strange place and marry someone ye dinna ken. I want to marry for love."

Love. If Ross had to do it over again, would he choose her? She had yet to tell him she loved him. A voice inside always stopped her. "I will help you," Juliet said. "But first you must tell me why your father agreed to let me be sent here." She would make a bargain with her sister-in-law if she wanted her help, and since Heather could not wait to tell the whole story, she decided to give her the opportunity.

"All right. I will tell ye." Heather huffed, as if Juliet had to bribe the story out of her. "Ye could be used for leverage, if needed. English soldiers wouldna hurt ye." Heather looked away. "Or we could hold ye for ransom."

"What?" Juliet's heart pounded against her chest. "I mean nothing to Donnach? Fiona?" She fell to the grass. "Or Ross?"

Heather crouched next to her. "No, sister, I dinna say that. I am telling ye the story because ye asked. I just want ye to help me."

"So you told me this just so I would help you?" Juliet asked through her tears. "Or so that I would leave and go back to England?" Juliet lifted her head, struggling to breathe. If war came, would the family use her as ransom? She curled into a ball. How could she go on living with people she did not trust?

"Heather!" Ross' voice made Juliet shiver. "What have ye done to her?"

"Nothing, Ross," Heather said. "I was trying to make her feel better."

"What did ye tell her?" Ross sounded angry. Juliet remained twisted around herself in the grass, unable to look at him. "I swear, Heather—"

"Ross! Dinna hit me!"

Juliet scrambled to her feet, placing her body in front of Heather. "She did not hurt me, Ross. She told the truth."

Ross glared at Heather. "Go." He pointed toward the path. "I will talk with ye later." He waited until the girl disappeared from sight. "Juliet? Tell me." He took her by her arms and looked into her eyes.

"You married me so you could have leverage with the king. I could end up being your prisoner or hostage if there is war."

He lifted one brow. "And do ye want to be?" His smile went higher on one side.

Juliet punched his chest. "No! Yes!" She made her hands into fists. "I do not know!" She fell against his body, sobbing. Mixed emotions swept through her. She did not know who was telling the truth anymore.

"Hey," Ross said as he held her away and looked at her. "Heather told ye a tale from before we met ye. We laughed and joked what we could do with an Englishwoman, a Sassenach. Da said he would let the king send the girl, and we would see what happened. He dinna want his loyalty questioned. Once she was here, he told me I could refuse to marry her. We would send ye back." He kissed her forehead. "When I saw ye, I ken ye were the one. The one I waited for all my life."

Her heart soared. Perhaps he told the truth. She placed her hand over his heart, sensing the steady beat, but said nothing. Could she trust him? Her mother's words came back to haunt her. *They will lie to your face and stab you in the back.*

He rubbed her back and waited until her breathing came back to normal. "So? We are good?"

"Ross, why did you not tell me?" Juliet blinked to fight back more tears as she looked up at him.

"It would just hurt ye, like ye are now." He pulled her to him again. "Dinna ye ken, I would protect ye with me life?" He kissed her hair and traveled to her neck. "I love ye, Juliet MacLaren, and if ye canna tell me the same, 'tis all right," he whispered in her ear. "Nothing and no one will ever come between us."

~ * ~

"Juliet, 'tis best if family stays out of this." Donnach crossed his arms. "Heather will wed who I say she should wed."

"Jamie MacGregor seems like a fine boy," Juliet said, doubting Donnach thought of her as family. She fidgeted with her hands, shifting from one foot to another. *I never should have come here.* Although, how could she not? Heather pushed and shoved her to the entrance of the receiving room as if Juliet owed her a huge favor.

"The MacGregors are troublemakers. He will bring her heartbreak in the end." Donnach swiveled in the chair to look at her better. "Anything else ye wish to discuss?" He glared at her as she stood in the doorway, never inviting her in.

"Yes. Why did you agree so quickly to Duncan and Eva's marriage? Was it because you could hold her hostage when the time came?" Juliet folded her trembling hands together.

Donnach lifted a brow. "Och, ye heard about that, did ye?" A sly smile crept across his face.

Juliet held her head up and straightened her body. "I am fine with being held hostage but not Eva. When the time comes, you have to agree to let her go."

Donnach let out a belly laugh so loud Juliet thought the whole castle heard. Tears ran down his cheeks, and he wrapped his hands around his stomach. Then he held up a hand. "Ye are a strong and stubborn lass." His hazel eyes locked with hers. "Ye found out from Heather, I am sure." He ran the back of his hand across his eyes as he shook his head. "Never tell that lass a secret."

"Was she right?" Juliet bit her bottom lip, waiting for the answer.

"Aye, we talked about it. We dinna ken ye, Juliet. We thought ye would have English airs about ye, a typical Sassenach."

Juliet widened her eyes. "So you judged me before you knew me?" She fought to stay composed. Could she trust the man seated before her? She had come to terms with Ross, but Donnach was a different matter. He was chieftain, laird of the estate, and would do whatever needed for his people and his land.

"If it ever comes to holding ye hostage," Donnach said so softly Juliet had to lean in to hear. "I hope ye will go with the plan."

Juliet had her answer. Her heart went back to a steady beat. The pulse in her neck stopped throbbing. To him, she was just a pawn in his game with the English. She swallowed once and said, "I hope I will be able." She turned to leave then looked back. "Please consider Heather's choice."

"Off with ye now," Donnach said with a wave of the hand, returning to the papers in front of him.

Juliet turned and almost crashed right into Heather, her body flat against the outer wall a few feet down from the receiving room. Heather's finger went to her mouth. She grasped Juliet by the arm and pulled her down the hallway. "I have a plan, sister, and ye are gonna help me."

Juliet closed one eye and stared at Heather when they came to a stop. She wanted no part in the new plan. "What do you have in mind?"

"I am gonna say I am with child, and ye will back me." Heather gave her a sly smile. "If ye ken what is good for ye."

"You … are…" Juliet stared at the girl.

"No! If Da thinks I am, he will insist Jamie marry me. We could take part in Duncan's ceremony." She wrapped her arms around her waist and twirled down the hall.

"Heather," Juliet said as she motioned to the girl to stop and rushed to catch up. "I cannot, in good conscience, do that."

"How about in bad conscience?" Heather grinned, showing her straight white teeth. "Please, Juliet! Jamie wants to marry me. He canna stand the thought of me being sent off to the Kinkaids. He loves me." She hung her head.

Juliet felt a tug at her heart and said, "I know how it feels to leave the person you think you love. You may find a real love at the Kinkaids."

Heather gave her a push. "No! Jamie is the man for me. 'Tis real." She looked at Juliet, and her brows crossed. "Ye loved another?"

"I thought I did. But I was wrong."

"Was it that man, John, that came with the soldiers? The one that ken ye?"

Juliet nodded. "He wanted me to return to England with him."

"Och! Jesus, Mary!" Heather pulled Juliet into hug, lifting her from the floor. "Ye stayed, sister. Ye are truly one of us." She set her down and stared into Juliet's eyes with a smile, one that did not reach her eyes. "So ye will help me?"

Juliet knew she was being manipulated by Ross' younger sister, but in that moment, it felt good to be accepted and part of the family so she nodded in agreement.

~ * ~

Ross spent more and more time away from Juliet as the month came to a close. "We have to be prepared for anything," he told her on their morning walk. "Grain needs to be stored. Meat is being dried and salted. It could be a long winter, especially if most of the men are not here."

"Not here?" She pulled him down next to her on the grass by the stream. "Has something happened?"

"Ye dinna need to worry. The men left behind will protect ye."

"Will they?" She had her doubts. "If you leave, I will feel quite alone. And where *are* you going?"

"To join the other Jacobites. Ye understand why I have to do this, lass." Ross tugged at her sleeve to pull her closer.

"No," Juliet shook her head. "I do not. You need to tell me."

He wrapped his arms around her, and she leaned against his chest. His hand traveled up and down her arm as he spoke. "As ye ken, the union between England and Scotland is quite new."

"Yes, I know the history. The two countries united eight years ago."

"Plenty of Scots were against it, especially in the Highlands. The number grows each day."

Juliet looked up at the trees, finding spots where the sun shone through the leaves. The morning sky promised blue skies and warmth, but she shivered at the thought of war. "The countries united as one," she said, "and now the Scots wish to dissolve the union because of a Protestant king." She turned her head toward Ross. "John Stuart could have been king. There were rumors at the castle. Queen Anne was ill at the time and knew she needed a successor. She offered him the throne if he would convert to Protestantism."

"Aye, there is that." Ross rested his hand on Juliet's shoulder. "He is a devout Catholic."

"He chose not to convert so she made George the king," Juliet said. "And since there is only one king and one country now, the Scots are not happy with that choice."

"Truer words were never spoken." Ross shifted position and drew Juliet to him. "Da canna go against King George. But it dinna mean Duncan and I have to be loyal to the English crown. We were never asked to sign the document."

A strange feeling crept over Juliet. "Is something going to happen?"

Ross looked around the cove as if spies were everywhere then said in a low voice, "John Erskine slipped into the country in disguise. He met with the Highland chieftains at Aboyne a few days ago."

"Lord Mar? The British Secretary of State?" *So that's where Donnach went.*

"The one and the same." Ross nodded. "He backs James the third, as James Francis Edward would be called when he takes the throne. It has begun."

"War?"

"Aye, soon. The Jacobite rising."

Fear, dread, and sadness filled her. Juliet did not know which emotion to conquer first as she rubbed her sweaty palms together. Suddenly she felt cold and sick to her stomach. She moved onto Ross' lap and lay her head on his chest. "Tell me what will happen here at Glenhaven. I need to know so I am prepared."

"Duncan and I will take most of the men from the village with us, leaving a few behind. Da will stay at Glenhaven. He knows the soldiers will come. He plans to say we are on a hunt or traveling. Whatever works at the time." Ross stroked her hair. "But really? We will meet up with the Kincaids and MacGregors to report for battle. Greer will come home to Glenhaven with Alec. Please help her with the bairn, Juliet. He is more like a MacLaren than a Kincaid—stubborn and strong."

Bairns. Children had been the furthest thing from her mind. Juliet realized she still had her sessions, and she had been married almost three months. The thought of having Ross' child made her eyes well with tears of happiness. "Ross?" She took his head in her hands. "You never say a word about children. What if—?"

Ross placed a finger on her lips. "Ye are enough for now. We have plenty of time." His green eyes blazed with passion. "Come to me." He placed his hands on her shoulders and slid her linen dress down to expose her breasts.

Juliet leaned against him, feeling his chest move up and down with every breath he took. She wanted to run her hands over his body and become one. "Ross," she whispered. "I cannot wait one more minute."

He rolled her onto his plaid and tossed his clothes aside. "Oh, Juliet, if only ye could see ye as I do. So beautiful—eyes like jewels of dark crystal blue, skin so creamy and soft begging to be touched. Yer mouth, soft, full and pink as if kissed by a wildflower." He glanced down at her body. "Ye are mine."

"And you are my Highlander husband. No one else's." Her heart soared yet she could not say the words he longed to hear. A small part of her held back, afraid of what was to come.

Ross' eyes glistened, and a smile crossed his face. "No one can tear me away from ye. Wherever I am, I will come back to ye."

He gently slipped on top of her, and they became one.

Chapter Seven

The preparations for Duncan and Eva's wedding had taken up most of her week. Juliet set the final vase of flowers on a table and smiled as she remembered how this had turned into a double ceremony. Heather threatened to become with child and not marry anyone. Her father nodded in agreement as he sipped his ale during her rant. "Would ye like me to help pick the man to father yer bairn?" he had asked.

Heather had stormed out of the dining room in a huff. She returned a few moments later to try her next tactic. "Jamie and I agreed to marry. That is all a Scot needs to do." She stood with her hands on her hips, waiting for an answer.

"Mutual consent? An irregular marriage?" Donnach tapped his fingers together. "I only recognize marriage by a priest."

"But 'tis the law. I sleep with Jamie and have his bairn then say we are married."

"I see ye have done some reading." Donnach's voice sounded calm, but his face turned several shades of red.

Heather threw her red locks over her shoulder. "We are handfasted, Da." She crossed her arms.

Donnach threw his hands in air as he stood. "Enough!" He leaned forward on the table. "Ye are married for a year and a day then?"

At that point, Juliet was thankful she decided not to help the young girl, although the wrath of Heather had come down upon her. Juliet did her best to avoid her sister-in-law until she came to her senses.

"No, Da, I would never go against ye. I am not handfasted." Heather let out a breath and hung her head. "I love ye and want ye to bless the union."

Fiona shoved her chair back and hopped to her feet. "I think ye two would go at it all day like fighting dogs!" she shouted and tugged on Donnach's arm. "Did we not say she needs a husband? Jamie MacGregor will be a fine blacksmith. Gordon will not live forever."

Donnach smiled down at Fiona. "Ye always make sense, wife." He looked at Heather. "Ye have my blessing."

The family cheered. Juliet gazed around at the people seated at the table. Eva and Duncan tapped their glasses together. Glynis lifted one side of her mouth in a smirk before reaching for her cup. Ross slipped his arm around Juliet and pulled her closer. He whispered in her ear, "May they be as happy as us." She turned and kissed his mouth, melting into the sweet warmth.

"Da," Duncan said as he leaned forward. "She can be married with us if ye get the banns posted."

"It may be hard to get done at this late date." Donnach cleared his throat.

"But not impossible." Fiona patted his arm.

"Then a toast is in order," Ross said as he stood. "To Heather and Jamie." He glanced around. "Where is the poor lad?"

"In the village, too afraid to come." Heather giggled. "He waits to learn his fate."

"Send a servant to fetch him." Ross waved his hand at her. "Tell him to join us for supper."

Heather ran from the room, and Juliet could tell she floated on air. "She does love him," Juliet told the room. All eyes settled on her as a lump grew in her throat. "I met him … once. I thought Donnach told you."

"Donnach has his secrets, dear." Fiona gestured at him with her cup. "Dinna underestimate him."

I will not. Juliet studied the man. She did not trust him, still unsure of his motives.

~ * ~

Juliet blinked a few times to bring herself back to reality and focused on the flowers. The blue skies with white, puffy clouds would make a beautiful background for the nuptials. She hoped a sudden storm would not interrupt the ceremony. "Oh! I need to get ready." She added one more stem of heather to the bunch then headed for the castle.

Voices came from the receiving room as Juliet made her way to the stairs. They grew so loud it caught her attention. She hesitated on the first step then changed direction. She leaned against the wall outside the room to listen.

"Ye need to tell us everything that happened, Da." Ross' voice had an edge of concern. "Now."

"All right. Calm yer nerves. Lord Mar has been deprived of his office. John Erskine is no longer the British Secretary of State. He came to Scotland declaring himself head of the Jacobites. He has pledged to help Scotland gain independence. He is in need of an army, and each clan has pledged to send men."

"Does he ken of yer problem, Da?" Duncan said.

"Aye, we spoke. He agreed I should stay at Glenhaven. He is grateful for yer support. After the wedding ye both need to get ready to leave."

Juliet held back the gasp that formed in her throat. Her knees wobbled, and she placed her hands against the stone wall for support. She had known the day would come, just not this soon. She would be left vulnerable if Ross left now, a puppet for Donnach to use.

"Erskine will send word. I will let ye ken," Donnach said, as his voice grew lower. "I wish ye both Godspeed."

No sound came from the room. Juliet tried to force her body from the wall, but she could not step away. Her heart felt as if it had slammed against the stone and back to the front of her chest. She had to force her feet to move toward the stairs, one painful step at a time. *Almost there. You can do it.* She climbed each step, dragging her heavy feet up and onto the stairs. *I have to pretend everything is fine. Eva is expecting me to help her dress for the wedding.*

"There ye are!" Eva placed her arm around Juliet's waist when she reached the second floor and guided her to the bedroom. "I am so nervous

I canna unlace the dress to get it over my head." Her face glowed with cheeks flushed pink. "I did my hair." She patted the upswept hair filled with flowers.

"It is lovely." Juliet smiled as she noticed an unusual glow coming from Eva. "Now where is the dress?" She glanced around the room until she spied it on the bed. Juliet busied herself with the gown, trying not to look at Eva.

"Juliet?" Eva touched her arm. "Are ye all right?"

"I am fine."

"Ye seem nervous."

Juliet took Eva by the arms. "I am happy for you. Let us get you ready. Duncan is waiting at the altar."

She slipped the dark green silk dress over her friend's head. Eva insisted on wearing the MacLaren colors and plaid just as Heather would. Juliet and the sisters would wear blue.

"I am so glad Heather will be with me." Eva squeezed Juliet's hand. "I do not like everyone's eyes on me."

"Well, it is going to be difficult not to look at you. You look beautiful." Juliet went to the cupboard for her dress. "As soon as I am dressed we will join the others."

When Juliet opened the door, the sisters stood in the outer hall. Heather beamed with happiness. "Och, Juliet! Ye look bonny."

Juliet shook her head. "Today is for the brides." She followed the girls down the stairs to the same doorway she walked through to become Lady Juliet MacLaren.

Glynis brushed past her. "Sorry. Just want to get this over."

Juliet had barely spoken to Glynis since her arrival. She never appeared to be in the mood to talk or acted as if she had somewhere to go. "Glynis." Juliet touched her arm. "I know we do not know each other well, and you may very well hate me. I do know you would rather be in plaid and kilt, but you look lovely." And she did. Juliet had a feeling Glynis had no idea how beautiful she was.

"Thank ye." She nodded her head. "And I dinna hate ye, but ye ken what ye are. So, can we trust ye?" Glynis closed one eye and stared at Juliet for a moment. Then she held up the skirt of her dress. "I dinna like this. Men have the freedom and women…" She looked at the ground. "'Tis not fair."

"I would love to hear more of your thoughts," Juliet said as her sister-in-law looked up in surprise. "But for now, we better start the wedding."

Glynis shrugged. "Why prolong the torture, eh?"

"Yes, exactly," Juliet said, feeling she'd had a breakthrough with Ross' sister.

The bagpipes began to play when the musicians spotted Glynis walking from the castle. Greer went next, followed by Juliet. Heather and Eva waited until the girls arrived at the altar. They walked together, clutching bouquets, appearing angelic in the late afternoon sun that shone through the trees. Juliet glanced at the men, searching for Ross. He smiled, giving nothing away.

Jamie, in red and green MacGregor plaid, stepped forward to meet his bride. Duncan waited for them to find their position by the priest before he greeted Eva. He took her hand, guiding her to the other side.

Juliet barely remembered her wedding day. She had been in shock and overwhelmed by new surroundings and people. This time she paid careful attention to every detail and stored it in her memory. If Ross went off to war, she wanted as many memories as she could find.

~ * ~

Ross spun Juliet around the dance floor. "Are ye having fun?" He squinted as he looked at her. "Ye seem sad."

She stared at him. "When are you going to tell me?"

His eyes flew open wide, and he brought her closer. "How do ye ken?"

"I have my ways." Juliet batted her lashes. "You men need to keep your voices lower."

"Ye heard."

"And when do you leave? Please do not say tomorrow. Give Eva and Heather more than one night with their new husbands."

"And what about me wife? Does she deserve more than one night?"

"Yes, she does," Juliet said. "Answer the question."

"In a few days. Lord Mar plans to announce James is king on the sixth of September." Ross danced to the edge of the floor and walked Juliet to a corner. His lips found hers as soon as they reached the darkened space. "I dinna want to leave ye," he whispered. "Tell me ye will wait. Ye will be here when I return."

"Where else would I be?" Juliet pulled back to look at him, a surprised look on her face. "You are my Highlander husband."

"Eh? Is that what ye call me?" Ross chuckled then grew serious. "The English will protect their people. Ye might be able to return home."

"Home?" Juliet saw her father's estate in her mind. The home had similar qualities to Glenhaven. Pale gray stone, rounded turrets, but the furnishings were more opulent. Tapestries and artwork hung on the walls; furniture imported from France decorated the rooms. She shook her head. It did not feel like home anymore. "My place is here." She lifted her head for one of Ross' kisses, her mouth slightly open.

Ross granted her wish, kissing her mouth with passion and tenderness. She stored away the kiss, along with the others. Juliet wrapped her arms around his neck bringing him closer. She slid her lips along his cheek and whispered in his ear, "I want to stay awake all night."

"Juliet," Ross murmured. "I will honor yer wish." He kissed her cheek. "For now, we need to join the festivities. Come." He took her hand.

"Ross," Juliet tugged on his hand. "One more question. Who will go with you?"

"Duncan," he said as he nodded toward his brother. "As will Ewan. But Jamie will stay."

"Why does Jamie stay?"

"He can help Gordon make weapons." Ross placed his hand under her chin. "Can we join the party now? I dinna want to waste another minute that I can spend with ye."

Nothing would be solved tonight. The family could experience joy this evening then heartbreak in the coming week. She smiled at Ross. "Yes, let us enjoy the night."

~ * ~

"I must speak with my family while we are all here," Ross said to Juliet as he escorted her back to the table after a few dances. He did not want to leave her side but had to attend to business.

"It's all right, Ross. Do what you must," Juliet said, and squeezed his hand.

Her hand felt small and warm in his. His heart broke at the thought of leaving her, but he planned to assure her safety tonight. He lifted her hand to his mouth and placed a light kiss on top. "I willna be long."

Ross found Donnach in the corner of the dining hall surrounded by men from the village. "Gordon, do yer best work. We need more guns and knives ready in just a few days. Put my son-in-law to work. He will have plenty of time to share my daughter's bed after the men have left." He slapped Gordon on the shoulder, and the group laughed.

His father spotted him on the edge of the crowd and made his way through the men to reach him. "Do ye want to speak to me, lad?"

"Aye." Ross nodded to an open spot away from prying ears. "Over there." He walked alongside Donnach and stopped, leaning against the wall.

"We are prepared … or as well as can be," Donnach said. "The men have weapons, and we have stored enough food to get through the winter. Just wish I was going with ye." He shook his head. "Bloody contract. That king?" Donnach put his finger in Ross' face. "Can burn in hell!" His face changed from its normal grayish tinge to a deep purple and back. "Those Sassenachs lay one finger on anyone here at Glenhaven …"

"That is what I wish to speak to ye about, Da," Ross said. "Juliet."

"Och." He waved his hand. "She will be fine. That Englishman? John?" He tapped his chin. "Alder!" Donnach seemed quite proud he came up with the surname. "He seemed quite fond of her. I could make a deal with him if the time came. The king," he said as he spat at the ground, "could care less what happens to the lass."

Ross' jaw clenched, his hands curled into fists. "Da!" he hissed. "I dinna wish anything to happen to Juliet. Ye will protect her like the rest of the family."

Donnach lifted his brow. "And who is asking?"

"Me, Da! Yer son. I ken we said this marriage could be beneficial, but Juliet is me wife. I … love her."

"Oh." Donnach straightened his back. "And I am still laird of this land, son. I will do what is best."

"Ye promise to protect her?"

"I promise to do what is best for her."

Ross hoped it meant Donnach would keep Juliet safe. "Then I have just one more question."

"Out with it." His father gave him a hard stare.

"These weddings. Ye gave yer permission so quickly. Why?" Ross scratched his chin as he waited for the answer.

"If ye must ken, and one day ye will be in the same position as laird, I gave me consent because the young Sassenach is with child. And Heather? I canna deny that lass. She could ask for the moon and stars, and I'd find a way to get them." Donnach gave his son a sly grin. "But dinna ye go telling her that."

"Ross! Ross!" Heather skipped over to where her father and brother stood. "Ye havena danced with me all night. Ye only have eyes for one lass."

"And is that so bad, sister? To love me wife?" Ross teased. He extended his hand. "May I have the next dance?"

The fiddler played a lively tune, and they wove in and out of the other dancers. Heather was always light on her feet, and Ross remembered spinning her round and round when she was young. For a moment, he fell back in time. When the song finished, Ross walked Heather to the table that held beverages to cool their parched throats.

"Juliet tells me ye have been kinder to her, Heather." Ross poured her some sweet wine and a mug of ale for himself. "Or did ye just use her to get what ye wanted? Now that yer married, will ye still be kind?"

Heather dropped her head. "Ross, I am sorry. I dinna mean to manipulate her into doing my bidding …"

"But ye did," Ross said calmly. "Ye sent her to Da to tell him ye wanted to marry Jamie." He looked into her hazel eyes, noticing tears. "Yer young, sister. I will give ye that. But if ye are not kind to me wife when I am gone? Ye will hear from me when I get back."

"I will try." Heather nodded. "She isna so bad for a Sassenach once ye get to ken her."

"And if ye dinna mind," he said with a bow. "I would like to return to her. I promised her a night of dancing and fun."

~ * ~

Juliet woke in Ross' arms. He still slept, snoring ever so lightly. She studied the curve of his lips, how his long, dark lashes lay against his skin. His hair, black and thick, framed his face, yet his chest was smooth with barely a trace of hair until his waist. She longed to trail her finger down his front to that hair but did not want to wake him.

She lay back on her pillow, recalling how Ross had carried her up the stairs to bed last night. He'd taken each piece of her clothing off with care and precision as she stood facing the window. His lips had grazed one of her shoulders then the other. She tried to turn into his arms, but he'd held her at bay. When his kisses traveled down her spine, following her waistline to her stomach, he'd spun her toward him and looked up at her from bended knee. She'd ran her hands through his hair and grabbed on to the locks at the back of his head, every nerve on fire. "Ross!"

"What is it, love?" He sat up, startled.

"I did not realize I said that aloud. I am sorry for waking you. You looked so peaceful." Juliet snuggled against him. "I was thinking of last night."

"The party?" Ross lifted a brow.

"No." She nudged him. "Of you and me."

"If ye have the time, I would like to kiss the spots I missed last night."

Juliet closed one eye and smiled. "You missed a spot?"

"Aye, I did." Ross pulled her on top of him and gestured to her neck. "And I think I will start right there."

Chapter Eight

"We are going to be late for the wedding breakfast, Ross." Juliet scurried around the room grabbing clothes for them to wear. "Donnach does not like it when we are late."

"He kens we danced into the wee hours of the night." Ross sat up as Juliet threw a shirt his way. "But ye are right. We best hurry."

Most of the men from the village sat at the tables when Juliet and Ross stepped into the grand hall. "Did they go home?" She looked at Ross in surprise.

"No. Da asked them to stay."

Breakfast had been served, and the men talked amongst themselves.

"Do they know?" she whispered.

"Aye," Ross said. "And they are ready to fight."

A shiver went down Juliet's spine. She'd learned the names of most of the men sitting along the benches on visits to the village with Ross. She knew their families, their wives, and children's names. Some of these men might not return whether the Scots won or not.

Eva ran up to Juliet. "Good morning!" Her face was flushed with excitement. "Duncan says Da has a big announcement."

"Oh, no," Juliet said. She could not let her friend be deceived. "It is not good news."

Eva's smile disappeared. "What is the news?"

Juliet stared at her. Eva must have surely heard the rumors. "The men are leaving. The war has begun."

"No! I just married him. No!" Tears welled in her eyes. "Do something, Juliet."

Juliet took Eva by the arms. "You must stay strong. Look at me." She waited for Eva to lock eyes with her. "We must be strong for our husbands and the family."

Donnach entered the room, Fiona on his arm. The men stopped talking when they saw him. He waved his hand in greeting as he guided his wife to her seat. Heather and Jamie rushed through the door, faces flushed red. Juliet guessed they came straight from their bed to the hall. A wave of heat traveled up her neck. *Did I not do the same?*

After they were seated and fed, Donnach rose from his chair. "My friends," he said as he looked out at the men. "And family." He glanced down the head table. "We are here for two reasons. One, to celebrate the consummation of two marriages." He waited for the shouting to die down. "And to discuss the Jacobite rising."

A gasp came from farther down the table. Juliet leaned forward to see Heather covering her mouth.

"As ye ken, I signed a document saying I am loyal to King George. I will stay at Glenhaven and oversee its running while most of ye are off fighting. I have already spoken to most of ye. Ye ken who stays, who goes." He glanced down the table. "Jamie, despite yer arguments, ye stay. We need ye here."

A scream came from Heather. She threw her arms around Jamie's neck, sobbing.

"Ross will be in charge of ye." Donnach changed his stance and looked out over the room. "He is yer leader. Ewan and Duncan will serve as his advisors and second in command. Ye have five days to get ready." He lifted his mug. "To Scotland!"

The men held up their cups and cheered.

A chill went through Juliet. The room may be celebrating, but the men's faces wore hard looks of determination. She told Eva to stay strong, now she must listen to her own words. If Ross did not come back, could she live another day?

Juliet glanced down the table and saw Jamie wiping Heather's tears away and kissing her cheeks. *Oh, how I long to be her.* She sank her teeth into her bottom lip as she watched the couple.

Ross touched her arm, making her jump. "Sorry, love. I want ye to ken I will spend most of today with my men." His thumb grazed her lips. "I would rather be kissing these."

"Ross, I want to help. Do whatever you need me to do."

"Talk to Greer. Stay with her through the day. She is not in the best spirits. Can ye do that?"

Juliet nodded. "But I need to *do* something, Ross. Help in some way. Please."

"Ask Greer to help ye pack food and ale onto the wagons. Ye ken where the supplies are." Ross took her chin in his hand. "Ye are a MacLaren, Juliet. Stubborn as the day is long. Dinna let it get ye in trouble whilst I am gone."

"I will not." Juliet did not feel stubborn. She held her ground when she needed to make a point. If that meant she was stubborn, she did not care. "If Greer's hands are busy, she will have less time to dwell on Ewan." She stared at Ross, waiting for him to acknowledge.

"Aye, it makes sense. Go and ask her." He nodded at Greer, who appeared to be leaving.

"Do you think your mum will mind watching Alec?" Juliet asked Ross as she rose from her seat.

"No. She loves the bairn. And if she tires of him? She has the servants." He smiled at Juliet.

She kissed the tip of his nose. "I have work to do. Greer!" she called to her sister-in-law.

"Aye?" She turned and smiled at Juliet, but her eyes appeared glazed over.

"I need your help. Ross has asked me to gather the women to do some work. We will fill the wagons with food for their journey." Juliet wanted Greer to get to know her and hopefully begin to trust her.

Greer blinked as if to focus. "Alec will be in the way."

"I am sure someone will watch him." Juliet looked over at Fiona. "Your mum?"

"She would love that. She says I keep him too much to myself. But I canna help it, Juliet. He is so precious."

"I cannot blame you, he is a handsome lad." Juliet studied the boy holding Greer's hand, thumb stuck in his mouth. His blond hair was almost white, and he had the MacLaren emerald green eyes. His chubby cheeks reminded her of Duncan. "Put wings on him, and he is an angel." She smiled. "He is two?"

"Aye, three soon. If they are gone for a long time, his da will miss his birthday." She glanced away.

"Come, let us ask your mum." Juliet did not want Greer to dwell on the war but help with the cause.

Fiona quickly agreed to take Alec for the day. Greer and Juliet headed outside to the storage huts across from the kitchen. The wagons sat in front, as Ross promised. Greer grasped Juliet by the arm when they reached their destination. "How do ye do it?"

"Do what?"

"Act as if ye are not hurting?"

"It is best to stay busy, Greer." Juliet pulled a bag of oats from the pile. "Take the other end." They walked out of the hut, tossed the bag on one of the wagons, and went back for another. "The men can make plenty of porridge and oatcakes from these." Juliet wiped her hands together when they finished.

"Turnips and potatoes next." Greer placed her hands on her hips and studied the wagon. "The baskets will fit well there." She pointed to a spot.

Juliet smiled at Greer. Work could be a good distraction from pain. "After we load the baskets, we take a break and get some food from the kitchen."

The two women did not stop until the sun rose high in the sky. Juliet wiped her brow with the back of her hand and gazed up at the heavens. How many suns would she count until Ross returned? A sharp pain went through her as she remembered he asked if she would return home to England rather than stay here if war broke out. He said he loved her but did not look upset or sad during that conversation. The lingering doubt she had about his love returned, and she would try to hide it the best she could until he left.

Greer and Juliet strolled to the kitchen. The day suddenly became overcast with dark, looming clouds. The cook served them lunch, and they sat on the grass outside the estate to eat.

"Thank ye," Greer said as she bit into some goat milk cheese.

"For what?" Juliet asked.

"Ye meant to distract me…and it worked." She gave Juliet a shy smile. "I dinna like ye at first, being a Sassenach and all. The English that have come to Glenhaven always put on airs, like they are better than us."

"I am sorry to hear that. No one is better than anyone else."

"Is that what ye were taught?"

Juliet shook her head. "No. That is just how I feel."

Alec came running toward them, Fiona following behind him. "Mum!" He threw his body into Greer's lap. She kissed the top of his head.

"So like his da," she whispered.

Juliet did not agree but stayed silent. With the exception of his hair, he looked like a MacLaren through and through. She could see Greer loved Ewan very much, even if it had been an arranged marriage. "Did you know Ewan before you were married?"

A bright shade of red crept up Greer's neck. "Aye. Since we were bairns. He was Ross' best friend even though he was older. We played right here in that field." She gestured to the grassy area behind the castle. "He was strong even then. Ewan would pretend to be a knight and rescue me from the castle."

Now it made sense. The families arranged the marriage knowing Greer and Ewan were in love. "Sounds lovely. I only have one brother, three years older. He never wanted to play with me. I was a girl."

"Did ye have friends?"

"School friends. Mother and I would visit their homes. She let me invite girls to the house once in awhile. She would say she did not like the shrill laughing when they came so they did not come too often." Juliet folded her hands in her lap.

"Well, now that ye are here, ye have us." Greer patted Juliet's hands. Her eyes had a sympathetic look.

Perhaps one sister finally cared for her. Glynis was still hard to talk to, and Heather was young and selfish. Maybe she and Greer would become friends.

"Mum?" She held up Alec. "Would ye mind? Juliet and I have work to do before the storm comes."

~ * ~

Each day, Greer and Juliet worked from sun-up to sundown to make sure the men had the supplies they needed. On the final day, they barely spoke to one another. Juliet knew they would break down and cry if they did, unable to work.

"Juliet!" Ross ran down a slope toward her. "We will be going soon. Ye have done a good job. Greer," he said as he pulled his sister into an embrace. "Thank ye."

Ewan came up the path with two horses. "These should do, Ross." He positioned them in front of one wagon. Ross helped him secure the horses in place. "Jamie's bringing the other two." He nodded at the second wagon.

Juliet stood by, watching. When they finished the job, they would be on their way. She heard Greer stifle a sob and reached for her sister-in-law's hand. "Stay strong."

Ewan, down on one knee checking a wheel, looked up at his wife. "Come here, lassie. Give old Ewan a kiss."

She rushed to him, and Juliet fought back the tears as they embraced. Ross walked around the horses. He stood in front of her, tall and proud in his plaid and kilt. The sun reflected off his dark hair and made his green eyes sparkle like gemstones. His grin lit up his face, making him all the more attractive. Juliet had to remind herself to breath as she gazed upon him. *My Highlander husband.*

Ross held out his arms. She fell into them, wanting to feel the strength of him one last time. Juliet lifted her head, eyes begging him to stay but knowing the answer. His mouth covered hers, and she felt the urgency of the kiss. She wanted him to know she loved him. How did she convey that in one kiss?

They parted, and Juliet's mind screamed for more. Just one more hug, one more kiss, one more time to be husband and wife. She looked up at Ross, expecting to see love in his eyes but instead found rage.

"Och, no! Ye are not going with us!" Ross yelled.

~ * ~

Juliet turned, thinking she would see Jamie MacGregor and gasped at the sight. Glynis stood before them, hair cut to her shoulders, wearing a white shirt. The blue and green MacLaren plaid was wrapped around her waist, with a dirk sticking out of a sheath on her belt. A broadsword hung in a holder strapped across her back.

"I am going with ye, Ross." Glynis stood with feet spread apart to hold her ground. "I can fight with the best of them. Ye said so yerself."

"Aye, when we were bairns, I did." Ross stepped toward her, and Glynis flinched. "I canna take a woman into battle."

Juliet noticed Ewan had slipped away. She wondered if he went to find some rope to tie her up. That would be the only way she would stay.

Ross and Glynis appeared to be at a stand-off. Neither spoke. They glared at each other for the longest time. Juliet prayed someone would speak and end the quarrel.

"What in bloody hell is going on?" Donnach's voice rang through the field. He bustled down the path toward them, Ewan in quick pursuit. Donnach's boots scrapped the stones as he came to a halt. "Glynis! Go inside."

"No, Da. I am going with them." She crossed her arms.

Donnach grabbed both sides of his head. "Where did I get these headstrong daughters?" He looked up at the sky. "Ye are testing an old man. 'Tis a test." Donnach turned to Ewan. "Get a rope."

So I was right. I cannot let them do that to her. "Glynis," Juliet said softly. "You look ready for battle."

"Aye, I am." She nodded at Juliet but kept a side eye out for Ewan, hand on her dagger.

"And Ross?" Juliet reached for his hand. "You said she can fight."

Ross stared at her, eyes round as saucers. She returned the look, begging for him to answer. "Aye," he finally said.

"So," Juliet said as she turned to Glynis. "That is why we need you here. Who will protect us?"

Glynis let out a breath. "There will be men in the village to do that."

"But what about the castle? Donnach cannot protect us all."

Juliet hoped Glynis saw that she gave her a way out. She did not want her sister-in-law tied up like an animal. "Please, Glynis, I want you to stay. I will feel safer if you do."

Glynis' shoulders dropped. "I will stay." She lifted her chin. "For now."

Donnach placed his arm across her shoulders. "That is a good lass. Ye would scare ye mum half to death if ye marched off with ye brothers. Now, go and change."

"No." She straightened her back.

Ross stepped forward. "Da, Glynis is ready for a hunt. Send her out to find a good grouse or boar." He lifted his brow, and Juliet's stomach flipped. She loved when he did that and locked it away with her other memories.

"Go! Before I change me mind!" Donnach waved his hand at Glynis. She flashed Ross a smile and rushed off to the stable. "Come up to the house before ye leave, all of ye. Yer mum wants to see ye off."

They followed Donnach back to the castle. Eva and Duncan stood with Fiona in the courtyard. When she saw Ross, Fiona let out a cry. She rushed to him and pulled him into her arms. "I told Duncan he has to come back … alive and breathing. I am telling ye the same. Come back to us, Ross MacLaren." She held him out and checked him over. "Watch over yer brother, he is not as strong."

"I will." Ross kissed her cheek.

Juliet could not hold back the tears any longer. They streamed down her face as she watched mother and son. Ross came to her, held her tight, and let go. "I canna keep saying goodbye." He kissed her once more then turned to Ewan and Duncan. "'Tis time."

They gathered together and shouted, "Now or never!" The cry of the Jacobites.

Donnach grabbed each one in a hug, slapped them on the back, and wished them Godspeed.

The three men mounted their horses and rode through the archway of the castle. Their wives ran after them, watching them disappear down the hill. Eva locked arms with her, and Juliet placed her arm across Greer's shoulders. None of them spoke. Juliet's heart tore in two. Nothing would mend it until she saw Ross ride up that hill and back into her arms again.

Chapter Nine

"They have taken Inverness, Gordon Castle, and marched onto Perth. Lord Mar has seized the town and made it his headquarters. 'Tis a good day to be a Jacobite." Donnach leaned back in his chair after finishing breakfast. "He has gathered more than 12,000 men, more than enough to defeat the Sassenachs." He smiled at the women at the table. Jamie had already left for the village. "We shall win the fight."

A month had passed, and Juliet relished any news sent to Glenhaven. She spent her mornings in the woods after breakfast, sitting by the stream, dreaming of Ross. She made plans to tell him how she felt on his return. She would finally say the words he longed to hear, and then maybe that small piece of doubt inside her would disappear. During these morning visits, Juliet had time to think about their relationship and realized she played a part as much as he did when it came to trust.

The trees had begun to show their autumn colors. She wished they could watch the changes together. On warm days, she went in the water, walked to the rock, and sat by the falls. Reality would call her back, telling her to get on with her day.

Glynis and Donnach went on daily hunts. The women waited for their afternoon return then prepared the meats—be it squirrel, rabbit, or deer—some for now, most for later. The people in the village continued to harvest the fields and stock the barns and storage huts with oats, potatoes, and turnips.

Juliet longed to leave the breakfast table and have that one solitary hour in the woods. She glanced down the table to check Donnach. He appeared to be finished with his food and announcements.

Alec slipped from Greer's lap and ran to her. "Auntie," he said. "Play."

She took his tiny chin in her hand. "I will when I return." She made a habit of chasing him around the outside of the storage huts once a day. He would disappear behind one, and when she rounded the corner, it always startled him into fits of laughter. For some reason, he loved the surprise every time.

Donnach stood after one last swig of ale, the signal they could leave. Juliet hurried away after kissing Fiona's cheek and thanking Donnach for breakfast. She had dressed for the walk so she made her way to the back of the castle and out the door, heading for the path that led to the woods. The same one she and John walked during his stay.

John? Why am I thinking of him? Juliet wondered if he was part of the fight. He had worn civilian clothes when he came in August. He never joined the Army that she recalled. She hoped he and Ross did not cross paths.

Juliet heard the water before she emerged from the brush. It calmed her, reassuring her it was still there. "Please be all right, Ross," she prayed.

A cool breeze blew around her. She dropped to the ground and wrapped her shawl tighter around her shoulders. The waterfall seemed to say his name as it flowed over the bank of smaller rocks and shale. She closed her eyes to picture him and longed for his touch as she crumbled into a heap on the grass. She begged for dreams of him, happy times when war did not exist.

Her eyes flew open. Juliet had no idea how long she lay there. She sat up, took one last look around, and ran for the path. When she stepped out into the sunlight, Juliet saw Heather running toward her. "Juliet! Come quickly!"

Her heart began to pound. Heather stopped in front of her, tears in her eyes. "One of the lads from the village is here. He was sent to tell us two men were spotted in the forest on the other side of the village."

"Ross?"

"He dinna say." She looked at the ground and kicked at the dirt.

"What? There is something else. What are you not telling me?"

Heather bit her bottom lip. She lifted her head and blinked. "There is a third."

Juliet's stomach rolled over, and her mouth went dry. She closed her eyes then opened them. "Just tell me."

"The third is wrapped in brown cloth draped across the third horse."

"Dead?" Juliet placed her hand on her stomach.

"The lad told what he ken," Heather said. "We have to wait and see."

"I am not waiting!" Juliet ran for the back entrance of the castle. She rushed down the hall to the receiving room off the grand hall.

Juliet recognized the boy standing in the room from the village. He lived with his mother and older brother next to the blacksmith. "Cowan!" She grabbed him by the shoulders and looked into his eyes. "Who are the men?"

"We dinna ken, Madam." He shrugged. "They were too far off to see. Me older brother was hunting in the woods and heard voices. He got scared and ran home but not until he got a look." He laughed. "I am not scared of anything. I wouldna run, but he ran like a scared rabbit."

"Did your brother get a *good* look at the men?" Juliet asked.

"No, he was too busy pissing his pants." Cowan smirked. "Mum said it wasna right for two men to bring a dead one here." He crossed himself. "We dinna need spirits in the village, unless," he said as he looked up at Juliet, "they are one of us. Then mum's eyes went like this." He closed his hands and opened them wide "She ken they were no strangers. They *were* one of us."

"How long ago?" Juliet stared at Cowan then at Donnach.

"They might be through the village and up the hill by now," Cowan said. "I had to finish my porridge and feed the goats before I could come. Mum thought they were far enough away. I had time." Cowan appeared to like being the center of attention. He put his hands on his hips and said, "But she told me when I left, 'Lad, run as fast as ye can to the castle. Dinna stop till ye get there.'" He smiled at the group.

"Thank ye, boy," Donnach said, and placed a coin in Cowan's hand.

The boy's amber eyes lit up at the sight of the shiny piece in his palm.

"Give that to yer mum." Donnach tugged on Cowan's dark hair as he placed another small coin in the boy's palm. "Now on yer way!" He waved his hand, and Cowan scurried out the door.

"Da?" Heather stood in the opening with Greer. "What do ye think?"

"I think we go and see who is coming."

"I need to find Eva and tell her," Juliet said.

"Already done." Heather stepped aside to reveal Eva behind her.

The girls grouped together, giving each other support and strength. Heather said a Gaelic prayer, and they parted.

"I say we go to the edge of the woods and wait," Donnach said. "Heather, go find yer mum."

The wives followed Donnach through the castle and into the courtyard. He headed for the main path that led to the village. The road disappeared into the trees making it hard to see. Sun poked through the leaves casting shadows on the path, but some areas seemed to be in total darkness. All they could do was wait.

Juliet squinted to see. Three horses and two men should be easy to spot. She paced back and forth across the road. A rustling of leaves and far-off voices made her stop. She heard the clop, clopping of the horse's hooves. Juliet strained to see through the shadows. A dark outline of men and horses grew closer as she watched. "It is them."

Donnach stood in front of her, sword raised in one hand, pistol in the other. "Get behind me. We have no idea who they are."

The figures hit a patch of sun. The man leading the first horse was too short to be Ross. *Duncan?* He appeared to have dark hair, but not as round of shape as her brother-in-law. Another man walked much farther back holding the reins of two horses. He appeared to be the same height as the man at the front, although it was hard to tell. *No! Ross is dead?*

Juliet could not wait any longer. She lifted her skirt and began to run. Her feet slapped against the dirt road, moving her toward the dark, shadowy figures.

"Juliet!" Donnach called out to her. "No!"

She did not listen. Her legs would not stop moving. The forms coming toward her hit another sunny patch. Juliet could finally see the man in front. She had been right. Duncan, who'd grown an inch and lost some of his baby fat in a month's time, led the way. "It is Duncan!" she yelled out, hoping Donnach heard.

"Duncan!" Juliet kept running, locked onto the slow-moving figure in front of her. "Please, Duncan! Is Ross all right?"

She stopped as the distance closed between them. Her heart pounded, sweat rolled down the middle of her back and beaded across her forehead. She smelled the scent of crisp autumn leaves and dry grass in the air as she put her hands on her thighs to catch her breath. She took one breath in and let it slowly out.

When she looked up, Ross stood before her. Her knees buckled, and he caught her as she fell. He lifted her into his arms and carried her through the forest.

They stepped out of the shadows to find Donnach had his arms around Greer. She knew who was wrapped in the cloth. Her face was screwed up into a tight ball as tears streamed down her face. She broke from her father and ran at Ross. He placed Juliet on the ground and reached for his sister.

Greer would have none of it. She pulled away and yelled, "Ye promised!" Her arms flayed in the air. "To keep them safe!" She pounded on his chest, and Ross did not move a muscle, letting her hit him as much as she wanted.

Juliet watched as Greer punched and struck Ross until she dropped from sheer exhaustion. Her shoulders hunched, arms dangling at her sides. Wet strands of hair clung to her face. She looked at Donnach then Ross. "We got word. We are winning. How could this happen?"

Ross lowered his head. "'Tis war, Greer. Even the winning side loses men." He took her in his arms. "We wanted to bring him home to ye, have a proper burial."

Greer buried her head in his plaid and wept. Long, soulful moans came from her. Juliet wanted to give her comfort but held her ground. Ross must take care of his sister.

Juliet noticed Eva had not made contact with Duncan. She nodded her head to tell her to go to him. Eva shook hers, and Juliet realized she was right. Now was not the time to celebrate a homecoming.

~ * ~

Ewan Kincaid would be laid to rest on his own land. Greer's slim frame could barely make it down the hill let alone to the church in the nearby town where the main chapel was located. Juliet had visited there once with Ross to buy spices and thread. She remembered he insisted she buy ribbon for her hair. The service would be held instead at the small chapel in the MacLaren village, and Ewan's relatives would take the body home.

A green and black tartan plaid covered the wooden casket. Bagpipe music played as the entourage walked behind the wagon from the castle. Donnach carried Alec in his arms. Greer had him dressed in Kinkaid green and black plaid. His white blond hair stood out as a beacon of light in the shadows of the forest. Juliet had her arm tucked through Ross', blinking over and over to keep the tears at bay. Heather had Greer by one arm and Jamie the other. Duncan held on to both his wife and mother. Glynis drove the funeral wagon, keeping the horses in check. The servants followed behind them in a silent procession.

People from the village waited outside the chapel with members from the MacGregor and Kincaid clans. Rows of Kincaid men with various shades of orange hair stood side by side, solemn looks on their faces. A small group of taller, leaner men in red and green plaid, made their way over to Jamie.

"Did the Kincaids come back from the fight for the funeral?" Juliet whispered to Ross.

"Aye, and a few MacGregors. Most will return to Perth tomorrow."

Juliet sniffed and held her breath then let out a sigh. "I do not want to think about tomorrow."

He squeezed her hand. "Then we shall not."

The priest stepped out of the chapel and held both arms in the air. He chanted a few words in Gaelic. The people said a phrase in return. Since she did not understand the language, Juliet picked up signals from Ross and others what she should do. She folded her hands when a prayer was given and crossed herself when the others did.

Jamie and Duncan held onto Greer for most of the ceremony. When the priest said the final blessing, she collapsed on the ground. She reached her arms toward the back of the wagon where the casket lay, sobbing. A man that looked eerily similar to Ewan climbed into the seat, taking the reins from Glynis. He shook the reins, and the horse trotted off down the road. Juliet stood watching with the rest of the family until the horse and wagon disappeared from sight.

During the service, dark clouds had assembled in the sky. A drop of rain landed on Juliet's cheek. She noticed wet, dark spots on her cloak. Dried leaves swirled around her feet as the wind gathered strength. "A storm is coming, Ross."

He nodded in agreement and walked to where his father stood. Far off in the distance, a bolt of lightning crackled in the sky. Juliet pulled her cloak around her, waiting for direction.

"We must head back," Donnach said as he glanced up at the sky. "By my account, we should be back before the storm comes."

Glynis swept Alec onto her back and bounced him up and down. "Pony!" Alec cried and showed a baby teeth smile. "Go!" Glynis ran for the road that led up the hill.

"Juliet," Greer called. "Would ye mind helping Glynis with him today?" Her green eyes appeared to have sunk into her face and had deep dark circles under them.

"Not at all. You take care."

The canopy of trees kept most of the rain from them until they emerged into the field. The drops came steadily now, but Juliet knew it was just the start of the storm. Thunder boomed behind them. Alec screamed and covered his ears. "Mum!" He held out his arms, but Greer did not respond.

"How about Auntie?" Juliet pointed at her chest. "Will she do?"

Distracted for a moment, Alec nodded and came to her. "Auntie." He snuggled against her body. Juliet's heart broke again as it had done all day.

Eva caught up to Juliet. "I need yer advice. I have something to say to the family. And I think it has to be today, before Duncan returns to Perth."

"Can it wait, Eva?" Juliet locked eyes with her.

"No." Eva shook her head. "I need the family to know I am with child."

Chapter Ten

Juliet's eyes welled with tears. She pulled Eva into a hug with her free hand. "I am so happy for you." Her stomach churned, telling a different story. "Of course, you must share the news. Duncan and Ross leave tomorrow."

"'Tis wonderful having them home." Eva sighed. "But the reason that brought them here…" She glanced over at Greer and shook her head.

"A baby may be just what we need." Juliet placed her arm across Eva's shoulders.

"Two would be better." Eva looked at her from the corner of her eye.

"I am starting to worry, Eva. I have been married since May, and you had five nights with your husband."

"Dinna worry, Juliet. It will happen."

"And what may ye lassies be gossiping about?" Duncan laughed as he wedged between them. "Och, I forgot my manners. I shouldna be joking today."

"It is all right, husband." Eva patted his arm. "Ye have been through hard times. I am sure ye had to use humor at the oddest times the past month."

"Aye," Duncan said as he stopped in front of the castle. "But now, we sit in Perth doing nothing. Lord Mar canna make up his mind. I dinna ken what he plans. Most of northern Scotland is under Jacobite rule. We need to keep fighting, but we do nothing. Ross says there is word we may attack Stirling Castle soon."

Fiona motioned for the group to come inside. "Why are ye standing in the rain? Ye need to come in. The MacGregors and Kinkaids will wait in the village until the storm passes. They will come to pay their respects to Greer before they leave. I need yer help."

A clap of thunder reminded them of the nearing storm, and they rushed inside.

"Juliet," Fiona said as she pulled her aside. "Do ye think ye can speak to Greer? She took to her bed as soon as we came home. She told me to watch the wee one." She shook her head. "So unlike her."

"She is in mourning. I am sure she will see that Alec needs her and be up and around in a day or two." Juliet patted her mother-in-law's hand. "I will tend to her."

Juliet found Greer curled on her side in the bed, facing the wall. "Greer? May I come in?" She took the silence for yes or that she slept. When she drew closer, Juliet saw Greer's eyes wide open, staring at the wall. "Greer?" She sat on the edge of the bed and waited.

"Juliet," Greer whispered.

Juliet wiggled closer to hear. "Yes? I am here."

"Take care of Alec."

"I will, but you are his mother."

"Aye, the only parent he has." Greer sniffed. "That is why I ask ye—ye and Ross—to raise my son if something happens to me." She rolled over and grabbed Juliet's hand. "Promise me ye will."

"I am only saying yes because it will not happen. You will live for a very long time." She bit her lip from saying more. Greer may even find another husband someday. "Do me a favor. Come to the grand hall and greet the guests."

"I canna." Greer rolled back.

"You can, and you will. Besides, you need to ask Ross if he is willing to take on Alec." Juliet crossed her arms, eyes on Greer's back. "I will not do it for you."

"I will come for an hour. That is all." Greer turned her head to look at Juliet. She had no color in her cheeks, and her hair lay flat against her head.

"Could I?" Juliet gestured to the brush on a table.

Greer gave her a nudge. "If ye get up, I will let ye fix me hair."

Juliet did her best to make Greer presentable. She changed her dress, brushed out her hair, and pinched her cheeks. She stood still as a post, and Juliet came in close to check if she breathed. "There! You are ready."

Juliet guided Greer through the hallway and down the stairs. Ross and Duncan were in deep discussion outside the receiving room. Ross glanced up when he saw them. "My two bonny lasses." He rushed to help Juliet maneuver Greer down the last of the steps. "I will take her, Juliet."

She followed them into the grand hall, and Duncan joined Eva who stood waiting by his parents. As she walked to her seat, Juliet smelled the smoked meat that had been prepared for this sad occasion. The burning peat fire had been freshly stoked, and the two smells mingled together. She wondered if she'd be able to eat after the day she had.

Juliet's eyes slid down the table. Glynis ate from a plate of food, sopping up meat juice with her bread. Donnach sliced into the large cut of venison and tore the chunks of meat from the bone. Little Alec had buttermilk around his mouth, dribbling drops from his cup onto the table. Heather and Jamie had their heads together, oblivious to the others.

Suddenly, a gasp came from Eva. "Oh, my!" She looked around at the family, ran to a bucket at the end of the table, and threw up.

Fiona set her glass of wine down and leaned forward to check on Eva. "Ye all right now, daughter?" she asked. "It will pass. It always does."

Juliet thought that was a strange thing to say to someone who felt sick. It could pass, but then again, she could be violently ill. *Oh! She is not ill. It is because of the baby.* Her hand went to her own stomach, and her heart dropped. *Will I ever get to experience that?*

Duncan brushed Eva's hair back and offered her his handkerchief. "I think we should tell the family, lass"

"I..." Eva took his hand then made eye contact with everyone in the room. "I dinna mean to announce this today." She turned to Duncan and whispered in his ear.

Duncan held up his hand. "Eva would like me to share our news. I am going to be a father!" He stepped back as a smile spread across his face. "Did ye hear that, everyone? Eva's with child!"

"'Tis good news on a sad day," Donnach said with a knowing smile.

Juliet studied Donnach's face. He did not seem surprised by the news. *Did he already know? And Fiona? Am I the last to know?*

Ross took Juliet's hand. She leaned against his solid frame, grateful he knew how much it hurt to hear the news. She prayed no one would look her way.

"Congratulations, brother! I will be next," Heather called out and nudged Jamie. They smiled at each other. "But today is not the day for us to talk of bairns. Greer and Alec are the priority." She looked at her sister. "Ye are staying at Glenhaven?"

She nodded. "I have talked to Ewan's da. He agrees it would be best for me. I will send Alec for visits."

"Greer." Fiona handed her a plate of food. "Eat. Please."

Greer shook her head. "I am not hungry, Mum."

"Ye havena eaten for days, lass."

"Then I will have a glass of wine."

Juliet poured a glass and took it to her. "You should sit."

"I have business with Ross first." Greer's eyes widened. "If I may talk to yer husband alone?"

Juliet went to her seat and watched the brother and sister from a distance. Ross' face changed to one of shock. He appeared to argue with Greer, and she placed her hands on her hips. He hung his head and nodded. She squeezed his arm then turned away. *He agreed.* Juliet glanced over at Alec, banging the cup on the table. He had no idea what happened to his father or that his aunt and uncle agreed to raise him if Greer should die. The day could not get any worse.

"Did ye ken?" Ross whispered as he slipped in next to her.

"She asked me earlier. Ross," Juliet said as she took his hand. "Why is Greer thinking of her death?"

"What better day?" He squeezed her hand. "Alec will grow tall and strong. He will take care of his mum. That is what I told her. But I said we would raise him if anything should happen. She plans to tell the family later, after she talks to the Kinkaids."

"Would they agree?"

"They would. They ken we wouldna keep the boy from them." Ross reached for his mug and drained the contents. He held it in the air, and a servant brought the pitcher. "Leave it," he told the young man. "It has been a long day."

~ * ~

After the funeral dinner came to a close, Ross took Juliet to their room. "There is something I need to tell ye."

Her heart started to race. "I have a feeling I do not want to know."

His face had a look of regret and sadness. "Aye." He took a breath. "I had a talk with Duncan. He is not going back with me tomorrow. I want him to stay here. Now that Eva is with child it seems best. If the English soldiers come—and they will—his presence can only help."

"No! Why do you go back alone? Duncan said you are sitting in Perth waiting for Lord Mar to decide the next move. Stay here until he does."

"If I go back, I may have his ear. Precious time is being wasted. We need to keep fighting. Now or never."

"I heard you say that before you left. Is that a battle cry?"

"Aye, and a good one. The Old Pretender wrote to the Duke of Berwick in August. Erskine," Ross said as he cleared his throat. "Or should I say, Lord Mar, passed along his message to the chieftains at the secret meeting."

Juliet cocked her head. "The Old Pretender? I believe that is the name people call James Stuart?"

Ross nodded.

"What did he, The Old Pretender, say in his letter to the duke?" Juliet asked.

"He wrote, 'I think it is now more than ever. *Now or Never*.'"

"Oh." That was a strong message. Juliet could see how the Highland clans would claim the words. "And what of Lord Mar? Why does he sit in Perth doing nothing?"

"I dinna ken. On the twenty-second of this month, James Stuart appointed Mar commander of the Jacobite army. He needs to take command. Mar has trouble making up his mind, deciding what to do next. The Old Pretender has to find a way to set sail from France and lead his troops. We are waiting for his arrival and are ready to follow him."

"Ross, I have an idea. What if you stayed until the festival of Samhain? You could make sure the crops are properly stored, the cattle slaughtered, and we are ready for winter. Alec would love to hear stories of the fairies. This is the time they can easily come into our world, or so I have heard from the people in the village."

"Ye make good points, Juliet. I will sleep on it." Ross pulled his shirt over his head and slipped into bed.

Juliet let her shift drop to the floor. "And it would give us more time for this," she said as she lifted the sheet to join him.

He pulled her toward him. "I want ye, Juliet." He breathed into her hair. "Now." He flipped her onto her back.

Juliet gazed up into his green eyes and saw his love for her. "Oh, Ross, you can have me every night if you stay."

"I will stay until Samhain. Then I return to Perth." His lips came closer, and her body tensed in anticipation. "My sweet Juliet, how ye tempt me." He covered her mouth with his.

The kiss made her come alive. Juliet wrapped her arms tighter around him, hoping he felt the urgency. Ross rose up on his hands to stare down at her. He lifted his brow and gave her a half-cocked smile. "Tonight, we start our family."

~ * ~

"Faeries?" Alec's green eyes widened in fascination.

"Aye." Ross tousled the boy's blond hair. "The gude faeries. If ye see a wee little person dressed in green running through the forest…" he said as he stared off into the woods. "Ye may have spotted a faerie."

Juliet sat at the edge of the water watching the two interact. They had coaxed Greer to come with them to the spring. She sat on a rock, staring into the water. Her willowy frame seemed thinner each time Juliet saw her. She had barely eaten since Duncan and Ross brought Ewan home.

"Greer?" Juliet rose from the grass and took the basket of food to her. "Would you like some bread? Cheese?" Greer shook her head.

"Take a look inside. You might change your mind." She placed the basket on the rock beside her.

"Cheese!" Alec ran to Juliet, holding up his arms. She lifted him, and he wiggled down to the basket to make his choice.

Instead of eating the piece of goat's milk cheese, he held it to his mother's closed mouth. "Cheese." He stared at her. She pretended to take a bite. "No." He moved it so it touched her lips. "Cheese," he said and waited.

Greer shut her eyes then opened them as a small bubble of laughter came from her. Alec saw his chance and popped the piece in her mouth.

"Ye have quite the lad, Greer." Ross took him from Juliet. He reached in the basket and tore off the end of the bread. "We will eat this as I tell ye more about Samhain." Ross gave Alec the end piece to chew on and settled him on the rock next to his mother. "Samhain marks the end of summer, wee Alec. 'Tis a sign to the farmers to harvest their crops and get ready for the dark days ahead. They also say 'tis the time for witches and faeries." He tickled the boy's belly. "But far more important, we need to make ready for winter. The cold dark days will soon be upon us. If we play and not work, then we have nothing to sustain us."

"A very good lecture, sir," Juliet said with a wink. "I think the boy may be more interested in the stories."

Ross bit his top lip, looked at the sky, and sighed. "Ye never cross a faerie, Alec. Ye leave them gifts and hope they like them. In return, they may do our chores, some threshing, or weaving in secret. The females are verra small, verra beautiful, but can be vicious to mortals. So ye have to be careful. They say the Faerie Queen wears green and rides a horse with silver bells plaited in its mane."

Alec mouth hung open. "I want one."

Ross threw back his head and laughed. "I think they are more trouble than they are worth."

Alec joined in the laughter. Juliet noticed a twitch in the corner of Greer's mouth.

"And we have to ready for All Hallow's Evening." Juliet counted in her head. "We have five days to make ready."

During the next few days, Juliet kept Greer and Alec busy hollowing out turnips for candles and making masks for the family to scare away the evil spirits. She talked with the cook about making soul cakes so Alec could go from room to room in the castle begging for the treats. The family came together to make it a special day for the boy.

"Ye are helping us mend our hearts," Fiona said to Juliet on the day of the event. "And ye will make a good mother one day." She left the room as quickly as she came.

Juliet longed to run after her. Fiona may have advice or a secret to help her. Was she doing something wrong when it came to love making and conceiving a child? It looked so simple from the outside. A couple married then announced the wife is with child.

"Argh!" A small masked boy ran into the room.

"Oh!" Juliet's hand flew to her heart as she pretended to back away in fright. "Please do not eat me."

"Auntie." Alec removed the mask. "'Tis me. Alec. I willna eat ye. I love ye."

Tears filled her eyes. That little boy may be the only one in the family who truly loved her. She crouched down and threw out her arms. Alec ran to her. "And I love you. I will do anything to protect you. Remember that."

Chapter Eleven

Ross and Juliet took Alec to the village for the All Hallow's Evening bonfire. They filled a turnip with embers from that fire to take back to the castle. Ross had Alec draped across his shoulder asleep before the night ended. The boy did not waken even as Ross mounted his horse for the ride back to the castle.

Juliet held the torch to light the way. She juggled the turnip between her legs praying it would not fall to the ground. Alec would be disappointed if it was not there when he woke.

Donnach had added extra lights in the windows and standing torches around the castle for the night. Juliet was not sure if he did it for Alec or really believed it kept bad spirits away. When they reached the stable, she waited for Ross to dismount. He laid Alec in a pile of hay. "He sleeps with the dead." Ross smiled.

"Do not say that on a night like this." Juliet handed him the turnip and slipped from the saddle. "Or around his mum." She jabbed Ross in the chest and shook her head. "Men."

"Oh, so I am a beef-head."

"Not as bad as that." Juliet stuck out her lower lip. "I would not have married you then."

Ross' hand slipped around her waist and tugged her closer. "I would have married ye, beef-head or not."

Juliet giggled. "Stop. You will wake Alec. Let us get him to his bed."

"And us to ours. 'Tis our last night."

The fun atmosphere disappeared. The walls closed in on her, making it hard to breath. Her stomach rumbled as if she were to be sick. Juliet placed her hand on it.

"Are ye all right?" Ross took her arm and led her to a bench.

"I am fine. You reminded me of something I tried to forget."

"I am sorry, lass." He crouched in front of her. "Forgive me?" He kissed the top of her hand then the other.

Juliet slid her hands out from his and reached for his face. "There is nothing to forgive. You did not ask for war." She ran her hand along his jaw, feeling the stubble that had already begun to appear after his morning shave. Her thumb traced the outline of his mouth. She ran her finger down the bridge of his nose, studying the straightness so she would not forget. "We should go."

Ross leaned forward and kissed her lips so lightly, she shivered from the touch. He pulled her cloak around her, lifted Alec from the hay, and guided her from the stable to the castle.

Fiona greeted them as they came down the hall. "Greer is in the drawing room waiting. She wants to see Alec."

Juliet followed Ross into the room. "I am sorry, sister. He is fast asleep. He will have to tell ye of his adventures in the morning. I will carry him to yer suite."

Greer tried to smile, but Juliet still worried. Her face showed no joy at their arrival. She did not speak as she rose from her chair. When they got to the top of the stairs, Juliet placed her hand on Ross' back. "I will wait for you in our room." She headed off in the opposite direction of Greer's chambers.

Juliet removed her dusty cloak and sat at her table in front of the mirror. She pulled pins from her hair and brushed it until smooth. The chestnut locks had a slight curl at the ends, not stick straight or thick waves. Her mother had told her how lucky she was to have such beautiful hair. She would sit and comb out Juliet's hair every night, telling her stories of when she was a little girl. Those were the only moments Juliet felt close to her mother. Once the day began, she had rules to follow and proper etiquette came first, above anything else.

After her hair was done, Juliet removed her dress and corset. She could breathe freely now. She glanced back in the mirror, studying the woman she saw. Dark blue eyes stared back at her. She puckered her lips. Plump and full, she liked that. Her mother made sure her skin stayed creamy white. An umbrella always had accompanied them when they walked in the sun. Juliet leaned closer to the mirror and swore her nose and cheeks had a bit of redness from being outside most of the day. "Mother would not approve."

"But I do." Ross leaned against the doorway, arms folded. "Ye look bonny in the candlelight." He slipped off his plaid and kilt, wearing only his shirt.

Juliet rose from her seat and took his hand. "Hold me all night."

"Dinna worry. I willna let ye go. I need to remember the feel of yer body to sustain me through the coming days."

Juliet buried her head in his shoulder. She sent Ross off to battle once before and never imagined she would have to let him go a second time. "You will be the only one to leave in the morning?" She met his eyes, trying hard not to cry.

"Aye, we spoke of it. Now we are done." His hands gripped her shoulders. Ross held her back and studied her face. "Ye are strong. I ken it the first time I laid eyes on ye. Ye are a MacLaren, Juliet. Let that guide ye through the coming days." His lips found hers as he guided her toward the bed.

They fell as one onto the goose down mattress, lips never parting. Ross rolled onto her, pulling her shift over her breasts. She felt his urgency and relaxed under his weight. He held her hands above her head and trailed kisses down her neck.

"Ross," Juliet whispered. "Get on with it."

He threw his head back and laughed. "There is my bonny lass."

They found pleasure in each other throughout the night, while Juliet pushed any other thought from her mind. She would not let darkness overshadow the night, not if this might be the last time with her Highlander husband.

~ * ~

The morning he was to leave, Ross chased Alec, who brandished a sword, around the courtyard one last time before he made his leave. The boy turned and set his feet in place. He held his sword high in the air, ready for a fight, reminding him so much of Ewan. He thought back to the day when he challenged his friend to a mock duel, fighting their way into the feast given for his bride.

Juliet. Ross let out a breath of air. *If I truly ken how ye felt. Do ye love me? Is it that hard for ye to say? No.* Ross shook his head. *I ken ye love me. I can wait for ye to tell me.*

"Och!" Ross had let his guard down, and a pain shot through his lower leg as Alec's whacked him with his toy sword.

~ * ~

"Be careful with Uncle Ross!" Greer called to her son.

Juliet linked arms with her as they walked into the courtyard. "He is growing too fast," she said to her sister-in-law. "He looks more and more like a MacLaren every day."

"He is a Kinkaid," Greer said. "But I can see how ye think that. His eyes."

As if he knew they spoke of him, Alec flashed a grin their way. Ross swooped in from behind and grabbed him around the waist. He ran to his horse as Alec squealed, threw the boy on the saddle, and then jumped behind him. Alec clapped his hands in delight.

"'Tis All Soul's Day." Greer looked up at the sky. "Do ye think he is here? Watching his son?"

Caught off guard, Juliet scrambled for an answer. "I think he is always watching." She squeezed Greer's hand. Her skin felt warmer than usual. "Greer?" Juliet faced her. "Are you ill?"

"No, I am just tired."

Juliet lifted her hand to Greer's forehead. Beads of sweat gathered along her hairline. Her cheeks were flushed pink. Earlier, Juliet had hoped it was a sign Greer recovered from the trauma of Ewan's death, but now, she was not so sure.

Ross rode around the courtyard with Alec while they waited for the rest of the family to join them. Juliet debated if she should tell him about Greer or let him go to Perth without any burdens.

Duncan, Eva, and Glynis finally appeared, followed by Donnach and Fiona.

"Heather stayed in the village last night," Donnach told his son. "She would like ye to stop by the blacksmiths on yer way."

"Aye, I will, Da," he answered. "Glynis." Ross lifted his chin, and she went to his side. The two had their own secret language, and Glynis always seemed to know what Ross meant. He dropped Alec down to her and dismounted.

Ross started the rounds of goodbyes. He spoke with his brother, now looking more like Ross after the weight loss and growth spurt. He moved on to his mother and father, hugging and kissing Fiona as she moaned in his arms. When he stepped in front of Glynis, she leaned her head forward. Without saying a word, Ross touched his forehead to hers, showing their powerful bond. Alec, still in Glynis' arms, wrapped one arm around her neck and the other around Ross'. Juliet wiped away a tear as she watched the scene unfold before her. Ross then held out his arms to Greer. She stepped forward, and he gently brought her to his chest. He kissed the side of her head and spoke only to her.

Juliet trembled as she waited. Her heart already felt torn in two and would not mend until he returned. Ross locked eyes with her, and she ran to him. He swept her into his arms, holding her so close she could feel his heartbeat. "I will send word every chance I can," he whispered in her ear. "Alec and Greer need ye. They all need ye." He kissed her cheek. "I hope the next time I see ye, a Stuart will be king."

She turned her face upward, begging for a kiss. Ross pressed his mouth against hers to take one last taste.

The last week had been filled with sadness, and Juliet decided it was not the time to tell Ross she loved him. He might take it wrong and think she only said it because he was going off to battle. Her heart ached as she held back, hoping she would get the chance one day. "Come back to me," she whispered.

Juliet stood frozen as he walked to his horse. Ross gracefully swung his body up into the saddle. He nudged the horse, speaking gently as they made their way to the road. Then he stopped, glanced back, and lifted his hand in farewell.

~ * ~

Even as the November days grew shorter and colder, Glynis and Juliet played outside with Alec every day. He never tired of chasing them around the storage huts and fighting Glynis with his sword. Juliet was drawn to the stables and the horses. She had not ridden as much as she liked. "I would like to teach Alec to ride. What do you think, Glynis?"

"That Da would say a man should be the one, but I am all for it. Besides," she said as she looked around. "Not too many men left around here." She shrugged. "What can he say?"

Juliet took that as approval. The MacLarens had a few ponies. She chose one for Alec's first solo ride. They followed the same schedule day after day—running, playing, riding. Alec would be so worn out that he would sleep until supper. In the afternoon, Juliet and Glynis would help with mending or any task Fiona needed them to do to help pass the time.

One unusual warm November morning, Juliet walked Alec around the fenced-in pen as he sat on the pony. She and Glynis had many conversations during that time. She began to feel closer to her sister-in-law.

"We have been doing this for weeks," Juliet said as she lifted Alec from the pony after the lesson. "Tomorrow I will let him have the reins."

"I think he is ready." Glynis nodded. "Ye are a good teacher."

"Thank you." Juliet looked at the ground. "You are the only one who does not ask if I am with child or when I will have one. Why is that?"

"First, 'tis none of me business. When ye are, ye will tell us."

"And second?" Juliet lifted her head to look at Glynis.

"'Tis nothing."

"I think it is." Juliet closed one eye and studied her. "Do you want to marry one day?"

"Perhaps." Glynis lifted a shoulder. "If I find the right man. I am perfectly happy the way I am."

"If you find this man, you will want children."

Glynis glared at her. "I am not saying that."

"Oh." Juliet's eyes widened. "Is the second thing, you do not want children?"

"Is that a bad thing?" Glynis glanced away. "I dinna ken what I want, Juliet, when it comes to family. I do ken I want a man who wants to travel the world and find adventure." Her face softened, and she smiled as she turned toward Juliet.

"That sounds wonderful. I hope you find someone who wishes for those same things."

"Aye! Before Da marries me off to the next man who stops this way." Glynis laughed.

Juliet giggled. "I hope he would let you have a say in the matter."

"Da? Och, no." Glynis shrugged. She took the pony's reins and walked it to the stable. "Let us get the wee one home to his mum."

Greer! She hid the fact she was not well. Only Juliet suspected. She picked at her food and sipped wine with the family. They were happy she sat at the table and ate. Juliet wondered if anyone noticed how thin she had gotten. Surely Fiona had if no one else. Why didn't she do something? Or maybe she had tried, and Greer rejected her help. Juliet took Alec's hand, and he grabbed Glynis' when she caught up to them.

Juliet glanced over at her. "Do you think Greer is all right?"

"No. She hasna recovered yet. I was hoping to see a little life in her by now." She cocked her head toward Alec. "For his sake."

"I think it is more than that." Juliet took a breath and whispered, "I think she is sick. She has had a fever since the day Ross left."

Glynis lifted her brows. "And ye are just telling me now?"

"I hoped she would say something."

"If ye ken ye should have told us," Glynis said in a stern tone as she put her hand on her hip. "Greer has kept to herself. We all are guilty of not noticing." She dropped her arm. "I shouldna be mad at ye. That lassie can act like a martyr. She has been doing it since she was a wee bairn. I will speak to Mum when we get back."

"Thank you."

Alec skipped ahead and into the courtyard. His white blond hair shone in the sun as he bounced along. Relief flooded through her, glad she told Glynis her suspicions. They followed Alec into the grand hall where cheese and bread had been set out for their return.

"There ye are!" Fiona said as she came into the room. "I will tell Greer ye are here."

"Mum! Wait." Glynis followed after her.

"It is just you and me, Alec. What would you like to eat?"

"Ye talk funny." He wrinkled his nose.

"What?" She touched the tip and smiled. "You just noticed?"

Alec giggled. "Donny call ye a 'bloody sassy'."

"Does he now?" Juliet's stomach flipped. *He is calling me a bloody Sassenach? Still?* She thought they were past their mistrust of each other. Donnach gave reports at breakfast whenever he got word from the Jacobites, sometimes asking her questions. *About England. How we think, what we would do in a certain situation.* Juliet collapsed in a chair.

"Auntie?" Alec tapped her arm and made a face.

"You are a little tyke." She took his chin and lightly shook it.

"Grrr," he growled as he held up his hands.

"What if we get this wolf something to eat?" Juliet petted his head. "He might not be so mean and nasty then."

Alec nodded and climbed in a chair next to her. Juliet had lost her appetite but filled a plate of food for him. She sat with the child as he ate, listening to his babbling. Some words made sense, and others did not. She tried to nod in the appropriate places. He blinked and rubbed his eyes, a sign she came to recognize as being tired. He laid his head on the table and would soon be fast asleep.

Glynis burst into the room. "Greer is taken to her bed, and Mum has sent for the doctor." She paused and looked at Alec. "I will take the wee one to Greer's room. But ye stay here, Juliet. Da has news. Tell him to wait for my return." She lifted the sleeping bundle into her arms and left Juliet alone in the room.

Juliet squeezed her hands together, wishing for good news. News that would send Ross home and make her feel safe again. She shifted in her seat as Donnach strode into the room.

"I have sent for Heather and Jamie. The rest of the family should be here soon," he said as he walked past her without so much as a look.

"Good afternoon to you, sir." If he had no manners, Juliet would still use hers.

Donnach nodded his head in affirmation, grumbling as he checked inside his plaid. "Here 'tis." He spoke to himself and smiled as he held up a long folded paper. "News we have been waiting for." His eyes lit up when he saw the others file into the room. "Och, there ye are, Duncan. May I have a word?"

Duncan walked up to his father, and Eva scurried over to Juliet. "I feel like I hardly speak with ye! Ye take young Alec out every morning then tend the horses. We sew in the afternoons, but we are not alone. Are ye all right?"

"As well as can be expected." Juliet sat back in her chair. "And you? Are you still getting ill from the baby?" She eyed Eva's stomach. With all the clothes, she could not see a bump.

"'Tis better. I dinna think Duncan could take much more." She giggled and looked over at him. "So handsome, but I think I like the rounder Duncan better."

"Oh?" Juliet lifted an eyebrow.

"More to love." Eva pulled up her shoulders and grinned.

The rest of the family, minus Greer, made their way into the room. Donnach took a head count. "We are all here." He glanced at Fiona. "Greer?"

"The girl is exhausted. The fever took her at her weakest. The doctor said she should be fine in a week or so."

"Good to hear." Donnach cleared his throat. "There is news. On the tenth of November, Lord Mar led his troops to Stirling castle where the English army had made their headquarters. Spies informed the British general of Mar's action. So the general, Duke of Argyll, moved his army to Sheriffmuir. The two armies finally met on the battlefield three days later."

"Who won, Da?" Duncan sat forward, eager to hear the news.

Juliet wondered the same. Donnach took too long to get to the most important part.

"We outnumbered them, but from what is written here, both sides claimed victory."

Glynis stood and placed her hands on her hips. "Ye mean no one won the battle?"

"Aye," Donnach said. "It seems so. The Jacobite army withdrew to Perth, although they claim victory."

"Any word of Ross?" Juliet's voice shook.

Donnach slipped his hand back in his plaid and pulled out another letter. "'Tis for ye." He held it out.

Juliet flew from her seat, grabbed the letter from his hand, and tore it open.

Juliet, My Love,

I am writing to let ye ken I am alive and well. I have also sent Da a letter. Hopefully, he has read it to the family by now. I survived the battle, but as in all war, we had losses. Our soldiers outnumbered theirs so we are claiming victory.

I am in Perth with the MacLaren clan. We all survived the battle. The Kincaids and MacGregors are not as lucky. Each lost men. I have heard James, The Old Pretender, is trying to raise money in France and find passage to Scotland, but it might not be until December when he steps foot on Scottish soil.

Be brave, my love. I dream of holding ye in me arms every night. One day soon, it will be real.

I send all my love. I love ye, wife.

Ross

She hugged the letter to her heart. *I love you, too. When you come home, I will tell you in person.* "He is safe." She smiled at the family. "But will not be coming home soon. James plans to come to Scotland to lead his army."

"'Tis about bloody time!" Donnach raised his mug of ale then took a long drink. "The clans need to see their leader. They will fight and follow him till the end."

Chapter Twelve

A light snow dusted the castle's hill and its valley below. Juliet wore her warmest wool dress and cloak as she headed to the stable. She promised to bring Alec's pony to the courtyard for a visit. He wanted to show his mother how he could ride on his own.

Greer's fever broke after a few days of rest and cool compressions. Juliet thought the leeches did no good, but the doctor insisted. He recommended she eat all meals in bed until she was strong enough to come down the stairs by herself.

"The MacLarens are strong," Juliet told the pony. "That is what Ross told me. Greer has had an awful time. Now that December is here, she can start anew." She glanced out the door. "Like the fresh fallen snow."

Juliet tugged on the reins. "Come on, Lil' Horsie." She smiled at the name Alec had given the pony. "You have a job to do."

Alec waited at the door of the castle, clapping his hands, as she stepped inside the courtyard. "Lil' Horsie!" He looked up at Greer. "Watch me, Mummy." He ran to Juliet's outstretched arms, and she slipped him onto the pony's back. After handing him the reins, she stepped back.

"Good job, Alec," Greer called out to him as he rounded the outdoor yard twice.

On the third lap, Juliet noticed Glynis had Greer by the arm. Her knees buckled, and she dropped to the ground.

"Greer!" Fiona rushed to her, followed by Donnach.

"Andra! Nessa!" He yelled for the servant girls.

They ran from the castle. “Sir?” Their eyes fell on Greer, and they ran to help.

Juliet jogged toward the pony and took the reins from Alec’s hands. His eyes were wide and round, staring at the scene at the castle door. “Come.” She put out her arms. “They will help your mum.”

He fell into her arms without a whimper. As she carried the boy toward the entrance to the castle, Juliet heard a voice call to her from the courtyard. “Madam!”

“Cowan?” The village boy seemed to appear out of nowhere.

“The Laird? Is he home?” Cowan panted and placed his hands on his knees. “I ran the whole way.”

“What? Tell me.”

“Is he here, Madam?” His voice quivered, and he shifted from one foot to the other. “Please.”

Juliet sensed his fear. “If you watch Alec, I will get him.”

She rushed into the castle and up the stairs. “Donnach? Cowan from the village is here. He needs to give you a message.”

“I will be right there.” He called out from Greer’s room then his gray head poked out the door. “What is it, lass?”

Juliet shook her head. “He will only speak with you.”

He followed her back down the steps to the waiting boy. “Cowan, how is ye mum?” Donnach slapped his shoulder.

“She sent ye these.” He handed Donnach a brown sack.

Donnach peeked inside. “Her biscuits. Tell her I much appreciate it. Nothing like them.” He held the sack out to Cowan. “Help yerself.”

“Mum will yank my ears out if she ken.” He gave Donnach a lopsided grin.

“We willna tell her then.” He turned to Juliet and held out the bag. “Daughter?”

Her stomach flipped, and she held up her hand. *How can anyone eat at a time like this?* “No, thank you.”

“Well then, Cowan,” Donnach said. “What brings ye up here on this cold day?”

“The soldiers are coming.”

Donnach lifted a brow. “The MacLaren clan returns?”

"No," he said as he shook his head, dark locks moving in all directions. "The English, sir. They are on the other side of the ridge. Gordon says they will be in the village soon."

"He kens to hide the weapons?"

"Aye."

"Thank ye. Now get home before the storm comes." Donnach looked up at the gray clouds gathering in the sky. He slipped coins into the boy's hand and gently gave him a push.

Juliet's body shook. Her hands trembled. She could not stop them, no matter what she tried.

"Look at ye. Shivering in the cold. Let us go inside." Donnach took her by the arm and guided her to his receiving room. "Sit."

"What do they want? Why are they coming here?" Juliet swallowed hard. Donnach poured two glasses of whiskey, handing her one.

"Drink." He nudged his chair back with his knee and sat on the edge. "We ken they would come. I told ye once, I would do what I need to do. Ye agreed to help. It may not come to that. We will wait and see what they want."

"How do they dare travel through Scotland? I thought the Jacobites had control of the northern section."

"There have been no skirmishes in the past weeks, and since Sheriffmuir, no major battles. They may feel it safe to travel. King George must have a message for me or is checking to see if I am here at Glenhaven." He folded his hands on the table. "All we can do is wait. Go to yer room, and I will send for ye when the time comes."

Juliet nodded and rose from her seat. She glided along the stone floor in a trance. When she reached the second floor, she did not head for her room, but turned and went up the next flight of stairs. She walked to the furthest tower and entered the rounded room. Juliet had a clear view from the higher vantage point and her wool dress and cloak would keep her warm as she watched for the soldiers. As she waited, cold air nipped at her cheeks, blowing her hair in every direction.

Watching the clouds gather over the woods, flashes of red suddenly appeared through the bare trees. *Five men.* The horses came out of the forest and into the field and would arrive at the castle in a few short minutes.

Juliet leaned out one of the little windows to get a better look. The soldier leading the group had a familiar stance. The color of his blond hair, plaited under the tri-corner hat, made her pulse quicken. "No," she whispered. "It cannot be." She waited until they grew closer. "John is a soldier? Why would he come back here?" Juliet pulled her cloak tightly around her body and slid down the cold stone wall. She drew her knees up and placed her forehead on them. Fear and grief overtook her. A tear, and then another, splashed onto the wool material draped over her legs.

"No!" Juliet lifted her head and gazed out the window at the winter sky. The gray clouds had thickened and taken on a darker color. She tried to hold the tears back but they came so fast she had no control. She brought her hand to her mouth to stifle the sound of her sobs and curled in a ball, hoping no one would find her.

~ * ~

"Juliet? There ye are! I've been searching the castle for ye. Juliet?" Eva's voice held concern.

Juliet did not want to open her eyes. "How long have I been here?"

"I have no idea. Maybe all day? It is past supper. Da has sent the soldiers to their chambers to wait out the storm. He said they will discuss business during breakfast." Eva crouched next to her. "I have to tell ye something. Yer not gonna like it."

"I know."

"Ye do?"

"I saw him." Juliet pointed to the window above her.

"Can ye sit up?" It sounded like more of a command than a question.

Juliet struggled to move her aching body. The cold floor was not the most comfortable place to sleep. She rolled her neck to one side then the other. "Did you see him?"

"From a distance. Duncan wouldna let me near him. We will have to wait till morning to see what they want." Eva tugged on Juliet's hand. "Come. I will take ye to yer room. We can speak there."

Juliet finally looked up at Eva. She wore a wool dress with only a shawl wrapped around her shoulders. "You must be cold. Sorry." She labored to stand. "I need time to get my legs under me." Juliet put her hand against the wall.

"I had Nessa bring some food to yer room," Eva whispered.

Juliet looked around to see if anyone else had come with her. She saw no one and had to smile. Eva liked to have secrets between them, and if bringing supper to her room was one, then let it be so.

A fire roared in the fireplace when they reached the suite. Nessa had done a good job making the room ready. "I did not realize how cold I was." Juliet rubbed her hands in front of the fire, taking in the warmth.

Eva slipped Juliet's cloak from her shoulders. "Like old times, Lady Juliet." She smiled.

Eva tried so hard to make her feel better, Juliet decided to play along. "I would have you draw me a bath if it was not so cold." They laughed together. "I have felt so alone, Eva. It is good to have you to myself." She went to the window and pulled the heavy curtain back to gaze outside. "The storm has come. Pray it stops soon. Otherwise we will have English soldiers living here for the winter."

"We wouldna want that." Eva chuckled as she set the table and began dishing food onto plates. "I am famished! When I saw John and couldna find ye, I lost my appetite."

Juliet joined her at the table. "I only saw John from a distance. How does he look?"

"As if he aged a hundred years. He is thinner. His face is lined, probably from scowling all the time." Eva smiled. "He is not the same John we knew in England. He has a determined look in his eye, as if he will get his way, no matter the cost."

"Ross told me to be strong." Juliet played with the food on her plate. "But he did not know I would have to deal with John."

"Ross knew the soldiers would come. He told Duncan to expect them. We are to say Ross is on a hunt, and Ewan died from measles."

"Ross would never go out in this weather."

"We are to say he left before the weather changed for one last hunt. Some of the men in the village went with him. Others went off to look for them. Can ye say that, Juliet? Can ye lie to John?"

"Yes, I can tell any story that will help the family. But I am still fond of John. He was my first love or so I thought. When he came to Glenhaven in the summer, he was so different. I never thought him to have a mean streak, but I saw it on that visit. Now I am afraid of what he might do." Juliet sipped the wine Eva poured. "Oh! I have not asked of Greer. Is she all right?"

Eva shook her head. "The fever's back. We canna send for the doctor in the storm."

"She got well once. She will do it again."

"We have to believe that is true. Oh Juliet, since Ewan died, Greer has not been the same. She has no will to live. I am afraid she may die." Eva covered her mouth, and tears welled up in her eyes. "When we first arrived in Scotland, it was like stories my mother told me of long ago—a prince and princess, a knight and his lady. Glenhaven castle beckoned me, and I knew I belonged. I dinna want all this sorrow to come down on the MacLarens. I feel we brought it upon them."

"I never thought of it that way." Juliet shook her head. "But the uprising or Greer's sickness had nothing to do with us." She looked at Eva and could read her face, see what was in her eyes. "You mean John. I brought John upon them."

"I dinna mean that. Ye are not to blame, Juliet! Yer family sent ye here. Ye dinna ask to come to Scotland."

"No, I did not. But I am here now. If John came here because of me, I will have decisions to make. If he is truly the king's liaison, then he will speak to Donnach and leave. We will not find out until the morning. So for now, we wait."

~ * ~

Eva stayed the night, curled up next to Juliet for warmth. Juliet woke and smiled at her friend. She wore a peaceful expression as she slept, reminding Juliet of their younger years. She recalled days in England when the two girls lay in bed talking late into the night under a warm down comforter. She slipped out of bed, careful not to wake her and stoked the fire.

"Juliet?" Eva sat up and rubbed her eyes.

"I am sorry if I woke you."

"Ye dinna." Eva stretched her arms in the air. "Do ye want me to help ye change yer dress?"

Juliet looked down at the brown wool outfit and smoothed the front. "No, I will wear this. I am not putting on a fine dress for John. I will just brush my hair."

"Let me." Eva placed her hand on her stomach as she slid from the bed, as if to protect the child inside. Juliet tried not to stare and ignored the tightening of her stomach every time she thought of someone having a baby.

"What is it?" Eva pulled her brows together. She took the brush from Juliet's hand. "Sit." She pointed to the bench in front of the mirror. "I know that look. Something is troubling ye."

"How did you do it?" Juliet whispered.

"Do what?" Eva cocked her head.

"That." Juliet waved her hand toward Eva's stomach.

"The bairn? Is that what ye mean?" She threw her head back and laughed. "Juliet, if ye havena lain with yer husband yet, I dinna ken what to tell ye." She looked at Juliet in the mirror. They communicated that way for so many years, each seeing the other in the looking glass as Eva worked on Juliet's hair.

Eva's smile faded. "Ye are serious?"

Juliet held her gaze, not answering.

"I believe there is only one way." She placed her hand on Juliet's shoulder. "It will happen. I am sorry ye are hurting."

"What if it never does?"

"What does Ross say?"

"He loves me, child or not. But will he always feel that way?" Tears filled Juliet's eyes.

"The way he looks at ye? Aye, he will." Eva ran the brush through Juliet's long, chestnut hair a few more times. "Ye are beautiful. Ye never see the way men look at ye. Those looks have nothing to do with bairns."

Juliet lifted one side of her mouth. "Thank you. But there is only one man I want to look at me that way." Her shoulders slumped. "I hope he is well, Eva. I worry so much."

"Since there has been no fighting, we know he is. Yer prayers will help him." She stepped back. "Would ye mind if I brushed out my hair and plaited it again?"

"Let me." She wanted to tease her friend about the way she spoke to break the somber mood, but her heart was not in it.

They changed places, and Juliet undid Eva's braid and brushed out her sandy brown hair. She sectioned it off and began the plaiting process. When she finished, she said, "We are ready. Let us go together to the grand hall. I hope the storm has passed so the soldiers can be on their way."

"To God's ear," Eva said as she crossed herself.

~ * ~

Before they reached the bottom step, Juliet heard a medley of men's voices. Her stomach churned, the pulse in her neck throbbed. She did not want to face John, afraid of what he wanted.

Eva took her hand and squeezed. "Chin up. Ye are Lady Juliet MacLaren. Nothing John can do about it."

"I miss him … the old John," Juliet whispered. "It would be so nice to have a visit, hear about my family. He used to tell me the funniest stories." She let out a breath. "It is not to be. I will be polite and hope he concludes his business today."

The girls stepped into the grand hall. Four English soldiers sat at a table, wearing white ruffled shirts, breeches, and dark boots that came to the knee. They appeared relaxed, laughing and enjoying their breakfast. Fiona sat with Duncan, Heather, and Jamie at the head table. Not in his usual spot, Juliet searched the room for Donnach. Farther down the table, he sat next to John in deep discussion.

When John saw her, he lifted his head in greeting. "Good morning to you, Juliet." He stood and bowed. "Eva." He said her name as if he stepped in horse dung.

"John, it is good to see you again." Juliet walked to where he sat and held out her hand. She would play the part of good friend until he left. He kissed the top and returned to his seat.

"Will you join us?" John pointed to the chair next to him.

"Thank you, but I must sit with my mother-in-law. I will speak with you later?" Juliet tried to use her sweetest voice, but noticed John's eyes clouded over.

"Of course." He gave a quick nod.

Juliet slipped into a seat next to Fiona. "How is Greer today?" she asked.

"Not well. I had hoped Alec would lift her spirits if he stayed with her during breakfast. Our best maidservant, Andra, is with them. She is to come and get me if there are any changes. We will send for the doctor as soon as the soldiers leave."

Juliet's heart soared. "They leave today?"

"Aye, as soon as Lord Alder is satisfied."

"I see he wears the king's uniform."

"He was commissioned by the king. He said he was a colonel, I believe." Fiona rolled her eyes. "Donnach spoke with him at length last night. He told the colonel that Ross is hunting somewhere in the forest and canna be found. Donnach gave Lord Alder permission to search the land for him if he so wished." She lowered her voice and said, "I am waiting for the bloody bastard to dig up poor Ewan's grave to make sure he is truly dead from the measles."

Juliet placed her hand on Fiona's arm. "The John I know would never do that."

Fiona did not answer and pursed her lips as Juliet made a small plate of food. "I may as well eat to pass the time." She smiled at her mother-in-law. "But it is hard. I wish the day to be over."

"And those soldiers gone," Fiona whispered, and flashed a fake smile their way.

Donnach and John rose at the same time. "We will continue our business in the other room." He gestured for John to precede him.

"A few minor details to work out, Laird MacLaren. Then we will be on our way," John said as he passed in front of Juliet.

Juliet could not bear to stay in the room one minute longer. "I am going to check on Greer and Alec, if you do not mind, Fiona."

Fiona nodded her approval, and Juliet hurried after the men. She planned to spy outside the room, listen to every detail discussed. Juliet checked the hall and glanced up the stairs. She positioned her body against the wall, inching closer to the open doorway.

"Lord Alder, I will tell ye one more time. I have been loyal to King George. I stayed at Glenhaven with my family as promised. I get word of battles just as ye do. A messenger is sent with news. 'Tis true, some of our men are missing, but I explained that to ye. They went looking for me son. Ross is a stubborn lad and insisted on one last hunt."

Juliet smiled when she heard his name. Ross was stubborn but so much more. His love and strength filled her heart.

"He insisted on going on this hunt before the darker days set in. He took some men with him. After the first snow fell, men from the village came to me and offered to search for them. Please feel free to join in the hunt. I want me son home."

That sounded convincing. Juliet's heart went back to a steady beat. John had his story to deliver to the king. The MacLarens were loyal.

"And what if I do not believe you?" John's voice sounded calm but held an air of arrogance. "What if I tell the king that Ross has joined the uprising, and you support the Jacobites? I am sure if I look hard enough, I will find evidence."

"That is yer choice, Lord Alder. I dinna ken what evidence ye will find, but I offer ye to look. Ye will find nothing."

"Your son? Duncan, I believe? Is he willing to come to England to assure the king?" The edge in his voice made Juliet shudder.

"Why does he need to report to the king?" Donnach growled. He had held his ground until one of his sons became a pawn.

"To join the British army and help win the battle against the Jacobites. We were outnumbered in some major battles. Every man counts. We have heard rumors that James Stuart plans to come to Scotland and lead his troops. We have to make ready for that final battle..." John paused. "Who knows when that will be?"

"And if I refuse?"

"I will have to give the king a most upsetting report. You are a traitor and have secretly supported the Jacobites. He will send more soldiers to Glenhaven to arrest you and the men of your village. Of course, I will have to leave some of my men behind now to make sure you do not escape."

"What do ye want to leave us alone? To let me son stay at Glenhaven? I have explained our position. I stayed loyal to George. For God's sake, man, what do ye want?" Donnach's voice grew louder with every word.

Yes! What do you want? Juliet bit her lip, not wanting to hear but knew she must.

"Juliet," John answered.

Chapter Thirteen

The scream forming in her chest had to be pushed down. Juliet bit her lip harder until she drew blood, and a metallic taste flooded her mouth.

"She is Ross' wife," Donnach said in a low voice.

"That can easily bc taken care of by an English judge. He will grant her a divorce."

"And who would want to marry a divorced woman?"

"I would, sir."

Black spots floated in front of Juliet's eyes. Her knees trembled and felt as if they could give out any moment. If she let herself, she would faint dead on the floor. *Be strong.* She heard Ross' voice. She blinked and placed her palms against the stone wall for support.

"So this is about Juliet?" Donnach asked.

"I have been given permission to bring any English citizen back to England who requests such action. They may feel threatened or unsafe in Scotland and wish to return home. That includes Eva." He said her name the same way as before.

"I assure ye, both women are fine. They dinna want to return home."

"Are you sure? Think long and hard, Donnach. If Juliet returns with me, I will tell the king he has nothing to worry about when it comes to the MacLaren clan. They are loyal to a fault. And between you and me, you know that is a lie. If I dug up your son-in-law, I am sure we would find a battle wound."

"The devil has filled yer soul, man! Ye will not touch that grave."

Juliet wanted to run, to hide from John, but could not move. His words were cruel as he manipulated Donnach.

"I do not want to, my laird. Give me what I want, and we leave tomorrow."

"Fine! Take the lass!"

Surprised at how quickly he gave her up, Juliet bolted for the stairs. She scrambled up them and into her room, flinging her body on the bed. "Ross! Oh, Ross! Please come home and save me."

"Ross may not be able to save ye, but I can."

Juliet lifted her head to see who stood in the doorway. She blinked away tears to focus. "Glynis?"

"Aye."

"You heard?"

"Every last word." She walked into the room. "I am sorry, Juliet. Ye have to go. But dinna worry, I will come for ye. I will rescue ye from the clutches of that horrid man."

"Juliet!" Donnach's voice boomed from farther down the hall.

Glynis slipped out of the room, finger to her lips. Juliet sat on the edge of the bed in shock. She locked eyes with Donnach when he entered the room. "Do you hate me that much?" she asked as she met his eyes, searching for some bit of sympathy but found none.

"I am sorry, lass, ye have to go back to England with him. I told ye I would do what needed to be done to protect the family. I asked ye if ye were, too."

"And I agreed." Juliet hung her head. "But not this. I thought you would say I was your prisoner, threaten to harm me if John did not leave. I never thought I would have to leave."

"It may be for the best," he said softly. "Ye will be back with yer own kind. Lord John wants to marry ye."

Juliet lifted her head, studying his face and eyes. She saw coldness and determination. Maybe Donnach did not hate her, but he would sacrifice her. "And what will you tell Ross?"

"That ye willingly went."

"No!"

"Ye ken it has to be that way. Ye never will come back, lass. Let him move on with his life. He will get over the pain."

Juliet threw herself on the bed, sobbing. "That is so cruel." She felt his hand on her back. "And do ye have a better way?" he asked.

Donnach was right. If she left Scotland, she would never return. She wondered how her parents would react when they saw her. Did they fear for her safety during the uprising? Would they be happy she returned? She never got an answer to the letter she sent with a band of travelers that stopped in the village. "Yes, I have a better way. I stay here, and you call his bluff."

Donnach chuckled then gave out a sinister laugh. "Bluff? That man has the look of a wild dog. He thinks he has been wronged. Ye, my dear daughter, were the prize and were taken from him. A rich man like Lord Alder always gets his way."

Juliet sat up and swiped at her eyes. "Then it is done. I leave tomorrow." She wanted to believe Glynis and hoped this was a temporary situation. But Glynis was one woman. What could she do? "I would like to say my goodbyes before I leave."

"Aye." Donnach lifted his hand as if he was going to take hers then thought better of it. "Ross said ye were a MacLaren, and I never believed him. Today I do." He left Juliet alone in her room.

She glanced around. "How can I leave? I never told Ross I loved him. He will be told I left him for John. I will go home and live with my parents. Then what? Marry John?"

~ * ~

John asked permission to visit Juliet in her chambers after supper. She paced the floor, wondering what he could want. A clearing of a throat drew her attention to the door.

"John, please come in." Juliet motioned to the small table where she and Ross often dined.

"We could not speak freely before," John said as he sat across from her. "But now we can." He helped himself to a glass of wine from the pitcher set in the middle of the table. "To us." He held the glass up and waited.

"To us?" Juliet shook her head. "I do not understand." She studied him carefully. Eva had been right. John looked gaunt, as if he had not slept in days. More lines and creases crossed his face from exposure to weather and sun.

"Then let me start from the beginning." John settled back in his chair. "When I returned to England I had much time to think. I realized you put on a good show for your Highland family. You wanted them to believe you were loyal out of fear."

"Fear?"

"Fear of them. And you also feared I would not come back for you." He took a long drink from the cup and refilled it. "I told you it was not over. Did you not believe me? Trust in me?"

"But it is over, John. I am married to another. I want to stay here."

"So you say. Once home, you will change your mind. Do you not miss afternoon tea? Walks in the garden? I have so many stories to tell." He lifted his eyes to the ceiling. "I cannot wait to hear your laugh again, Juliet. How I missed it."

"All those things were lovely. I remember them with fondness. I will always be fond of you, John."

"Fond?" His voice rose. "What happened to love? You once told me you loved me and no other. I still love you. I want you more than ever."

"I love my husband."

"And you will love your new husband."

Juliet's eyes widened. "And who would that be?"

He chuckled and set his glass on the table. He reached for her hand and kissed it softly. "Me, my dear. Who else?"

Juliet's jaw dropped, and as much as she wished to close it, she could not. His determination to marry her—against all reason—had finally set in.

"Surprised? We will get you a divorce and marry on your birthday. I thought you would like that." He held up his cup in a toast then drained the drink.

"My birthday is March first. You have planned this all out?" At one time, Juliet would have been thrilled to marry John, especially on her birthday. What a gift that would have been! She was always impressed by his organizational skills and how quickly he could make things happen. He had studied in Germany and France as a boy and appeared comfortable in any situation. Three years older, Juliet had been in awe of his knowledge, sometimes wondering why he had chosen to pursue her.

"Yes, we need time to make the preparations. Three months should be enough. I have already set some things in motion."

"What if I do not want a divorce?"

"You have no say."

Juliet sat straighter. "And what if I do not want to marry you?"

"You will come around to my way of thinking, I am sure. All these months you should have been in my arms, not that barbarian's. New clothes, new surroundings are all you need. You will live with me until the wedding. Father is ill and since Abigail passed…" He looked away. "The house is empty. We will fill it with children."

A stabbing pain shot through her heart then relief. She may not be able to fill his house with children. "I am sorry about your sister. Her passing took a toll on you. I loved her, too. We were the best of friends."

Juliet pictured the blond girl with blazing blue-gray eyes, always laughing and loving life. Two years younger than John, he considered her a friend as well as a sister.

"Then come home and honor her memory. Our first girl can bear her name." His eyes pleaded with her, and for an instant, she saw the John she knew.

"I am coming home whether I like it or not. Donnach does not want me here anymore. He will tell Ross on his return that I abandoned him for you. I have no choice."

John's expression changed from shock to anger. "You will never say his name again. Do you hear me? And you will come to love me again! Say it." He stood and knocked over the glass of wine he had just poured.

Juliet did not have time to think. He had her by the arm and yanked her from her seat. John slammed her body against his. "Say it."

"I will come to love you again." Juliet's voice sounded so high-pitched she did not recognize it.

John grabbed a handful of her hair and tugged her head back. "Like. You. Mean. It."

His face came so close that Juliet could smell the sweet scent of wine on his breath. The fragrance of lavender wafted from his clothes.

Juliet trembled but could not move and had nowhere to go. John placed his body so she could not escape. "Better yet." He pulled her arm and threw her on the bed. "Say it there."

"I ...will ... love you," Juliet whispered.

"That is all I needed, my love." His face softened, and he licked his lips. "I will treat you as my queen always."

John's body pushed her into the soft mattress. His weight held her down so she could not slip free. He took her arms and pinned them over her head against the velvet quilt that covered the bed. "Since you are not a virgin, why wait?"

She turned her head from side to side, trying to avoid his advances. Juliet had no time to think or process what just happened. John had her life planned out, and she felt like his prisoner. Now he lay on top of her, expecting more than she could give. "No, John. Please no."

"Ye heard the lass," a voice above them said. "She said no."

The dimly lit room made it hard to see, but Juliet caught the reflection of the fire on the dirk's blade at John's neck.

"Get off me," John shouted as he struggled to get up. He pushed at the arm holding the knife. "Juliet had too much to drink. I was helping her to bed."

What? I had one glass. You had six or seven. Juliet locked eyes with Glynis. She longed to throw her arms around her and thank her. "That is true, Glynis. Could you show Lord Alder to his quarters? I am quite tired."

Glynis nodded and grabbed John by the arm. "Happy to serve ye." He stumbled along after her.

Juliet sat in the middle of the bed and wrapped her arms around her waist. One lone tear traveled down her cheek. "Who will be there to protect me when I leave this place?"

~ * ~

Juliet packed her belongings the next morning, readying for the trip. She went from one task to the other in a daze.

"May I come in?" Eva's voice brought tears to her eyes.

"Yes, of course."

"I have something to tell ye." Eva stared at the floor. "John stopped me in the hall after supper last night. He told me to be packed and ready to leave with ye in the morning. Duncan heard him as he came out of the dining hall and almost choked the man to death. He said not to speak to his wife that way. I wasna going anywhere."

"I am so sorry," Juliet said.

"He pushed past me and called me a whore." Eva's cheeks turned pink. "No one ever called me that before."

"Stay away from him, Eva. Do not come to the courtyard to see me off. We will say our goodbyes here."

"Do ye mind?" Eva wiped away a stray tear. "I canna believe ye are leaving, Juliet. We have been together all our lives."

"I know. My heart is broken in two." Juliet took her friend's hands. "John says I have to marry him after I get a divorce. I hope I can get word to my parents before it happens."

"That is a strange thing to say, Juliet. Ye are going to yer parents' home, are ye not?"

"No, John is taking me to his estate. I will not be going home."

"He canna force ye to live in his house and marry him."

Juliet would never tell Eva that was exactly what he planned to do. She would insist on coming to England with her—baby or not—or have Duncan interfere on her behalf. She could not risk their lives. She had to go through with Donnach's plan to keep the family safe. "I am sure it will all work out."

The two friends wrapped their arms around each other and stood in silence.

"Well," Juliet said as she pulled away. "I think I am ready."

"Juliet," Eva said. "If it is a girl, we are naming her Juliet. We know what yer doing for us."

She may know more than she is letting on, but I will not give the plan away. "Thank you, Eva. That is very kind. And keep working on that brogue." Juliet tried to give Eva a smile as she walked her to the door. "I am going to stop in and see Greer before I leave. Will you send word to the Alder estate when she is better?"

"Yes." Eva squeezed her hand. "I will."

"Go. If you do not, I will start to cry and never stop." Juliet watched until Eva turned the corner, disappearing from her life.

She slipped back in the room and glanced around. Her eyes came to rest on the paper and quill at the reading desk. "I can write a letter, hide it, and hope he finds it."

That one nugget of hope pushed her on. Juliet dipped the quill into the ink and began to write.

My dearest Ross,

No matter what you are told, I left in protest. I would never leave you willingly. John Alder gave Donnach no choice. Know that I love you, will always love you, and will think of you, day and night for the rest of my life. I wanted to tell you in person how much I love you, but now I will never get the chance. We will never see each other again, and for that, I will regret each day I have to face without you. My heart is filled with pain, but I will do anything to protect the family. You are all safe now. Do not come for me, I beg you.

Juliet

Tears splashed onto the paper as she wrote. Juliet stared at her words, reading them over and over again. "You can start again, Ross. Find a girl who will give you as many children as you deserve." She folded the paper and looked around the room. "Where can I hide this?"

"Ye can give it to me. I will make certain he receives it." Glynis leaned against the doorframe.

"Glynis!" Juliet ran to her and pulled her into an embrace. "Thank you. Thank you so much."

Glynis wiggled away from her grip with a snort. "'Tis a piece of paper, Juliet."

"Not just for that." Juliet took a breath. "For last night."

"He is no better than a pig." Glynis pretended to spit over her shoulder.

Juliet held back a laugh, not sure if Glynis was serious. "I have to marry that pig."

"Perhaps not." Glynis lifted the MacLaren eyebrow. "I could come with ye, be yer maidservant. I would protect ye from his advances."

"I wish you could come. Your father would never allow it."

"Then ye need an excuse or a story to tell the bastard until I rescue ye."

"And how do you plan to rescue me? One lone Highland girl?" Juliet wished Glynis could rescue her but knew better.

"I have lived in the woods for weeks at a time. I can make me own camp and ken how to hide. No one would take a woman for a soldier. I could walk the streets of London if I wanted. Men would bow and women would curtsy." She gave Juliet a clumsy dip.

"Oh, Glynis," Juliet said as a smile formed on her face. The girl was unaware of her beauty. She would stand out wherever she went. "You have taken a terrible day and made it better."

"And let us make it even better. Ye tell John Alder that ye are a proper woman. The day he marries ye is the day he shares yer bed."

Juliet let out a sad laugh. "I never would have thought of that. Thank you, Glynis. I will keep you forever in my heart."

"Until we meet again." Glynis pointed at her chin as she walked away. "Dinna forget this face." She flashed a grin and went down the stairs.

Her heart fluttered as she watched Glynis disappear as suddenly as she had shown up at her doorway. She had hoped they bonded during the days spent with Alec, and now, she felt a connection. But it was too late. Too late to befriend the rest of her sister-in-laws and win over Ross' parents. They viewed her as an outsider, even though at times she felt she made progress. Her shoulders dropped. and the heaviness returned to her body.

"Now where was I?" Juliet turned toward the room. "Right. Hide the letter." She looked down at her hands. The folded paper she held was gone. *Glynis took the paper? Please God, let her keep her word.*

Juliet stepped into the hall and headed for Greer's quarters. She heard Alec's little boy voice coming from the suite as she drew closer.

"Just a sip, Greer," Fiona said as she held her daughter's head. "Broth, 'tis good for ye."

"Auntie!" Alec's cry of joy broke her heart as she entered the room. Juliet would never see those emerald green eyes again. She would always wonder if he kept the white blond locks or if they grew darker as he aged. Some of his chubbiness had left him over the last few months, replaced by a small boy's figure.

"'Tis his birthday, Juliet," Greer whispered.

"Oh!" Juliet had forgotten after the ordeal of the last few days. "You get Donnach to take you to the village, Alec. Auntie and Uncle had a surprise made for you. It is waiting at the carpenter's." She hoped he liked the sword with the MacLaren crest she ordered.

"When ye get back, ye can take him." Greer forced the words from her mouth. "He can wait."

Juliet looked at Fiona, eyes wide.

"That is a good idea, Juliet. Ye willna be gone long? A month perhaps? Weather permitting, of course. I told Greer how much ye wanted to see yer family for Yule." Fiona did not flinch as she told the simple lie. Juliet wondered if her mother-in-law would miss her or had just been polite all these months.

"Yes. Christmas," Juliet said. The Yuletide season had not crossed her mind. Living in Scotland, she knew it would not be celebrated. The Church of Scotland had banned the celebration, one more thing to add conflict between the English and Scots.

"But she must be here for Hogmanay," Greer said as she struggled to sit up.

Juliet rushed to the bedside. "I will try my best. Please, Greer, rest."

Fiona sat on a chair next to Greer's bed and reached for Juliet's hand, pulling her closer. "The lass may need to stay longer, Greer. We canna expect her to travel through storms and deep snow just for Hogmanay."

"For the end of the year celebration? I will try." Juliet smiled. "Tell me what you do on that day, Greer, so if I am not here, I can picture it in my mind."

"We sing and dance. We bless the house," Greer whispered. "And throw fireballs to welcome the new year."

"Sounds wonderful." Juliet took her hand and patted the top. "I must be on my way but shall see you soon." As she held Greer's hand, she realized Greer had been the first one to accept her. Juliet had grouped the family into one unit, not seeing them as individuals. Greer had trusted Juliet with her son, asked her to raise him if anything should happen to her. Tears filled her eyes. "I will miss you, sister. Get well."

Little Alec tugged on Juliet's skirt. "Lil' Horsie miss ye."

"And I will miss him. But do you know who I will miss the most?" She touched the top of his button nose as he wrinkled it. "You." She lifted him in her arms one last time and kissed his cheek. Juliet buried her face in his hair and took in his sweet little boy scent, something to remember him by. Tears welled up in her eyes as she thought of the wonderful times she'd had with her nephew and what she would miss in the days to come.

"Goodbye," she whispered. "Be good for your mum." And with that, she was out the door.

Chapter Fourteen

"Juliet?" John offered his hand to assist her.

She cringed inside but smiled. "Thank you."

"My men are quite adept at making a secure camp. We will be outdoors for seven days, but I hope to make you as comfortable as possible. Within three days, we should be safely in our own borders."

Juliet swung up onto her horse, the same one she had ridden from England. Donnach and Duncan stood by expressionless, arms crossed. She had said her goodbyes to the women, and Duncan caught her in the hall.

"I will take care of Eva. Ye can count on that, sister. Thank ye for what ye are doing." He bowed his head.

"And I will thank ye not to let your brother believe I left him." Juliet waited for him to look at her.

"I canna, Juliet. Da would—"

"Yes, well, I do not have to worry what Donnach will say or do anymore." She sniffed. "He never wanted me here and would have loved to see me gone as soon as I arrived. He got his wish."

"Och, Juliet, he dinna wish that."

"I think he did."

Duncan reached out and rubbed her arm. "He was wrong."

Juliet shook her head and focused on the two men in the courtyard. She stared at Donnach, trying to read him. *Does he care I am leaving? Is he glad? Of course, he is glad. He will lie to Ross and say I left him.* She lifted her hand to say goodbye, and he nodded once.

The horses headed out single file. Juliet rode in the middle with John trailing behind her. The weather had cleared, and the sun reflected off the new fallen snow. When they reached the forest, the bare trees provided some shade from the blinding light.

Heather stayed in the village with Jamie and did not return to the castle to say goodbye. She had sent word for Juliet to stop by the blacksmith's shop. John argued it would take too much of their travel time, but she stood firm.

The horses picked their way through the snow. Although the storm howled and whistled all night, not much snow fell. The road had begun to show through the thin layer of white. Juliet stared off into space until the bottom of the hill came into view. They would be in the village soon.

"Juliet," John called. She turned her head to acknowledge. "Stay on the horse and wait for the girl to come out. Say your farewells, and we will be on our way."

Juliet snarled, knowing he could not see. She suddenly realized that he would make demands, and she would have to follow them for the rest of her life. Why did she not notice that before? She strained to think back in time. "You need to put up your parasol, Juliet. The sun is peeking out from behind that cloud. We do not want anything to happen to your fair skin." John would then duck behind her as if she blocked the sunlight for him. It made her laugh at the time. She began to recall other incidents—not wearing the right dress, disdain for her friends, saying they were immature and silly, never following her wishes—that John now seemed selfish or demanding. He had hidden his commands with humor.

The village appeared before her, and Juliet's heart raced. She would get to see one more MacLaren before she departed for England. She spotted Heather's tall frame and red hair as they approached the blacksmith's shop. The girl sat on a bench outside the house wrapped in a cloak and jumped up when she spotted Juliet.

"Juliet," Heather said as she hugged her leg. "Come in and warm yerself."

"I have orders not to dismount." Juliet cocked her head back toward John, far enough away he could not hear.

"Bloody bastard," Heather said under her breath.

"Heather!" Juliet bit her bottom lip to keep from laughing.

"Ross will come for ye. I will tell him as soon as he rides through the village that the devil took ye." She cast an evil glance at John.

"Good day to you, too, Madam *MacGregor*." John tipped his hat as he guided his horse next to Juliet. "You know the MacGregors have lost favor with the king. Watch over your husband."

"John!" Juliet was startled by his response. *What could the MacGregors have done?* Hadn't she done enough to protect the family? Now he made a threat against Heather's husband.

"Juliet?" John stared at her. "You have said your goodbyes?" He lifted his eyebrows. "Then we shall be on our way."

Juliet extended her hand down to Heather. "Take care."

Heather kissed her hand. "Ross made me see I have been a little selfish. I have ye to thank for Jamie."

"No, Heather, I do believe it was all you. You and your stubbornness." Juliet smiled at the girl. "A favor?"

"Anything."

"Eva's birthday comes on the twenty-ninth of January. Wish her a happy birthday from me."

"And I will give her a few soft smacks from ye, too." Heather winked at her.

"One more thing. Do not tell Ross to come for me."

Heather's smiled faded. "He will want to."

"Not after your father tells him I chose to leave with John."

"That is a lie!" She put her hands on her hips.

"Please, Heather, promise? I have written him a letter. Let that be enough." Juliet did not want any of Donnach's children to get in trouble. All she could hope was that Glynis gave Ross the letter.

On the ride through the woods, Juliet had made up many stories about her fate. But this reality was the best one. Leave with John, beg Ross to start a new life. Yet she couldn't be so cruel to let him think she left willingly. Was she thinking of only herself when she professed her love? That would give Ross hope and the will to find her. It also gave her a ray of hope, and perhaps that was why she did it. She'd always have that to cling to when life in England became unbearable.

"Och, aye, I willna tell him. But I willna stop him either." Heather huffed and flipped her red hair over her shoulder.

"Juliet!" John's voice held a stern tone.

She nudged her horse and followed after him. They made their way through the village and into the forest. Soon she would be on the ridge overlooking the MacLaren land. She remembered stopping there the day she arrived, gazing into the valley, wondering what lie ahead.

Once the group passed the ridge, they followed the main road to the last large town in Scotland. Juliet had visited once with Ross, excited to shop and meet new people. He had described the layout of the land once they arrived. The MacLarens, Kinkaids, and MacGregor estates encircled the town, making easy access for all three clans. They'd spent the day walking the cobbled streets and a night in the inn. Ross spoiled her and bought colored ribbons for her hair. She tried not to think of him as they rode through the town now. People peered out their windows then slammed them shut. Obviously, they had gotten word English soldiers were coming through their town. She longed to call out to be rescued but knew it was fruitless.

From there, they would ride to the English border. John said they would make camp after they passed through the town. Juliet thought he did not trust the Scots and chose to travel through instead of stopping at the inn. *No, we are still too close to MacLaren land. The sky is still light. We can ride for another hour or two before the sun sets.*

"Juliet," John said as he pulled up beside her. "May we start over? I would like permission to sleep in your tent tonight."

Juliet gave him a look she hoped convened her loathing and refusal.

"For warmth only." He smiled.

She swallowed and looked away. "Your request is denied." December nights were cold enough inside a home. She had never slept outdoors during that time of year. Yet, she'd shiver and freeze rather than let him in her tent.

"As you wish. My men will build a bonfire and maintain it through the night. Deerskin will be laid down in your tent. We have brought many wool blankets and some quilts. I assume you will be keeping your dress and cloak on."

Juliet swung her head his way in time to see a wink and a genuine smile. The John she knew returned for a moment, but for her it was too late. She did not love him anymore and could not stand the thought of marrying him. She had less than three months before the marriage took place and hoped it would be enough time to change his mind.

Chapter Fifteen

The Alder estate loomed ahead. Dark skies with thick, gray clouds had made the day's journey long and depressing. The house did not look welcoming as they approached. Almost the same color as the storm clouds, it cast off an eerie glow and at times seemed to disappear in the mist. Juliet should have felt grateful to be there after riding a horse in the cold for seven days, but instead she felt a lump grow in her throat and her heart pounded. *This will be my home now.*

She turned to John. He sat on his horse, gazing at the house. "It feels so good to be home," he said as he glanced over at Juliet. "Our home."

Juliet lowered her eyes. She'd wait until they were settled to ask her questions. Servants greeted them at the door, and Juliet followed John up the marble steps to the second floor.

"I thought you would like this suite." He bowed as he extended his arm. "Mother decorated it."

She entered the room and surprisingly found it to her liking. The house may have looked cold on the outside, but the suite was warm and inviting. It had simple yet elegant furnishings of gold, cream, and blue. "It is lovely, John. I know how fond you were of your mother."

He stood behind her and brought her body against his as he slipped his arms around her waist. "And in a few months, you will share my bed," he whispered in her ear. "You will forget all about him."

Juliet's heart raced at the thought of Ross but knew not to speak of him. Each time she mentioned Ross during their trip, John would give her a stern warning. "Do not speak of him, Juliet, ever again. There will be consequences if you do." *A beating, perhaps? Locked in my room?* She shivered at the thought.

"See, you are coming around already. You quiver at my touch." John let her go, and she faced him.

"I am cold, John. I would like to get my shawl."

"Of course." He left the room, and Juliet heard him call to the servants. "Why in the bloody hell are you dawdling down there? Get the trunks to Lady Juliet's room."

"You told us to wait, sir," a girl's voice answered.

"Now I am telling you to bring them," he said in a stern voice.

"Yes, Lord Alder."

Juliet heard pounding on the steps and a slight young girl around the age of fifteen appeared in the doorway. She curtsied, lost her balance, and banged against the wooden frame. "Sorry, milady, I am a bit clumsy."

"It is quite all right." Juliet smiled at the brown-haired, brown-eyed girl. She had a plain face, but when she smiled, a look of beauty overtook it. "I am Juliet."

The girl curtsied again, this time with more success. "I am Ann. At your service, Lady Juliet." She walked to a rope by the door. "All you need to do is pull this, and I will come running."

"You do not have to run," Juliet said with a giggle. "I can wait."

"But Lord Alder cannot." She looked away.

I have learned more about this man in seven days than in all the time I knew him. "I will speak to him about that," Juliet said.

"Oh please, no. Do not do that." Ann held up her hands as if adverting a blow, her face turning red.

"All right, I will not." Juliet decided to use that to her advantage. "Then I have something to ask you. If I do not tell John about you, then you will not tell him about me?"

The girl nodded. "Your secrets are safe with me. I like having a woman in the house."

"There are no other women servants?"

"No… well, yes. What I mean is a woman *of* the house. There needs to be one since the duchess and Lady Abigail passed." Ann moved away from the door as Juliet's trunks were brought in. "I best get to this. I have said too much."

Juliet searched for her shawl as Ann put her clothes in the dressing room. She longed to ask more but did not know if she could trust Ann, having just met the girl. *She is not Eva. Remember that.*

A footman appeared at the door, dressed in a fancy velvet green coat, black silk knee breeches, white silk stockings, and powdered hair. "Lady Juliet? Lord Alder requests your presence in the parlor. I have been sent to escort you."

"I have not changed from my riding clothes. Would you be so kind as to wait in the hall?" Juliet asked. He nodded and retreated to the hallway.

"I heard!" Ann rushed from the dressing room and shut the door. "The lord loves gold. I found a yellow dress he will admire." She helped Juliet remove her clothing, poured water in a basin, and handed her a towel.

Juliet washed her hands and face the best she could, wishing she had more time to look presentable. The dress Ann chose had not been wore during her time at Glenhaven. The gold silk with intricate beading had seemed out of place. She slipped it over her head and waited as Ann laced up the back.

"I heard you are to be married. It is quite exciting. The servants cannot stop speaking of it." Ann clapped her hand over her mouth. "There I go again."

Juliet laughed. "It is fine, Ann. I enjoy hearing gossip and talking to another woman."

Ann's eyes widened. "You think I am a woman?"

"Yes." Juliet patted the girl's face. "Now would you open the door?"

The footman bowed and said, "Follow me." He walked to the stairs, and Juliet trailed after him.

The steps and grand foyer floor were made of white marble with black and gray swirling through it. The area looked quite regal and reminded Juliet just how much money the Alders had. The parlor was located to the right of the foyer, and the footman bowed as he gestured for her to enter.

"Thank you." She stepped into the room. A richly carved white wood and marble fireplace was the main focal point of the room. John sat by the fire, staring into it. "John?"

He sprang to his feet. "Juliet, please come sit by the fire. May I get you a brandy? Sherry, perhaps?"

Juliet crossed the hardwood floor to reach him. "Whatever you are drinking."

"Sherry, it is."

He returned with two glasses and settled in a chair across from her. "We will have so many nights like this. I dreamed about you living in this house as my wife. At first, I thought it was not to be. Your father put up a good fight when I asked for your hand before they sent you off to Scotland."

"I would like to hear about that day. You are not a pauper. You could provide for me. So why did Father tell you no and send me away?"

John brought his glass to his lips, staring at her over the top. Juliet fidgeted in her seat. He took his time and savored each sip. "You do not know?" he finally asked.

Juliet shook her head.

"Oh, my beautiful Juliet, I can see how your father did not want you to know you were collateral."

"Collateral?"

"He offered you as security against a loan he owed the king."

Her head began to pound, and Juliet's stomach tightened. She placed her hand to her forehead and rubbed the spot between her eyes. "I was used as payment?"

"In a way, yes. Collateral means you were security in the deal your father made with—"

"I know what collateral means. I would be the payment if he did not come up with the money he owed. Get on with it." Her eyes locked on his, and she hoped he saw the fury in them.

"Tsk, tsk," John said as he waggled a finger at her. "Hold your temper." He leaned back in the chair. "A payment was due the king, and your father did not have the money. So he sent word to the king that he had a way to ensure peace with the Scots, and perhaps George would pay for the advice, maybe call off the debt. Your father is always looking for ways to make money the easy way, Juliet. He piqued the king's interest and was invited to the castle. Luckily, he speaks French. As you know … or may not … the king speaks little English."

Juliet recalled the trip. Her mother had new dresses made for the visit and a special wig for her father. They were gone for a week. When they returned, her father was in better spirits than he had been in months. "The king does not speak English?"

"Only a few words. He refuses to give up his heritage and is still tied to Germany."

"So how does he conduct business?"

"He speaks with his ministers in French. Although, he has stopped going to cabinet meetings, and they meet in private without him. Poor man. I do not think he wishes to be king of England. Although, he does try hard to fulfill his obligations to the country."

"Since you speak German, I am sure you have a good relationship with him." Juliet could tell he liked the compliment so she asked, "What happened during my parents' stay at the castle?"

"Your father laid out his plan to the king. Offer an English lady of good breeding for marriage to a Highland chieftain's son." John placed his hand next to his mouth. "Of course, your father knew Laird MacLaren had two sons of marrying age. He did his research. According to your father, once the union took place, peace would prevail. The king would have a bond with the laird. He, in kind, would keep the other chieftains in check. Very well thought out, if I say so myself." John crossed his leg over his knee, settling in to finish the story.

"How did the king know Donnach would agree?" Juliet asked.

"He did not. He sent a courier to Scotland with the message and waited."

"And the laird agreed," she whispered, knowing full well Donnach did not want an English bride sent to Glenhaven.

A month after her parents' trip, the king sent orders for Juliet to go to Scotland. He had chosen her to marry the son of Donnach MacLaren or so she had been told. Her mother said it was her civic duty. Juliet would help maintain peace among the English and the Scots. Her sister-in-law, Heather, became the first to tell Juliet the true story. Donnach never wanted the marriage. He was a Jacobite, a Scot who wished for independence and his own king. He only agreed to the marriage as a cover and hoped the king saw it as a sign of loyalty. Down the line, she could be used as a hostage or bargaining tool.

"Yes, the MacLarens agreed." John closed his eyes for a moment as if in thought. He opened them and smiled at Juliet. "Your father's hope that the king would forgive the debt did not happen. He knew he could not pay the money, so he volunteered you as the bride to be sent off to Scotland with no thought at all to your future or ours," John said with a wave of the hand. Then his eyes flashed in anger. "Selfish man!" He ran his hand through his hair and took a breath as he leaned forward. "When the time came to collect the debt, your father did not have the money. You became collateral, Juliet, and paid it off. He would have gone to debtor's prison. You saved him."

A tear fell from her eye and ran down her cheek. She fought the rest back, but they slowly came trickling down her face. John handed her a handkerchief.

"If you knew, why did you not tell me?" Juliet accepted the handkerchief and dabbed at her eyes. "Use it against my father when you asked for my hand?"

"I did not know then, Julict, you have to believe me," John begged. "I only found out since I have been at the king's side. George did not care if a MacLaren married an Englishwoman, but after hearing your father's presentation, he liked the idea. Not enough to pay for it, but he thought it might work. Anything to prolong the peace and give him time to strategize against the Scots. So he agreed to the plan. But he added an addendum. You had to stay in Scotland and wed the laird's son. He'd forgive the debt, but only if you married. You, Juliet, fulfilled the obligation without ever knowing." John lifted his glass to his nose and sniffed, taking in the aroma. "Your father knew you would not go unless it was a royal command. He asked the king to order you to Scotland."

Juliet wept into the handkerchief. Sorrow filled her heart, hate took over her mind. "How could my father do that to me?" She peeked at John over the handkerchief.

He shrugged as he stared at her. "I *am* sorry. People do strange things when it comes to money."

Juliet thought of the MacLarens. They traded and bartered, little money ever exchanged hands. The villagers paid taxes to the laird, but he accepted whatever they gave him—a goat, bushels of wheat, five chickens. As long as the family could eat, were safe and happy, money did not seem to matter. She dried her eyes. "I would like to see my parents."

"I have invited your mother to tea tomorrow."

"Oh."

"You did not think I would keep you prisoner?"

"You told me stories of the Tower of London, John. I thought you might lock me away." Juliet smiled, pretending to like him, humor him. She would do that every day to stay on his good side.

"Juliet," John said as he leaned across the tea table to take her hand. "Do not think me a beast. I love you and did this to protect you. The king was done with you. He did not care if you were safe in Scotland, only I did. One day you will understand and come to thank me. I cannot wait to marry you and make you my wife."

Juliet swallowed hard, not able to speak. If she had heard those words a year ago, her heart would have leapt with joy. Now it felt as if someone squeezed it into a tight ball, making her dizzy and unable to think. She had been forced into the situation and had no way out.

"Dinner is served, sir." The same footman came to the door.

"Thank you, Joseph." John rose and offered Juliet his arm. "The first of many dinners to come, my love."

Juliet slipped her arm through his as she stood. "Yes."

He leaned toward her and kissed her cheek. She wanted to recoil and slap his face. Instead, she let him lead her from the room with a smile.

~ * ~

"Your mother is here, Lady Juliet." Ann rushed into the room. "Such a fine lady! The fur she wears is of such good quality. And her dress! The deepest of blue silk!"

"That is mama's favorite color. It matches her eyes," Juliet said.

"You must have her eyes." Ann looked at her. "You have the bluest of eyes. I always wished for ones that color."

"Yours are a fine brown, Ann."

"If you like a dull, dirty brown." She smiled as she went to the dressing room. "Yours are like little gemstones, all glitter and sparkle." Ann sighed as she came back in the room. "You only have one yellow gown, milady. Lord Alder is having more dresses made for you in that color."

"My mother always told me to wear blue, to bring out the eye color."

"Will she like that you wear the same color?"

"You said she is wearing dark blue?"

"Yes, I am sure."

Juliet went into the dressing room and came out with a sky blue silk dress. "This will do fine."

After Ann helped her dress, Juliet sat in the vanity chair in front of the mirror so the girl could do her hair.

"Your mother's hair is much darker than yours." Ann held up Juliet's chestnut locks. "You must have gotten this from your father."

"My father's hair is closer to red. I guess I have a little of both of them." For a moment, Juliet felt as if she talked with Eva. The two girls would gossip until her mother sent a servant to say she must come to dinner. She fought back the tears, wishing she could see Eva now.

"There you go. Done." Ann patted her shoulder. "Are you excited to see you mother after all this time?"

"Yes," Juliet lied. "I will go down on my own, if you do not mind."

"I do not. But Joseph may." Ann giggled.

Juliet wished for some time alone with her thoughts. John had filled her day with activities, never leaving her side. She fell into bed exhausted last night. *This has to change. I am sure he has work to do.*

She heard voices coming from the parlor when she reached the bottom of the stairs. Juliet lingered in the hall, hesitant to join them.

"So you know about William's financial woes." She heard her mother's voice.

"Yes, I know everything," John answered. "I heard the king forgave your debt, so things are well?"

"They could be better." Juliet still waited outside the door as a pause came in the conversation. "Now that my daughter has returned, I will take her home with me."

"Now, Constance," John answered. "We both know that will not happen."

"And why should it not? She is my daughter. You have no hold over her."

"But I do."

Her mother gasped. "What ever are you saying?"

"That the Kingstons will do anything for money, even sell their own daughter. How could I let her go home to people who treat her so callously?"

"I take offense to that! The king ordered my daughter to go to Scotland. He chose her. It was a privilege and an honor."

"Ah, but as I told you, I know better." John's voice remained steady.

"What could you know?" Her mother sounded angry. "You have no idea how bad it was. William did not mean to lose his money in that copper deal. The mine failed. He could have gone to jail if he did not pay his debts. We had to do something."

"Yes, you did. You sold your daughter to the highest bidder. Something I would never do. I love her." John let out a breath. "You probably are still in hard financial times. Am I correct?"

"As I said, we could be in better straits."

"Then let me help."

"How?" Her mother's voice went up an octave.

"If Juliet becomes Lady Alder, the future Duchess of Essex, I will be your son-in-law. Family helps family."

"Why that is so kind of you, John." The sound of Constance's voice had changed to overly sweet then became lower in tone. "But there is always a price to pay. What do you want?"

"Help."

"Help? Whatever can I help you with?"

"Juliet seems hesitant to marry me. I think you can nudge her in the right direction," John said.

"That is all?" Her mother laughed. "Of course, I will help."

"Mama?" Juliet decided to make her entrance. She could not stand to hear another word. At least she knew her mother would not be on her side.

Constance flew from her seat and embraced Juliet. "My dearest girl, I dreaded the start of each day, knowing I would not see your sweet face. Sent away to that horrible place." She made a face.

Juliet bit the insides of her cheeks. She swallowed before she spoke, hoping a sarcastic tone would not come out of her mouth. "I missed you, too."

"Was it horrid? Those awful Scotsmen and those strange clothes they wear?"

"It was not that bad." Juliet accepted a cup of tea from a servant who had been standing by the table.

"I want to hear all about it, especially the part when John rescued you."

"He did not rescue me, Mother. Donnach, my father-in-law, told me to leave. I was happy there."

John cleared his throat, and Juliet noticed his hand clenched into a fist.

"But I am happy to be home." She longed to make an evil face at him.

"And we are happy to have you!" Constance set her cup in the saucer. "I am glad you will get to marry the man you love."

Juliet did not know how long she could keep up the pretense. "Yes, I look forward to the day. I would love to come home, Mama. I should not live in my husband's house before the wedding. It is not proper to be here."

"Well," Constance said as her eyes went to the ceiling. "That would be wonderful, but your father is sick … very contagious. He would not want you to become ill. Can you stay here for a while? Until he is better?"

Juliet saw a sly smile cross John's face. "I will be happy to have Juliet here as an invited guest, Constance. That is, until William is well."

"Is father going to be all right?" Juliet felt a twinge of sadness and worry for him then realized her mother did not tell the truth.

"He needs rest and attention. I will not be able to visit as often as I would like."

"But what about Christmas? It is next week."

"John?" Constance glanced his way, looking for an answer.

"We will work something out, Juliet."

"Whatever you say, John." Juliet turned to her mother. "Since I am a soon-to-be divorced woman living under another man's roof, I would not want a scandal. What will you say when people find out?"

"For now, no one is the wiser. John has assured me no one knows you are here. The servants have been sworn to silence." Her mother smiled. "But you are right, people will soon find out you are back. I do not want our family's name tarnished. We can say you are here due to illness in our home, but that excuse will last only so long." She again looked at John for help.

"After William is well, we will think of something, even if you have to move in here, Constance." John laughed, his gray eyes shining.

He is happy when he is in control. "Mama, since I am staying here I have one more concern."

"What is it, my child?"

"Since I have been married, John thinks it is all right—"

"No!" Her head snapped in John's direction. "I may agree to some of your terms, but not that. Juliet should be married to you if she sleeps in your bed. Any sense of impropriety and she will come home. Illness or not!"

"Calm down, Constance. Would you like some brandy in your tea?" John reached for the bottle next to his cup and held it up. "Juliet has been given her own suite. I stand by my word as a gentleman. Juliet will not be in my bed until our wedding night."

"Or mine," Juliet grumbled.

"What was that, my love?" He glanced her way.

"I said that is fine."

"Fine. That is agreeable." Constance stood. "I have overstayed my welcome. I should be going."

John tugged on the rope that hung on the wall. "Joseph will see you out."

~ * ~

As Juliet slipped into bed that night, she swore she heard a noise. “Who is there?” When no one answered, she blew out the candle. She lay on her back, staring into the darkness. She had been at the house two days, and it seemed like an eternity.

A click drew her attention to the door as a gleam of light shone through a small opening. “Who is it?” She sat up and pulled the sheet across her breasts.

“Only me, my love,” John answered as he shut the door behind him.

Chapter Sixteen

"I promised your mother not to take you to my bed, but I said nothing about yours." John sat on the edge of the bed, placed the candle on the table, and removed his shirt. He reeked of alcohol, and she wondered how long he had been drinking.

Juliet swallowed her gasp. After removing the shirt, he wore nothing at all. John reached out and pulled the sheet from her hands, his eyes staring up and down her body. She felt violated and cornered. "We agreed, John. We would wait for our wedding night."

"You are forgetting the most important words, Juliet. In my bed." He crawled onto the mattress and put one leg over her. "Arms up."

"What?" Juliet shivered, and her teeth began to chatter.

"Cold? I will warm you soon. Come on now, do as I say."

"This is how you want our first time to be? You give commands, and I follow them?"

"Do you like to play games, Juliet? I like to win. I like to be in charge. You liked that about me. So first rule of this game, arms up."

Juliet had nowhere to run, no one to save her. She lifted her arms in the air and felt her shift lift over her head.

"Ah, that is so much better, is it not?" She felt his breath on her neck working his way down her body. "You are beautiful, Juliet. I wanted to do this from the first time I saw you. You wanted me, too. I saw it in your eyes."

"Ooh!" Teeth nipped at her breasts.

"You like that?"

"Please, John."

"I like that, Juliet. Keep asking for it. Or is it you cannot wait a moment longer?"

She felt him spread her legs apart, and he wiggled between her thighs. Her mind raced with thoughts of Ross. If she pictured him, she might make it through the ordeal. She had no idea what would happen if she resisted.

"Wait!" Juliet struggled to get out from under him. Her mind raced, trying to come up with a quick plan. "I would like more candlelight. The better to see you."

"Hmm," John brushed her hair back from her face and kissed her lips. "I like that."

A pounding at the door stopped the action. "What the bloody hell?" John grumbled as he stumbled from the bed, pulling his shirt on. He placed his finger over his lips, a smirking grin on his face as if it were a game.

"Who is it?" Juliet called. Her voice sounded shaky, but whoever it was might think they woke her from a deep sleep.

"It is Ann, Lady Juliet. I am sorry to wake you, but there is a fire in the parlor. For your safety, you need to come out of your room."

Juliet scrambled for her shift. "I will be right out. Go downstairs. I will meet you there after I dress."

John reached for her and pulled her to him, kissing her tenderly. "I love you. I am sorry for the interruption."

"John," Juliet said as she caught her breath and looked into his glassy eyes. "I am disappointed. I thought you had more respect for me." She smelled the brandy on his breath. *I am trying to reason with a drunken man.* "Were you in the parlor drinking before you came to my room?"

He rubbed his head. "I believe so. I cannot remember." He looked down and laughed, running his hand through his hair. "I need to go to my room and get some breeches." He staggered toward the door, barely able to stand.

Juliet waited until he left, threw on a wool dress, and ran down the stairs. Joseph was bringing out a pair of burnt breeches on a poker as she reached the parlor entrance.

"Half in the fire? I wonder how that could have happened?" he mumbled.

"Yes, I wonder." Juliet watched him walk to the front door and toss them into the snow, smoke billowing up in the air.

"We have the fire out," Ann huffed as she emerged from the room out of breath and blew a wisp of hair from her face. "Thank the Lord, it snowed last night. We did not have to go far for water." Ann took her by the arm. "Are you all right, Lady Juliet?"

"I have been better." She gave the girl a sad smile. "But happy there was not a larger fire."

"Good night then." Ann turned to go down the hall.

"Ann?"

"Yes, milady?"

"Is there a key for my bedroom door?"

"Why, yes. Would you like it?"

Juliet nodded.

"Wait here."

Juliet was not sure if John had keys to all the rooms, but hopefully this would work for the rest of the night. She would make another plan in the morning.

Ann returned with the key and curtsied. "Please do not be angry with me."

"For giving me a key?" Juliet wrinkled her nose.

"No, milady, for not telling you sooner there was a package tucked in your clothes. In all the excitement, I laid it aside and forgot to tell you."

"Where is it?"

"On the floor of the dressing room, next to the trunk."

Juliet rushed up the stairs, locked the door behind her, lit a few more candles, and headed for the closet. A brown cloth package tied with string lay on the floor just as Ann said. Her heart raced as she reached down to pick it up. *Whatever could it be?*

She took the wrapped item to her bed and set the candle on the table next to her. Juliet slipped a piece of paper out from under the string. Her fingers trembled as she unfolded the letter.

Something to keep ye safe.

G

Juliet pulled the end of one of the strings, and the tie fell away. She grabbed the edge of the cloth and lifted, laying each layer flat on the bed until she exposed what was inside. "Oh." She reached out and touched the gleaming blade of the dagger. "Glynis, you said you wished you could protect me. You will never know that wish came true."

She slid the dirk under her pillow, blew out the candles, and slipped under the covers. Her eyes grew heavy with sleep, her heart beat at a normal pace. "Thank you, Glynis," she whispered right before she fell into a deep sleep.

~ * ~

"You do not have to keep locking your bedroom door, Juliet. I learned my lesson. I have a pair of burnt breeches to remind me." John chuckled as he sipped his tea. "I blame the drink." He gave her a cavalier smile.

Juliet sat across from him in the parlor while they waited for her parents to arrive. It had taken until Christmas Day to clean the room and remove the smell of smoke from the furnishings. "I am sure you have keys to all the rooms in the house, John. A locked door would not stop you." She lifted the corners of her mouth.

"I put everyone at risk that day. My father would have never made it out of the house, let alone down the stairs." John shook his head. "I had too much to drink and was not thinking clearly. Forgive me?"

Juliet nodded as she pictured him pulling off his breeches that night, throwing them aside and running up the stairs in his hurry to make love. The pants landed in the fire and slowly started to burn. It made a humorous scene, but the end of the story was no laughing matter. If concern for his father kept him at bay, so be it.

Her thoughts were interrupted when Joseph appeared in the doorway with her parents standing behind him, their faces flushed from the cold.

"Oh, Lord John," Juliet's mother said as she strolled into the room. "I love what you have done with the house. So festive!" She leaned over and gave him a kiss on the cheek then the other. "Juliet, you are quite ready for celebrating in that ruby red dress!"

John had the house decorated for the holiday season with evergreens and holly. The staircase had evergreen trophies with green ribbon entwined through them. Everywhere Juliet looked she saw something framed in the green scented pine or adorned with red holly berries. Mistletoe hung in the doorways, and John made sure he and Juliet ended up underneath the green balls with white berries quite often. With each kiss, she tried to accept her new life, but all she could think of was Ross. She wondered if he was alive and well and said a pray for him each night.

Joseph led the family into the dining room, seating her mother across from Juliet. John sat at the head of the table, her father at the other end. Juliet found it rather odd her father's health improved so quickly that he could attend the dinner, although she doubted he was ever sick. She could barely look at him and wished for the dinner to end before it had started.

The cook had made a Christmas feast of mince pies, Yorkshire Christmas pie, and plates of cheese. The Yorkshire's crust stood tall and proud, encasing the finest meat money could buy. The cook explained how she started with a pigeon and stuffed it into a Cornish hen. The hen went inside a goose. The goose was put inside a turkey.

"Father's favorite part of the meal. I will take him some after we finish." John smiled at his guests around the dinner table then cleared his throat. "I know we give gifts in the new year, but I could not wait. Since you are all here, it is the perfect time." He placed a black satin box in front of Juliet. "For my future wife."

Juliet stared at the box. She had no desire to open it, knowing the contents.

"Juliet, do not be rude," Constance said.

"Thank you, John." Juliet steadied her hand and reached for the container. She lifted the top to see a ruby and diamond ring inside. "It is lovely."

"Your engagement ring," John said as he took it from its resting place. "Let me put in on."

Juliet had left the MacLaren emerald and diamond ring on the table in Ross' room. He would find it on his return home. Her heart broke as she pictured the look on his face when he discovered it. She felt the cool metal of the new ring slid along her finger and looked down as John kissed the top of her hand. The square cut ruby surrounded by tiny diamonds fit perfectly. "It is beautiful."

After dinner, footmen marched into the room, each carrying a dessert tray. One plate had figures made out of sugar, another held chocolate cream in fluted glasses. Pineapple and oranges were on the final dish. Juliet was glad for the distraction.

"I so like those Ratafia cakes. Did the cook prepare any of those?" Constance looked up at one of the footman as he served her.

"I will check for you, Your Grace." He nodded his head once and left the dining room.

"After dinner, you may want to retire to the parlor, Juliet, with your parents while I will visit Father," John said as they finished dessert.

Juliet had only seen the duke once since her arrival, John standing by her side the entire time. He never gave her a chance to visit again. She had hoped John's father might listen to reason if she could see him alone.

"I would so like to see him," William said.

"He is not up for guests today," John said with a hint of disdain as he studied the wine in his glass. "Or any time soon."

"Oh." Constance covered her mouth. "From the way you speak, he does not seem long for this world. I will pray for a full recovery."

"To God's ears," John said as he gazed up at the ceiling.

"You would be lord of the manor, Duke of Essex," William announced what the rest were thinking.

"Father!" Juliet scolded him with her eyes.

"Sorry, John, but it is something you have to prepare for."

"We should not speak of such things on Christmas Day." Juliet rose from her seat. "Mother? Would you care to join me in the parlor for a glass of sherry?" She brushed past her father and went down the hall.

"Juliet," Constance said as she followed her into the room then stopped and sniffed. "What is that smell?"

"We had a small fire."

"Oh my! Was anyone hurt?"

"No, Mama, we are fine. But thank you for asking." Juliet rolled her eyes. *If only she knew*. She poured the sherry into the glasses. "Happy Christmas."

"In the spirit of Christmas, can you find it in your heart to forgive your father?" Constance raised her brows as she touched her glass to Juliet's.

Juliet drew in a breath. "And should I forgive you, too, Mother?"

"What?" Constance's eyes widened.

"I heard you speaking with John. He asked for your help and you gave it to him…after he offered money."

"I did not! And he did not!" Her mother's face flushed red. "How can you say that? John reminded me that family helps family. That is all."

"Is that all I am to you, Mother? Something to barter? Do you even love me?"

"Yes, we do, Juliet," her father said from the doorway. "I beg your forgiveness. I will do anything to make amends."

"Help me get back to Glenhaven then. Tell the king Donnach MacLaren is loyal." *Will Donnach welcome me back?*

"That I cannot do." William folded his hands behind his back. "I will not send you to a place where there will always be war or dissent. You are safer here. Marry John, Juliet. You will have a good life."

"But I do not love him, Father," Juliet said with tears in her eyes. "I love Ross. I am married to him."

"Not for long. The judge will hear your case at the end of January, and in a few weeks, you will be free to marry John."

"Ah, William, are you speaking of my upcoming nuptials?" John swept into the room. "Father is resting so dinner will have to wait." He poured sherry into a larger glass than Juliet used. She hoped he would not drink too much. That side of John terrified her. She could not reason with him when he became a pompous and entitled drunkard.

John motioned for everyone to sit. As they settled around the fireplace, Juliet turned to her mother. "I have yet to see David. Is he well?"

"Your brother is fine, dear. In fact, he is spending the holidays in London with Charlotte Cosgrove and her family. They are a perfect match and will wed soon. As you know, her father is in the House of Lords, and David hopes to follow in his footsteps one day."

Juliet pictured her brother, so opposite of her. His dark good looks came from their mother, and he went after what he wanted just like her. "I am happy for him."

"Will they attend the Frost Fair?" John leaned forward, excited at the prospect. "Father took Abigail and me to London six Christmases ago. We stayed at the finest hotel and ate the most wonderful Christmas dinner there, but Abigail could not wait to get to the Thames."

"The river has to be frozen, does it not?" William asked.

"Yes, they cannot have it every year. But when they do, it is a sight to behold." John's gray eyes became clear and bright. "Juliet, you should have seen it. It was a few years ago, I believe the year was 1709, but I remember it like yesterday. I was sixteen at the time. Merchants set up stalls and booths on the ice to sell their wares. So much to see! Toys, copper, earthenware, and Abigail's favorite—coffee. That girl loved her coffee. There were food stalls and entertainment, too." He locked eyes with Juliet. "I will take you next year if the river freezes in time. I want you to see it."

"It sounds quite remarkable," Juliet said. She longed to roll her eyes and say she would never go anywhere with him.

"I would love to go!" Constance smiled at John, and Juliet thought she noticed him grimace.

"That could be arranged, Your Grace. We would love to have you." John appeared less excited about the fair and poured another drink.

"John, is it true the Old Pretender has left France for Scotland?" William asked. "What have you heard?"

"He landed on Scottish soil on the twenty-second. Our spies have kept track of his movements. He must have gotten word that Lord Mar was an indecisive bastard, and the Jacobite campaign had become stagnant under his leadership. James Stuart needed to be seen in the flesh and rally his army. Pity." John shook his head. "Those bloody Jacobites outnumbered us at times. They should have won back Scotland by now. Instead, we will prevail."

"You seem so sure," William said as he walked over to the table. He took the decanter of sherry, filled his glass, and then did the same for Constance.

"Thank you, dear." She looked up at him and gave him a smile that did not reach her eyes. "Let us not speak of soldiers and war on this day."

"Of course, Constance. You are quite right."

John held his glass up for another pour. Juliet's father walked to John and filled it to the top then glanced out the window, "It is starting to grow dark. We should leave soon, Constance."

"I just started my drink, William." Juliet's mother appeared out of sorts. She brought the glass to her mouth and took a huge gulp.

"I will let Joseph know." John jumped up to pull the cord a little too eagerly.

Juliet fought back a laugh. John wanted them to leave as much as she did. She glanced at the doorway, surprised Joseph already had arrived with her parents' coats.

"Mother? Father?" She stood. "It was so nice to share the holiday with you." She hugged Constance.

"Oh!" Her mother appeared startled. "We are leaving now?"

"Juliet," her father said as he walked toward her with open arms. She hesitated but remembered it was Christmas. "I am sorry," he whispered in her ear. "I never thought it would have come to this. I was sure I would have the money in time. Believe me."

She pushed away, not knowing what to believe. "Happy Christmas, Father."

William kissed her cheek. "It is so good to have you home. The life you wanted is now yours."

Joseph helped them on with their coats while guiding them from the room. Juliet and John followed them to the front door where their carriage awaited.

"A nightcap, Juliet?" John swept his hand back toward the parlor after the door closed.

Juliet accepted a half glass more and settled in on the chaise closest to the fire.

"Cold, my love?" John slipped in so close she could barely move.

"I am fine, John, thank you." Juliet lost count of his drinks and feared a repeat performance of a week ago.

"I would like to kiss you."

A memory flashed through her mind. Ross asked if he could kiss her the night they met. She recalled the tenderness then the passion of his mouth on hers, making her want more. "Ross," she whispered.

"What did you say?" John's eyes went dark, like two cold stones. Juliet felt his hand tighten on her shoulder.

"I said, of course." She swallowed as her eyes darted around the room. Juliet sat between the fire and John, trapped.

John let out a sigh and pulled her toward him. She smelled the sherry on his breath mingled with the lavender scent he liked to use. "I want your present to me now." He licked her lips, starting on the bottom lip, and working slowly to the top one. "I want to taste all of you," he murmured.

Juliet sat still, letting him explore her mouth, her neck, and down to her bosom. The tip of his tongue did not stop sliding over her body. She wished to push him away and ask for a napkin. He rested his head on her chest and looked up at her. "Kiss me."

She lowered her head until their lips touched. Juliet felt his mouth move against hers then slowly fall away. She opened her eyes to see him slumped in her lap and smiled as she gently pulled her body out from under the snoring man. "You rest, John. Happy Christmas."

Juliet headed for the stairs. "You may have wanted me as a present, John." She stopped at the top of the steps. "But you gave me the best one instead. Sweet dreams."

Chapter Seventeen

A pounding at Juliet's door woke her from sleep. "Juliet," John shouted. "Open the door. I have bad news."

Her heart slammed against her chest as she threw on a robe. "Whatever is it?" She flung the door open wide.

John stood in the hall, dressed in his uniform. "The king has called up my regiment. We are to report as soon as possible. I will lead my men to Perth."

Juliet gasped. "Perth?" Thoughts of Ross flashed through her mind.

"The Old Pretender is on his way there." He looked down at her nightclothes. "Change quickly and come to breakfast. We will continue our conversation in the dining room."

Juliet tugged the rope hanging next to the door and waited for Ann to arrive. She could not believe her good fortune. John would leave for Perth, giving her time to escape. But where would she go? "Perth. If Ross is there, that is where I shall go."

"Did you say Perth, milady?" Ann curtsied and went to the dressing room. "I believe that is where the Jacobite headquarters is located."

"Ann, please do not tell a soul what you heard. I need to stop talking to myself." Juliet joked to distract the girl. "People may think I am a bit daft."

"You are anything but daft, Lady Juliet. I think you are smart and beautiful. If only I could be half the woman you are." Ann emerged from the closet holding a blue wool dress over her arm.

"Ann," Juliet said as she placed a hand on her arm. "You are a lovely girl, do not ever forget that. You have been a kind friend." She tucked a stray piece of Anna's hair back under her maid's cap.

"Friend?"

"Yes, a friend." Juliet wiggled into her corset and turned to let Ann tied the laces.

"Arms up," Ann said as she giggled, holding the blue dress in her hands.

Those words gave Juliet a chill down her spine, and she froze. The hellish night with John swept through her mind. *Do you like to play games, Juliet? Arms up.*

"Milady?" Ann waved a hand in front of Juliet's face.

"Oh! Yes." Juliet let her slip the dress over her head. "I have to get to the dining room, Ann. This is fine." She picked up a brush and ran it through her hair.

Juliet heard John's voice before she entered the room, giving instructions to the servants. "And by all means, she is not to go outside alone. The stable boy has been told not to saddle her horse for any reason. If her mother visits, make sure she does not try to leave with her. It will be January soon, and winter is upon us. I do not think she will try, but if anyone lets her slip by, there will be hell to pay."

Juliet leaned against the hallway wall to catch her breath. John threatened the servants. They would be watching her every move, not wanting his wrath to come down on them. She placed her hand on her stomach, took a deep breath, and put on a smile. "Good morning, John." She swept into the room in a fluid motion. "I see everyone is assembled. Are we all to get instructions?" She batted her lashes.

"No, we have finished here. Dismissed." He nodded at the row of people. They shuffled to the servant's entrance and disappeared, leaving Joseph, the footman, the lone servant in the room.

"Juliet," John said as he walked over to her. "You are lovely, as always." He guided her to the seat next to his at the head of the table. "We have much to discuss. Coffee?"

"Tea would be fine." She leaned back as Joseph served a steaming cup.

John took her hand and kissed it. "I am sorry to be leaving you, my dear. The king agreed to let me have this time at home, but duty now calls."

"John," Juliet said as she retrieved her hand and reached for the teacup. "How did you get your position in the army? You are in charge of a regiment and make agreements with the king. That is quite impressive."

He smirked. "Money speaks many languages, especially to those in dire need of it."

"So you bought your commission?"

"For you, my love." John nodded at Joseph, and waited for coffee to be poured into his cup. "I needed power when I arrived at Glenhaven. I could not just be the king's courier like my first visit. I was given the authority to make decisions deemed fit for any English citizen. I felt you needed to come home for your safety. Donnach MacLaren would not challenge a colonel in the British army."

He went to such extremes to bring me home? I have to be careful. "That was kind of you to do, for my sake. I am curious, how long will you be part of the British army?"

"Until this bloody uprising ends. Then I am relieved of my command."

"But if you already have money and position—?"

"Why stay and fight? At first, it was done for you, Juliet. But now that I have led my men into battle, heard them call out my name as we charge..." John puffed out his chest and said in a deeper tone, "Lord Alder's Regiment! Charge!" He smiled at Juliet. "I have become loyal to the cause and my men."

"Do you know how long you will be gone?" Juliet asked, trying to look worried.

"Until it is over. I am afraid, my love, we will have to postpone the divorce hearing until I return."

"That is fine. I understand." Juliet stared into her teacup, hoping to mask her hopeful expression.

"We may not marry on your birthday, although I so wanted to." John leaned back, looking at Juliet over the cup he held to his mouth. "Would you consider giving your husband-to-be a farewell to remember?" He wiggled his eyebrows.

Juliet choked on the tea she sipped. She grabbed for her napkin and spit the liquid into it. "John! How many times have we discussed this? I am a lady and will wait till my wedding day."

"But think of our past interludes and the tender kisses. The time we were interrupted in your bedroom. We were as close as two people can be. Do you not want that with me?"

Tender interludes? Juliet folded her hands in her lap to keep herself in check. "When the time is right," she answered.

"Sir." Joseph clicked his heels together and bowed. "Your escorts are here."

"Already?"

The footman nodded.

"Give them some breakfast and tell them I will be down shortly." John turned to Juliet. "I have to finish packing. Will you see me off?"

"Of course. Just let me know when." Juliet brought the teacup to her mouth as John rose from his chair, hoping to avoid a kiss.

"Go to your bedroom. I will seek you out there." He left the room with Joseph, leaving Juliet alone.

"Why can I not stay right here? Why the bedroom?" She brought a fist down to the table. "A few more hours then he will be gone." She looked up to see Ann staring at her, mouth hanging open.

"Sorry, milady. I came out to see if you needed anything. I did not realize you felt the same about the lord as I do." A smile crept across her face.

"Then you will help me?" Juliet's heart leapt in her chest. She had an ally.

"I can wait in your dressing room. No one would know I am there. I can come out at the appropriate time."

"You would do that for me?" Tears welled in her eyes.

"I know you love your Highland husband, Lady Juliet. I can see it in your eyes. You sit at your window and stare out as if you are in another place and time. My heart breaks for you. I am sorry Lord John is forcing you to marry him."

"I loved him once, Ann, but that is a fond memory. I wished I could still think kindly of him. I do not know this John. He has changed."

"Since you left for Scotland he has not been the same. That is what they say." Ann cocked her head toward the servants' door. "The boy inside him left and a raging man took his place." She shrugged. "As cook would say."

Can I trust her? Juliet sighed. *I have no one else.* "Let us go up and get ready." She slid the chair back and made her way up the stairs to her room with Ann.

~ * ~

John appeared in her bedroom doorway, still dressed in uniform, ready to take his leave. Juliet rose from her vanity chair and rushed to greet him, hoping to keep him from entering the room. He swept her into his arms, slammed the door shut behind him, and walked her backward to the bed. "Have you ever taken a soldier to bed? A commander of the British army?" His lips found hers before she could answer. He pulled back and said, "Take off your dress and on your knees."

Juliet's heart raced. She wondered what he had in mind. Her hands fumbled with the back laces of her dress as her mind spun out of control.

"Here." John twisted her around. "Let me. I know you are upset I am leaving." He ripped the gown from her shoulders after loosening the laces and let it drop to the floor. The corset flew across the room. Her shift gave little protection against the cold chill in the room. His hands fondled her body as he turned her toward him. He pointed to the floor. "Get down."

"Why?"

"To make a promise."

Juliet sank to her knees and waited.

"Say you will be here on my return. You will marry me without delay and love me until the end of our days."

Juliet's mouth went dry. She fought to find her voice. "I will wait for you."

"And?"

"Love you to the end of our days." Her voice shook.

"Get up." John removed his belt and laid a pistol on a table next to the bed. He slipped his red jacket off. "There. Much better." He took Juliet by the arms. "Please, I want something to remember you by, to think about during the cold nights in camp."

When Ross asked, Juliet wished she could give him everything and more. John's words did not move her. She could do as he asked, but when she thought of his arms around her a feeling of nausea swept through her.

"Juliet?" John whispered as he gave her a light shake. "Did you hear me?"

"Yes."

"Then join me." He motioned to the bed as he gave her a nudge.

She fell back onto the mattress and slid to the middle of the bed. John lifted one knee, resting it on the edge.

"Lady Juliet, I found the necklace you asked for!" Ann rushed from the dressing room. "Oh, pardon me." Her eyes widened in a mock look of horror and shock.

"Get out!" John yelled and pointed to the door.

"But Lady Juliet—"

"I do not care what Lady Juliet wanted you to do. Do it later! Get out!"

Ann looked at Juliet and back at John. "I need—"

Before she finished, John turned toward the table and picked up the pistol. He aimed the gun at the maid. "Did you hear me?"

Ann's eyes sent an apology to Juliet as she rushed for the door. The plan had failed miserably but gave Juliet enough time to slide her hand under the pillow. When John faced her, she brandished the knife at his throat.

"Now you get out," she said through gritted teeth. Her heart pounded but her thoughts were clear, and she would not hesitate to use the weapon. Let them throw her in prison if she stabbed him. Juliet did not care. "I will make no promises to you," she hissed. "I will not marry you. My husband is a good man. He would not aim a gun at a servant. He would not threaten me in our bed. You will never be my husband."

John threw his head back and laughed. "Enjoy your little game while you can, Juliet. You will be here when I return. You have nowhere to go. Go ahead. Try to leave. You will see."

"Sir?" A tap came at the door. "We need to head out to make camp before we lose light."

"I am coming." John brushed off his coat and went to the mirror. He checked front and back before adding the belt. "I look quite good for an officer, do you not agree, Juliet?"

She had quickly dressed while he primped at the mirror. "You are a handsome man, John. I always thought that."

"There is my girl." He flashed a wicked smile.

Juliet still held the blade in one hand and would not put it down until he left. "Stay safe, John. I wish no harm to come to you."

"Thank you." He bowed and headed for the door. "You know," John said as he stopped at the door, "this will not happen again. You *will* come to my bed and also become my wife." He lifted his chin and stared into her eyes. "Until then."

Juliet followed after, watching until he reached the bottom of the stairs. "I will never be your wife!" she called after him. "I have a husband, and his name is Ross MacLaren." She shuddered as he flashed a look of anger in her direction then went out the front door.

~ * ~

One cold, gray day blended into the next. Juliet never left her room and had no idea how much time had passed. She had lost track of the month and even the day. When she allowed herself to think, her thoughts went to Ross. *Would John and Ross meet up in battle? Is Ross still alive?*

As she sat alone in her room, Juliet had much time to think. She played out scenarios in her head. In one, she married John and tried her best to make it work. After all, she had agreed to come back to England with the promise the MacLarens would be safe. Juliet would dig deep to find the feelings she once had for John but could not. John would grow bitter after they wed, and they would live the rest of their years in a loveless marriage.

In another daydream, she escaped and went to her childhood home. Her father protected her this time, and she lived out her years as an unmarried spinster, longing for a love she never could have.

Finally, in the best scene, the one she played over and over in her head, took her home to Glenhaven. The family rejoiced when they saw her. Juliet never had sisters and her brother had been distant. They never had a serious conversation in all her years living at Norchester. Ross' siblings were quite the opposite, loving and boisterous, showing their emotions by fighting and laughing together. "If only that dream could come true." She sighed as she stared out the window.

A knock on the door signaled Ann's arrival. She brought Juliet meals and coaxed her into eating.

"Milady? I have some tea and biscuits." She set the tray on the table. "Please come and eat. You sit and stare out the window all day. I do not think it is good for your health."

Juliet turned and smiled at the girl. "Only if you will join me."

Ann slid out a chair and settled in. She poured tea in Juliet's cup. "You have to eat. Don't just drink the tea," she said as Juliet came and sat across from her.

"Has there been any news?" Juliet asked Ann the same question every day. John had instructed the staff to only pass along positive information, but the girl willingly told her more.

"Yes, from what I have heard, the British are claiming victory," Ann said.

"The Jacobite army was so strong in the beginning and fell apart so quickly." Juliet shook her head. "Ross told me there were problems." She had been torn over who she wanted to win the war. Her English side wanted things to stay the same, as they always were. Her loyalty to the family in Scotland wanted freedom for them, something they wanted so badly. In the end, she never made a final decision.

"As our soldiers advanced on Perth," Ann continued, "Lord Mar had given orders to burn villages between Stirling and Perth so our men would have nowhere to get supplies. but we carried on. The Jacobite numbers have dwindled, milady, and our army has grown and acquired heavy artillery." She leaned forward and whispered, "Or so says Joseph. I heard him talking to the cook when I was preparing your breakfast."

"When did that happen? The burning?"

"The end of January."

"Ann?" Juliet leaned forward. "What day is it?"

Her eyes widened. “You do not know? You have been in this room too long, milady. It is the tenth of February. I came up to tell you Lord Alder has sent word he is on his way home. The English have claimed victory. You did not hear me before? Lord Mar led the Jacobites out of Perth on the fourth of February. The British army has been busy taking prisoners to try for treason.”

“Ross!”

“If he is caught, that could be his fate.”

Juliet covered her face with her hands. The news couldn’t get any worse.

“Do not cry, Lady Juliet. I should have never given you that letter. You haven’t been the same since,” Ann said, shaking her head. “I stole it for you from Lord John’s pile of mail, hoping it would make you happy. Instead you have been depressed for weeks. Now I wish I had never seen it.”

“Do not blame yourself, Ann.” Juliet pushed her plate of food toward thc middle of the table. “I would like some time to myself, if that is all right.”

“I will clear this and be on my way.”

Juliet waited until Ann closed the door behind her then slid the letter she always kept tucked in her sleeve from its hiding place. She sank into her chair by the window and unfolded the paper, now worn after many readings. The handwriting on the paper flowed along in a familiar style. “Eva.” She sighed as she smoothed the letter in her lap and began to read.

Juliet,

I hope this letter finds you in good health. The cold has set upon us, but we have enough supplies to get through the dark days. Little Juliet is kicking my belly daily now. I wish you were here to share it. Duncan insists it is a boy and his name will be Donnach or Campbell, after his grandfather. I know in my heart that it is a girl. The good Lord would not deprive me of that simple request.

I promised to write and let you know the progress of Greer’s health. She never left her bed again after you left. We lost our sister on the third of January. For some reason, she thought you were coming home for Hogmanay and fought to live to the new year. Little Alec cries for her daily, and we do our best to comfort him. Each day he goes to the courtyard to wait for your return. That seems to give him hope and calms his spirit.

I am not writing this to hurt you. I want you to know that we still think of you and wish you could return to us. I hope this letter finds its way to you and not into Lord John's hands. I will have Duncan take it to the village as soon as I finish. He said someone will take it into town and hopefully to England from there.

Your friend and servant,
Eva

"No! No! No! She was not supposed to die." Juliet clenched the letter in one hand and pounded her leg with the other. Tears welled in her eyes as she ran to the window and stared into the dark gray sky. "Poor little Alec. I need to be there for him." She let out a scream as she ripped the paper to shreds and threw it into the fire. Of all the terrible events she had been through, not being there for the child was the worst.

A shiver ran through her, and it felt as if a hot poker stabbed her heart. Juliet had no words, only moans and sobs as she threw her body onto her bed. Tears streamed down her face. Her whole body ached with grief and pain. "Please make it stop," she whispered. "I cannot live another day if it does not."

Chapter Eighteen

"Lady Juliet? Are you awake?" Ann's voice came through the door.

"Yes, come in." Juliet struggled to sit up.

Ann looked at the table where trays of food sat. "You did not eat."

Juliet barely noticed Ann come in and out yesterday, bringing her lunch and dinner. "I am sorry. I could not eat."

"You will waste away to nothing, milady."

"Then Lord Alder will not be able to find me." Juliet tried to smile.

"Your letter?" Anna asked. "Do you want to talk about it? Every time I ask, you never answer. Did you receive bad news?"

Juliet let out a long breath. "Ross' sister died."

"The one you said was ill."

"Yes. Greer."

"She wanted you to raise her son if something should happen to her," Ann said.

Juliet bit her lip and nodded.

"We will just have to find a way to send you back then." Her maid put her hands on her hips. "A child needs a mother."

"If only it were that easy." Juliet sighed. "Donnach would not welcome me or protect me. Ross is my home, not Glenhaven, and he is not there."

"That sounds so romantic." Ann hugged her body as she wrapped her arms around her waist. "I can almost picture Ross. You have told me so much about him." Her face changed to one of panic. "Oh! I have something to tell you." Ann's voice went to a whisper. "There is word the lord will be home tonight."

Juliet flew out of bed. "No! It is too soon. I have not made a plan. I sat by the window all these weeks, feeling sorry for myself, mourning Greer, and acting helpless. How could I be so stupid?"

Ann looked at the floor. "You will have to let him into your bed. I am sorry."

"Do not be sorry, Ann. I may be able to leave before he gets here."

"But where would you go? You will not survive the cold on your own. Let me help."

John had aimed a gun at Ann. No way would she involve her in an escape plan. Juliet dropped her shoulders. "You are right. I am doomed." She locked eyes with Ann. "As soon as he arrives, you are to tell me. I will just have to make the best of it."

Ann gave a nod and closed the door as she left the room. Juliet rushed to the closet and chose the warmest clothes she could find. A travel bag sat in the corner, and she packed what she could fit inside. She combed the room, looking for necessities and items to help her stay warm. "I will need food. Do I dare visit the kitchen?"

Juliet decided to boldly walk into the kitchen as she made her way down the stairs. She was the lady of the house, or would be, so she had every right. The cook curtsied as she entered. A few servants bowed and stepped out of her way. "Ann has been wonderful," Juliet said to the cook. "She brings good food to my room, but I have a craving for those little biscuits. Where do you keep them?" Juliet pretended to search the room with her eyes, turning her head to the left then right.

The cook scrambled around the kitchen, opening containers to show Juliet what she had baked.

"Lovely. I will take them all."

The cook appeared surprised but did as she asked. While she waited, Juliet searched the kitchen for utensils and a cooking pot. She already had the knife Glynis gave her, but another one would be useful. Juliet slipped one up her sleeve and placed a small pot under her shawl. To light a fire, she needed flint and steel. She knew it was not an easy task to start one and hoped she could learn fast. Woe to the servant who let a fire burn out in the fireplace.

Juliet walked to the back of the room where a fire blazed in the huge kitchen fireplace. *They certainly must keep a stockpile here.* She spied a tall tin box next to the hearth. Her heart pounded as she approached the container and lifted the lid. She glanced over her shoulder making sure no one watched. Her hand slipped in and out quickly, squeezing the flint and steel in her palm. *Where do I hide them?* She looked down at her chest and slipped them into her bosom.

"Milady?" The cook tapped her shoulder.

Startled, Juliet jumped and let out a gasp.

"I am so sorry, madam. I did not mean to scare you. I just wanted to tell you I have wrapped the biscuits. They are on the table." She gestured to the spot. "Is there anything else you would like?" She smiled, showing crooked teeth. Two were missing on either side of the front four.

"No, you have been quite helpful. I will let Lord Alder know."

The cook curtsied. "Why thank you. I do my best."

Juliet hoped she did not make too many strange noises as she left the kitchen. The metal pot tapped against her arm where she had hidden the knife up her sleeve. She let out a breath when she reached her room, spreading the secret loot on her bed. Her next step was to pack it all away. She would have to wait for dusk to steal away, and prayed she would survive the cold night ahead of her.

~ * ~

Juliet sat on the edge of the bed making final plans in her head when something thumped against her window. Her heart skipped a beat as she rushed to the curtain and pulled it back. The gray morning had turned into a darker afternoon, and she could not see below the second floor. A white ball hurled toward her window, causing her to step back in fright. "Oh!"

Gaining her composure, Juliet realized someone threw that snow on purpose. *Do I dare open the window?* She took a few steps toward it and loosened the latch. *I have nothing to lose.* She lifted the bottom of the sash window and stuck her head out into the foggy air. "Who is there?"

Instead of an answer, a rope flew at her. Pure instinct caused her to reach out and catch it. The sturdy rope looked strong enough to support a climber. "Who ever is out there, thank you. I will securely tie it and let you know when it is ready."

Juliet glanced around the room to find the best spot to tie the rope. *The bed? The dresser?* Her nerves took over. *Hurry! Ann must have arranged this, and I do not have much time.* She chose the leg of the sturdy mahogany bed. Her hands trembled as she coiled the rope around its leg and tied it as tightly as she could. She gave a gentle tug and waited.

A dark head appeared at the base of the window. A hand grasped the frame and finally a body wrapped in dark clothing tumbled into her room. The soggy lump sat up and pushed the cloak from their shoulders.

"Glynis!" Juliet rushed to her side and knelt on the floor. She wrapped her arms around her. Tears stung her eyes." I have never been so glad to see someone in my life!"

Glynis lifted the MacLaren brow. "Ye done?" She stared down at Juliet's arm around her body.

"Yes, yes, of course." Juliet lifted her hands in the air. "I cannot believe you came. Is it really you?"

"Aye." Glynis scooted back and leaned against the wall, pulling her knees up to her chest, catching her breath. "And now we need to get ye out of here and take ye home."

"I cannot go with you," Juliet cried as she realized she could not go with her liberator to Glenhaven. She thought of the Cosgroves and her brother. "I will go to London. Will you help me get there?"

"No." Glynis shook her head as she straightened her plaid. "Ye will come with me—"

"And me," a male voice said from the window.

Juliet froze. She knew the voice but was afraid to look. "It cannot be."

Glynis smiled. "Ye best look before the beef head falls from the window."

"Ross!" Juliet ran to the window as he climbed in. She fell to the floor, grabbing for him, wanting to feel his body to make sure he was real.

"My bonny lass," he said as he brought her to him.

Juliet wept in his arms, relieved he was alive and not in the hands of the British Army.

A knock came at the door. "Milady?"

Juliet whispered, "It is my maidservant, Ann. She can be trusted, but I do not want to involve her." She put a finger to her lips and went to the door.

"Yes?" Juliet said as she opened it a crack.

"He is home, milady. The cook is preparing dinner. He would like you to join him."

Juliet swallowed. "Tell him I will be down in a minute."

Ann curtsied. Juliet shut the door and leaned against it.

"I willna let ye go to him, Juliet." Ross stood in front of her, eyes filled with tears. "He had enough of ye already."

Juliet locked eyes with her husband. "You do not think I let him in my bed, do you?" A wave of anger spread through her. She wanted to recount the times she had to fight off John's advances or give in to a kiss or two and longed to make Ross feel the humiliation and helplessness of her situation. But he was a man. He would never understand.

"Not if ye used the dagger I sent ye." Glynis chuckled, still leaning against the wall, arms dangling over her knees. "Trust her, Ross. Let her go. She may have her reasons."

"Thank you, Glynis. I want him to see me. He threatened the staff and there would be consequences if I was not here when he returned."

"If yer not back in a short while, I am coming for ye," Ross said as he bent to kiss her. "For luck."

Juliet placed her hands on his chest. "Before I go, Ross MacLaren, I am not waiting another minute to say this. I love you."

A smile spread across his face. "I ken."

"You do?" Juliet crossed her brow then glanced at Glynis. "You gave him the letter?"

"Aye." Glynis nodded without looking at Juliet. She was too busy adjusting her cloak for comfort.

Juliet kissed Ross and slipped out the door. She could hear her heart beating in her ears as she descended the stairs, all her senses were on edge. Every nerve tingled, and a range of familiar scents caught her attention as she walked through the house. The aroma of flowers in the foyer, the faint smell of smoke from the parlor, and a waft of fresh baked bread coming down the hallway from the kitchen. John's voice carried from the dining room, stinging her ears.

"More wine, Joseph! A celebration is in order." He raised his eyebrows when he spotted her. "Well, I see my wayward fiancée did not get too far. I thought you planned to not be here on my return."

"As you see, I am here." Juliet jutted out her chin. "I was about to change for dinner when I got your message so if you will allow, I will return shortly."

"No need to change. Come, greet your husband-to-be." He pushed back his chair and rose to greet her.

Juliet dreaded each step she took that closed the gap between them. *I have to be convincing*. "John!" She extended her arms in welcome.

A look of surprise spread across his face then relief. Juliet embraced him and pulled back, kissing him as if she was welcoming Ross home. Guilt swept through her but there was no other way.

"Well." John straightened his coat. "Just as I expected. You doted upon my very absence."

"Shakespeare. You always loved reciting from his plays. And were quite good at it, if I remember." Juliet looked up at him and batted her eyelashes.

"Fine! Your flattery worked." He waved his hand. "Go and change. I can wait. But do not be too long."

Juliet kissed his cheek. "Thank you." She restrained every muscle to keep from running through the hall and up the steps. When she reached the top of the stairs, Juliet rushed into her room.

~ * ~

Ross wrung his hands, pacing back and forth on the Persian rug that covered the hardwood floor in Juliet's bedroom.

"I swear yer going to wear a hole in that fancy rug, Ross," Glynis said. "Sit down, ye pigheaded mule."

He stopped and glared at her. "Why are ye calling me names, sister?"

"The lass just told ye she loved ye, and yer fuming over Lord John instead."

Ross walked to where his sister sat and slid down the wall next to her, coming to a stop when his backside hit the floor. "Yer right. I couldna stand the thought of that bloody arsehole touching her." He buried his face in his hands. "When Da first told us of his plan, I wanted no part of it. He said I could refuse to marry the lass once she got to Glenhaven. But …"

Glynis pulled his hands away from his face. "Ye loved her once ye laid eyes on her?"

"Aye." Ross took a breath and let it out slowly. "At first, I thought I was taken by her beauty. I wanted to deny the feeling. How could I fall in love with a Sassenach? But I only saw her … nothing else. And once I got to ken her? I swore I would protect her for the rest of my life." He glanced at Glynis. "But she..." He shook his head. "I could never tell if she loved me. Every time I thought she would say it, something stopped her." Ross nodded toward the door. "I thought she was thinking of him, the fecking piece of shite."

Glynis let out a hearty laugh. "That he is."

Ross studied his sister's face. "Ye ken something I dinna. Why did ye give her that knife?"

"For protection, Ross." Glynis lowered her eyes.

"Ye were never good at lying to me, sister." Ross placed his hand under her chin, lifting her head. "What happened?"

"The bastard tried to have his way with her at Glenhaven before they left." Glynis pretend to spit over her shoulder. "I happened by the room. The door was open. I heard Juliet trying to reason with him, but he overpowered her. When I saw him throw her on the bed, I had to do something. The day she left I hid a dirk among her clothes in the trunk before the servants took it downstairs."

"Thank ye for that." Ross took Glynis' hand. "Ye and I are connected in some mysterious way, ye ken. Ye felt my love for her."

"Mum said it was the faeries." Glynis smiled. "We were born in the month of All Hallow's Eve when they are ready to come out and play. Me first then ye the year after. She thinks they bonded us together to cause her extra grief. At times, I think Mum was right. I ken what yer thinking before ye do."

"And what am I thinking now?" Ross teased.

"That yer wife said she loved ye, ye beef head." She nudged him with her elbow. "And I am glad she does. I can tolerate her more than some of the women in the village."

"Ye can? That is progress." Ross lifted his brow. "When I left for Perth, I thought my sisters were still not fond of me wife."

"Greer liked her. Maybe not at first, but Juliet was there for her when ye went off to war the first time. She helped with Alec, and the wee one likes her."

"And what about ye? When did ye come to like her?"

"She helped Alec learn to ride. Juliet is good with the horses. And…" Glynis looked away. "She listens to me and thinks I have a right to live as I choose."

"Aye, to see the world." Ross placed his hand on her arm. "I wish that for ye also."

Glynis laid her head on his shoulder. "If we bring Juliet home, Da will not be happy. Having one Sassenach forced upon him was enough, but two?"

"Ye mean Eva? I thought he gave his blessing after he found out he would be a granda."

"Ross, ye can be dumb as a post at times. Eva was Juliet's maid and a Sassenach. Do ye think Da was happy about that? But she was with child, and Duncan said they would run away if Da did not agree to the marriage."

"Our little brother has grown this year," Ross said then looked down at her, brows crossed. "Eva was with child before they married? I had forgotten that after all these months." He felt a blow to his side. "Och! That hurt!" They both started laughing.

The door flew open, and Juliet stood in the doorway, hands on her hips. "I hope you two are enjoying yourselves."

"Aye," Ross said as he smiled up at her. "Glynis tells me how she hid the dirk in yer trunk. I am glad ye found it, Juliet, and it didna get in the wrong hands."

"Are you two done with storytelling?" Juliet teased, but Ross noticed her eye twitch. "I would like to leave this place, the sooner the better."

Glynis popped up to her feet. "Sorry, lass, I was just getting comfortable. Thawing out my boots." She pointed to her feet and the puddle of water that surrounded them.

"I have our horses hidden in the brush just beyond the house. Let us go." Ross offered his hand to Juliet. "Glynis will go out the window first then I will help ye down."

Juliet went to take his hand then hesitated. "Wait! I planned to escape tonight." She rushed in the dressing room, and brought out her travel bag plus a brown sack. "Food." She held up the bag. "I went to the kitchen earlier."

Glynis nodded her approval as she climbed over the window frame. Ross wrapped Juliet's cloak around her and held her close. "Ye love me?" His heart soared with happiness. "I never thought ye would."

"I am so sorry, Ross. I have waited months to tell you. I will tell you more, but first I would like to leave this awful house."

"I can wait." He bent down and placed a gentle kiss on her mouth. She tasted so good, sweeter than he remembered. "My love," he whispered. "Ye are mine, and mine alone. John Alder will never lay eyes on ye again." He walked to the window to check on Glynis' progress and motioned for Juliet to join him.

"Wait!" Juliet showed him her left hand.

An angry roar went up inside him, but Ross did not let Juliet see his hatred. Instead he gently pulled John's engagement ring from her finger. "Where do ye want me to put it?"

"Anywhere. I do not care."

Ross placed it in the middle of her bed. He lifted his brow and gave his wife a one-sided smile and a wink. Then he guided her to the window, placed the rope in her hands, and lifted her through the open space.

~ * ~

"My things!" Juliet's eyes widened as the cold air hit her face. She began to slide down the rope whether she wanted to or not. Her stomach flipped, and her scream caught in her throat.

Glynis broke her fall, placed her to the side then spread out her arms. Juliet's bag flew out the window. Ross' legs came next. He had tied the food satchel to his belt, and it dangled to one side. Juliet followed the silent instructions Ross pantomimed when he reached the ground and followed him to the place where he hid the horses.

The night air was extra cold, but Juliet felt a bead of sweat trail down her spine. She wiped her forehead and let out a sigh of relief when she saw the horses.

"My horse?" Juliet wrapped her arms around its muzzle. "How did you manage?" She turned to Ross and saw him smile.

"I ken ye loved and trusted him, Juliet. I stole him from the barn before I climbed up to yer room."

Glynis looked up at the full moon. "We have some light to travel by." She glanced at Juliet. "Are ye ready to ride through the night? We have a spot picked out to camp, but 'tis miles away."

"I will ride day and night to get away from here." Juliet mounted her horse. "What are you both waiting for? Let us go."

Chapter Nineteen

The trip from Alder Estate to Scotland had been grueling. The first night and into the next day they rode quite a distance, never stopping until they reached the spot Glynis deemed safe. The three fell into a makeshift tent and slept soundly side by side. Then, on the following night, Glynis feigned illness and insisted on heading into the woods to find pine needles to chew on. Not much talking or sleep happened that night. Ross pulled Juliet into the tent as soon as Glynis disappeared into the night. They made love then clung to each other until morning light. One day merged into the next until they reached the border. The last two nights of the trip, the trio camped on Scottish soil. Now, so close to home, Juliet saw relief in both their faces.

"Ross?" Juliet settled in next to him by the fire on the last day. "I am sorry to hear what happened at Perth. Did you—?"

"Help set fire to the villages? Aye." He played with a few sticks he held in his hand and threw one into the flames. "Some of the clans had already left for home. I sent our men home after the fire. I saw the defeat in their faces, the slump of their shoulders. They had given their all for naught."

"You did not go with them?" Surprised by the information, Juliet looked at Glynis. "Then how did you end up together?"

Glynis lifted her shoulders. "When the men came back to the village without him, I began to question each and every one of them, gathering bits of information. Most believed he was still with the regiment. I set out in the direction of Perth and hoped to find him."

"And ye found me." Ross nodded his head. "On the road home."

"Why did you stay behind?" Juliet wrinkled her brow.

"I helped escort James Stuart to his ship after my men left. He is safely on his way back to France. There was nothing left to do but go home or be captured by the British."

"Are they aware the MacLarens were in the fight?" Juliet bit down on her bottom lip.

"They may. I dinna ken. The only proof is John's word. He can say I wasna at Glenhaven during his visit."

"That is not enough evidence!" Juliet met his eyes and watched him shake his head.

"'Tis." He put his arm around her shoulders and drew her to him. "I love ye, but ye have to believe it. An Englishman's word against mine? Who do you think they would believe? We may be in danger for a while, Juliet."

"Like the MacGregors," Glynis said as she chewed on a small stick. "We have to tell Jamie he canna go home to visit his returning clan. Even if he dinna fight, 'tis not safe."

"What did the MacGregors do?" Juliet wished the war never happened. So many people she loved were in danger.

"Do ye ken the history of the MacGregor clan?" Ross asked.

Juliet shook her head. She never studied Scottish history. "Please tell me."

Ross poured a cup of whiskey and offered her a taste. "To keep ye warm." He waited as she sipped before he started the story.

"In 1602 the MacGregors ambushed the Colquhouns and others who rode with them … with good reason. That group of men had been commissioned by the king to punish the MacGregors for raids on settlements. The MacGregors had been persecuted for centuries, sometimes deservedly so, and they finally decided to fight back. Outnumbered, they split their forces in two. One group attacked from the front." Ross held up one hand. "The other came up from the rear." He raised the other one. "They caught the Colquhoun group between them," he said as he clapped his hands together, "slaughtering them. The king was outraged, and in a fit of anger, abolished their name. From then on, any person bearing that name had to choose another and renounce the old. No one could call themselves Gregor or MacGregor thereafter under pain of death."

"How did the clan name survive?" Juliet asked.

"Those who refused to change their names went to Ireland or across the sea to the colonies. Sympathetic clans helped them too. But for over fifty years, those people had no home and were on the run. They were considered a rebellious tribe. Laws were made against them. When caught, they were imprisoned or sold as slaves."

"What happened to the MacGregor men who fought in that battle?" Juliet asked.

"Captured and hanged."

She shuddered at the thought. "But there are MacGregors now, Ross. The name has returned. I do not understand."

"The name ban lifted in 1660, but there are still laws against the clan. The MacGregors proudly took their name back." He drained his cup. "They are a hearty bunch. Many families had fourteen children or more to carry on the name."

"But it seems their bad reputation is in the past. What does that have to do with the Jacobite rising?"

"Ever hear of Rob Roy?"

"I have heard tales of Rob Roy, yes." Juliet nodded. "He is an outlaw and a cattle rustler but also a romantic figure."

"Aye, so I have heard." Ross laughed. "He has many names and lives and dies to see another day. *He* is a MacGregor."

"He is?" Juliet lifted her brows in surprise. "Did he fight alongside you?"

"No." Ross slowly moved his head back and forth. "At times, I wondered whose side he was on. His clan sat by and watched the fight at Sheriffmuir as if waiting to see who would win the battle. There were rumors he might side with the British. He has an ally in their leader, the Duke of Argyll."

"You tell me of only one man, Ross. And it sounds as if the British have no problem with Rob Roy, especially if he did not join in the fight. Please explain why the MacGregors are in more trouble for the uprising than the rest of you. I still do not understand."

"Ye dinna have patience, wife, or an ear for a good story. I am getting to it."

Glynis threw a stick at him. "I could tell it faster, brother."

Juliet turned to her. "I also want to hear *your* story, Glynis. Whatever possessed you to leave home to look for Ross?"

"Mum would say the devil made her do it." Ross threw his head back and laughed.

Juliet smiled. She wondered if Ross knew how Glynis felt about marriage and children. How she longed for adventure. If he did, what would he advise her to do?

"No one can stop that one," Ross said as he pointed at Glynis. "Stubborn, like all the MacLarens."

"I admire her," Juliet said. "Glynis has saved me more than once." She reached out her hand toward her sister-in-law.

Glynis slipped her hand into Juliet's and squeezed. "We better let Ross get on with his story, or we will freeze into statues before he is done." She laughed and threw another stick at Ross.

"Verra funny, sister." Ross caught the twig and tossed it in the fire. "Where was I? Och, I remember. Telling Juliet why the MacGregors are in more trouble than the rest of us." He refilled his cup of whiskey and settled back.

"In September, the MacGregors came out in support of Lord Mar in hopes he would rescind the act against them." He turned and looked at Juliet. "As I said, although the ban against their name was lifted, there are still laws against them. Then, they broke out into open rebellion that month. On their way to join up with the other clans, the MacGregors passed through the town of Dunbartonshire, robbing them of weapons, horses, and whatever they deemed useful for the uprising. Those who resisted were punished."

Ross stretched his arms and shifted his body to find a comfortable spot. "When they arrived at Inversnaid on the twenty-ninth of September, the MacGregors decided to take possession of the villagers' boats and pulled them up on dry land. If people did not cooperate, they were threatened. They tend to use violence to get their way." Ross lifted a shoulder.

"Oh." Juliet hated to hear how people treated each other in war.

"Then the MacGregors marched home after Sheriffmuir, a show of defeat. We ken in our hearts it was the end, but we stayed … some of us, that is." Ross rubbed his face. "I dinna understand. We had them outnumbered. Most of Scotland was back in our hands, but they won."

"Ross," Glynis stood. "We have to get ye home. If the soldiers come, ye have to be there. The family will do whatever it can to protect ye. We dinna want ye to hang for treason."

Juliet stood and said, "I will leave now if you want." It was the dark of night, but she would do anything to keep Ross safe.

"I ken ye would, sister," Glynis said. "As soon as we see light, we will be on our way." She lifted the door of the makeshift tent and crawled inside.

"Ross," Juliet walked over and took his hand. "Thank you for finding me and bringing me home."

"Ye think of Glenhaven as home?" He rubbed the top of her hand with his thumb.

"No, Ross." It came to Juliet as if someone whispered in her ear. "*You* are my home. Wherever you are, that is where I want to be."

~ * ~

The horses picked up their pace as if they knew the end of the journey drew near. Juliet followed Glynis down the road that took them toward home. Ross pulled up his horse when they reached the ledge where Juliet first sat on the day she arrived at Glenhaven.

A dusting of white snow covered the village, and gray smoke poured from the chimneys of the houses. The animals huddled in their pens. Early morning risers had been hard at work, clearing paths and tending to the sheep, goats, and other livestock.

Juliet turned to Ross. "Does it feel good to be home?"

"Aye," he said, taking a breath then letting it out, "but if I had found ye gone when I got here, I may not have been so happy."

"Your father is not going to be happy to see me. I can tell you that." Juliet looked at him from the corner of her eye.

"If he is upset, we will deal with it. For now, let us enjoy the view."

Juliet's eyes traveled up the road to the castle. The pale gray stone of the building stood out against the dark gray afternoon sky. Inside the walls, she knew sadness prevailed. Glynis disappeared one day, Ross was at war, and Greer had died. So different from the first day she arrived. "I am ready if you are, Ross."

He glanced at Glynis. "Ye lead the way, sister. Bring us home."

Cowan ran from his family's pen as they rode through the village, the first to spot them. "The laird's son and his lady! Lady Glynis!" He wore a giant grin, exposing all his teeth as he vigorously waved his hand.

Juliet pulled up her horse. "Hello, Cowan." She always had a fondness for the boy.

"Did ye stab ye captor and escape?" He pantomimed a recreation of the scene.

"No," Juliet said, shaking her head with a laugh. "Nothing like that. My husband came for me and brought me home."

Glynis cleared her throat.

"Oh! And he could not have done it without Glynis." Juliet smiled her way.

"Ye are home just in time for the winter's thaw. See?" He pointed at the ground. "The snow will be gone soon."

Juliet had lost track of the days again. "That sounds wonderful, Cowan. Come and visit soon. Little Alec would love to see you."

"I will." He lowered his eyes to the ground and kicked the gray, mushy snow. "I am happy ye are back, Madam."

"Thank you." Juliet nudged her horse and headed down the road. Her heart began to beat faster when they reached the woods. She had no idea if she would be welcomed at the castle. They came out into the field as the sun broke through the clouds. "I hope that is a good sign, Ross," she said to him over her shoulder then gazed up at the sun.

He helped her from her horse as Glynis rode on to the stable. "I want to get the horses settled in the barn. They deserve a good rest." He spoke softly to the animals as he led them away, leaving her to wait outside.

The longer Juliet stood in front of the castle, the more anxious she became. During their nights around the campfire, the trio had discussed many issues. Juliet told of Eva's letter and that she knew Greer had died. She and Ross spent hours talking about Alec and how they would help him grow into a fine young man. She took deep breaths, in and out. *I know the truth about everything now. Let that help guide me.*

"Juliet!" Ross waved as he emerged from the barn, and she ran to meet him. "Ye are shivering." He wrapped her in his plaid and pulled her close. "Glynis is tending the horses. Let us get ye inside."

When they reached the courtyard, a little boy dressed in green and blue plaid played in a dry corner. The sight of him made Juliet's heart leap with joy. He threw small rocks at the wall, aiming at a certain spot. She swore he had grown two inches and had lost the baby fat from his arms and legs.

"Good shot!" Ross called out to him.

Startled, the boy turned to face them. He squinted in the sun and cocked his head. "Auntie?" He dropped the stones to the ground and began to run.

Juliet's eyes welled with tears. "He remembers me," she whispered to Ross.

"Of course he does. Ye are his aunt."

She crouched down to greet the boy, almost knocked over from the force of his blow. Juliet laughed and lifted him up with her. "Yes, love, it is Auntie. And look," she said and turned Alec to face Ross. "Uncle."

Ross placed his hand on the boy's head and stroked his hair. "We are back and will never leave ye again."

Alec's little face crumpled, and he began to cry. Juliet held him close, rocking back and forth to soothe him. "Do not cry, little one. I am here now."

Ross took Alec from her. He wiped the boy's face with his plaid then held him high in his arms. "Ye are going to be all right now."

Alec reached out for Juliet. "Auntie."

"No, boy." Ross shook his head. "She is not yer aunt. From this day forward, she is yer mum, and I am yer da. Never forget that. We will protect ye with our lives. Ye never have to worry. Ye mum and da are here."

Juliet wrapped her arms around the two. She felt Alec's hand in her hair. She had a son. It was the most wonderful feeling in the world. "Your da is right, Alec. We will be here for you always."

~ * ~

Glynis joined them and took Alec from Ross' arms as they walked indoors. The halls in the castle were silent. "I will find Mum and Da. Go to yer room, and I will come for ye. Andra kept the fire burning in yer chambers, ready for the day ye returned, Ross."

Juliet followed Ross up the steps in a dream-like trance. *You are really here. Ross is a touch away.*

The suite had been kept clean and warm during their absence. Ross strode to the table and picked up Juliet's ring. He slipped it onto her finger without saying a word. The round emerald surrounded by diamond chips twinkled in the firelight. Juliet had left the MacLaren necklace next to the ring. When Ross reached for it, she placed her hand over his. "I am not ready to wear it."

The gem reminded her of a happier time when she thought Donnach received her into the family. Now, it stood for lies and deceit, and she wanted nothing to do with it.

"I can see why ye are hesitant. Da is old and set in his ways. He never truly let ye into his heart. If he did, he never would have sent ye away." Ross turned away and under his breath said, "The old fool."

"Ross," Juliet said. "I will never stay here alone again. If you leave, I go with you."

"Aye, and Alec too. We made the bairn a promise, and I intend to keep it." Ross faced Juliet. "We are a family, Juliet." He placed his hands on her cheeks and kissed her lips with a passion she had missed. "I have a son."

"Is that good enough?" Tears welled in Juliet's eyes. "Another man's son is now yours. He may be the only child we ever have."

"Then 'tis God's will. We were meant to be his parents." Ross kissed the tip of her nose. "Dinna ye ken how much I love ye? Och, Juliet, the first time I saw ye, I ken it was meant to be. Alec took to ye like a mother. He saw it before I did."

"What did he see?"

"He was to be with us. Our son."

Juliet's heart burst with happiness. "Our son. I love those words, and I love you." She slipped her arms around Ross' waist and gazed up at him. "I missed you so much. I thought I would never see you again."

"Tell me again. Tell me ye love me."

Juliet poked his chest. "I think you would let me tell you all day."

He lifted his brow. "And not during the night?"

"Oh, yes." Juliet nodded. "Especially at night."

Ross' eyes peered up and over her head. "Glynis? Did ye find them?"

"Aye, everyone will wait for ye in the dining hall. Alec is with Mum. He is the happiest I have seen in a long time."

"Let us go to them." Juliet slid her hand into Ross'. Her heart pounded at the thought of seeing Donnach. She swallowed and placed her hand on her throat. "I am not expecting a welcome like Alec's from the rest of the family."

"We will see about that." Ross went out the door and down the steps, never letting go of Juliet's hand … until he saw his father.

Chapter Twenty

"Ye bloody bastard!" Ross lunged at Donnach, hands around his father's neck. "How could ye send me wife off with that fecking piece of shite?" He pushed Donnach up against the table. "I should squeeze the life out of ye right in front of the family, ole man."

"Ross!" Fiona yelled. "Take yer hands off yer da now!"

Startled by her voice, Ross looked up. Donnach slid his arms inside Ross' and pushed with all his might. He slid his dirk from his holder at his waist and held it at his son's throat.

"Dinna threaten me like that ever again," he said through gritted teeth. "Ye were not here. Ye dinna ken the facts. Yer wife saved the family and yer hide."

"Enough!" Fiona shoved her way between the two men. "No more fighting!" She turned to Donnach. "And do ye plan to murder my son so I only have three bairns left?" Tears streamed down her face. "Och, ye stubborn MacLarens." She wrapped her arm around Donnach's waist. "Yer son is home. Greet him as ye should."

Donnach tossed the knife on the table. "Ross, laddie, ye are home." He placed his arms around his son and slapped him on the back. He leaned back and looked at Ross. "Forgive me?"

Ross looked at Juliet out of the corner of his eye.

No, I do not want him forgiven but for the sake of the family, I will pretend I do. "Ross, it is all right. He did what he had to do." Juliet's expectations would always differ from Donnach's. She wanted him to protect her, but instead he sacrificed her. By the look Donnach gave her, she knew nothing had changed. He did not want her here. She felt as if he thought she had brought the wolf to the henhouse and would do so once again. When John realized Ross rescued her, he would not be far behind.

Ross nodded. “If me wife forgives, I will also.”

Eva, who had stood in the background, ran to Juliet. “I am so glad to see ye!” She hugged Juliet tightly.

Juliet felt the baby under Eva’s clothing. Her heart did not ache this time, and she did not chastise herself for not giving Ross a child. Alec somehow filled the void inside her, and she gazed over at the boy with love. “You look lovely, Eva. The baby will be here soon?”

“Two months.” Eva smiled, then a redness crept up her neck that Juliet found odd and would question later.

“And you do not have to name her Juliet now that I am back.”

“Och no, I still plan to give the bairn yer name.” Eva winked.

“I do not think Donnach will like that very much.” Juliet held back a giggle. “She will be a constant reminder of me.”

“Aye, that was the plan,” Eva whispered.

A servant brought out a tray of food for breakfast. Fresh hard-boiled eggs, salted herring, and smoked beef adorned the plate. Another maid followed with milk, cream and honey, sea biscuits and oatmeal cakes. Juliet’s stomach growled. She had not eaten much on the journey.

“Tea, milady?” Nessa carried in a steaming pot. Ross had arranged a shipment to be brought in when he discovered how much she liked it.

“Mum,” Alec said and tugged on her skirt. “Hungry.” He held up his arms to her.

“The lad is too big to be held,” Donnach said.

Juliet looked at him defiantly and lifted Alec up into her arms. “He has been through so much and needs tender care. As his mother, I will say when he is too big.” She carried him to the table and settled him in her lap. “Have you ridden little horsie since I have been gone? I hope someone helped you.”

“Glee-Glee did.” He pointed at Glynis.

“Thank you,” Juliet mouthed.

Glynis nodded. “He had to learn to ride in the snow and cold like a man."

"That he is," Juliet said as she brushed his hair from his face. "But we have to remember he is still a boy."

Alec snuggled against her as Juliet prepared a plate of food for him then slipped him on the bench next to her. "Now, you will show everyone what a big boy you are. You will sit at the table and eat, just like the rest of us."

His little mouth hung open as he looked up at her, listening. "I can do that." Alec reached for an oatcake and dipped it in his cup of milk.

"That is my good boy." Juliet smiled at Ross as he took his seat on the other side of her. "He will grow up tall and strong. You promised your sister, and we will make sure he does."

Ross took Juliet's hand and said, "My mum, Glynis, and Eva have been looking after the boy. He stays in a room next to my parents. I would like to move him into our chambers."

Juliet began to configure the space in her mind. "The small space next to the dressing room would be perfect. I will make him a new quilt for his bed and let him choose the colors."

Ross leaned over and whispered in her ear, "But tonight is ours. We will let the lad stay in his room for one more night."

A warm sensation traveled up her neck, flushing her cheeks. "Whatever you say, husband." His love for her radiated from him. During her stay at the Alder estate, that was missing from her life. She placed her hand on Ross' cheek. "I love you. I cannot stop saying it."

"And I love ye. How would ye like to spend the rest of the day with Alec and me, the three of us? After all ye been through, ye deserve some fun."

Juliet met his eyes and saw the twinkle returned. Ross had been so serious during the trip, she wondered if the war had affected him. He held back pent-up anger against John, too. Glenhaven brought out the best in him. "Yes, I would like that very much."

"Then I will ravage ye tonight and every night after that if ye give yer permission," Ross said as he pulled one side of his mouth into a sly smile.

"Oh, I agree, Mr. MacLaren, but we have to learn to be quiet. We have a little one to think about." Juliet returned his look.

Ross broke into a full smile. "We certainly do." He leaned across Juliet. "Alec, are ye ready to go outside and throw some snow at yer mum?"

Alec's eyes widened. "Can I?"

"Aye, but ye have to let her throw some back."

Alec nodded his head up and down so fast, Juliet had to giggle. "And when I say stop, we stop. That is the rule." She tried to look stern as the little boy slipped off the bench. "Ross?" Juliet looked up at him. "You should stay and speak with your father. John may not be far behind us, and we need a plan."

"There will be time for that later. I wish to celebrate our homecoming, if only for a short while."

"As you wish." Juliet bowed her head. She would let him have his fun then remind him to seek out his brother and father afterward.

"Come, Da." Alec took Ross' hand, and they left together.

"We will meet ye out there!" Ross called over his shoulder.

"Juliet," Fiona said in a strict voice. "Before ye leave, I want to speak with ye."

"Yes?" Juliet looked at her mother-in-law. She had aged over the winter from the stress and grief. Her eyes had lost some of their spark, and her hair was streaked with more strands of white.

"I understand why Ross wants Alec to consider ye his parents. But the lad seems to have taken to the idea verra quickly." She stopped and reached for her mug of ale and took a long drink. "But I want him to remember that Greer and Ewan were his parents."

"I agree." Juliet reached out her hand to Fiona. "I will never let him forget them and always be grateful that Greer thought me good enough to be his mother."

Fiona took her hand and gave Juliet a sad smile. "That is all I ask."

~ * ~

"Tell me everything, Juliet."

She lay in Ross' arms, content after making love. "What do you want to know?"

"Was he kind to ye?"

"John? Yes and no. He made sure I had what I needed and was comfortable even though I was his prisoner. I was not allowed to speak your name or about my time in Scotland. If I did, he became cold and distant, almost threatening. I was afraid one day he might strike me if I forgot and said your name."

His arms grew tighter around her. "I could kill him, ye ken."

Juliet sat up and stared into Ross' eyes. "No! Do not say that."

"If he took ye again, I would."

"Could he? Take me?" Juliet sank her teeth into her bottom lip. "Would he come for me again?" *Of course he would. We will be in danger again. Nothing has changed.*

"Ye ken the man better than I. Ye tell me."

"I can tell you this. The man I thought I knew when I was a young girl in England is not the same one who came to Glenhaven. Or maybe I just did not know him. This man is capable of anything." Juliet shook her head. She did not want to admit she knew the answer. John *would* come. "Ooh, it makes me so angry every time I think of what he did." She snuggled back into Ross' arms. "His father is ill, and I am afraid will not live much longer. John will inherit the estate and become very rich. He bought his commission in the army and has the king's ear."

"That makes him a verra powerful man," Ross said. "When he comes, and ye ken he will, I will be arrested." He leaned back and looked at Juliet.

"I will not let him," Juliet said sternly. "Besides, we have no idea when he may come. As I said, his father is very ill. Ann, my maidservant, kept me informed about what went on in the house. The Duke almost died while John was gone, but when he heard his son was on his way home he rallied, perhaps to see him one more time. Knowing John, he will want to stay by his father's side until he passes. They were very close, especially after the duchess died."

"And when the duke dies?" Ross made a noise in his throat. "John becomes a duke, giving him even more power. Ye said he has the king's ear already."

"Did you know the king speaks very little English and refuses to use the language?"

"A German king not wanting to speak the English language?" Ross laughed as he ran his hands through Juliet's hair. "I didna ken. How does he communicate?"

"He speaks French. John is fluent in both German and French which I am sure helped his cause."

"So the English would rather have a king that speaks no English over one that can because he is Protestant. Just like the uprising, 'tis more about religion than politics." Ross shifted his body and lay on his side, facing Juliet. "I heard King George has great respect for the British army. He can use them to counter his enemies, even in Germany."

"John did mention the king planned a trip back to his homeland. Even if he has enemies there, he probably misses it."

"As I missed ye." Ross rolled on top of Juliet, resting on his elbows. "I could look at ye all night."

"I do not want you to waste the night looking," Juliet said as a smile crossed her lips. She lifted her hands and pulled his face to hers. "I want your lips on mine, Ross MacLaren."

He brushed her mouth with his, teasing her. "Like that?"

"No." Juliet stuck out her lower lip.

He dipped his head and kissed the pouting lip. "Or this?"

"Ross!" Juliet playfully punched his arm.

Ross lowered his body onto hers, not letting his full weight bear down. His mouth covered hers as he rolled to his back, bringing her with him. Juliet broke the bond of their lips for a moment. "Make us one, Ross," she whispered.

"Until the morning light," Ross said as he made her wish come true.

~ * ~

"Happy birthday, Juliet!" Eva squeezed her as best she could with her rounded stomach then ushered her into the dining hall for breakfast.

"Sister," Duncan said as he kissed her on the cheek. "May ye have a great day."

Heather and Jamie rushed into the room, hand in hand.

"We slept here so we wouldna be late!" Heather spun Juliet around.

"So happy to have my sister home." She hugged Juliet tightly. "I really mean it," she whispered.

Glynis carried Alec in on her back. "Horsie!" he called to Juliet. "Glee-Glee is a horsie."

"Well done, Glynis," Juliet said. "Thank you for watching him."

She slid Alec to the floor. "We have to stop feeding the lad so much. He feels as heavy as a horse." Glynis tickled Alec's side, and they laughed.

Juliet tensed when Donnach and Fiona entered the room. Donnach had not spoken to her, except formally, for the two weeks she had been back. Fiona said as she passed by, "Twenty. I wish I could remember that age."

"Ye were bonny then and still are," Donnach answered. "Juliet." He nodded his head and went to his seat.

The cook had added sweet cakes to the morning menu. The table overflowed with jelly and bread, fresh eggs, oatcakes, smoked beef and milk, cream and honey.

"This looks wonderful. Thank you." Juliet made eye contact with everyone in the room. "There seems to be one person missing." She looked at the doorway. "Ah, there he is."

"Cowan!" Alec ran up to the boy and pulled him by the hand. "Sit by me." He commanded as he pointed to the spot next to his.

"Madam." Cowan smiled at Juliet, showing his crooked teeth. "Thank ye for inviting me. I wish ye a special birthday, and by all means dinna want to ruin it. I have been on this earth eight years and would like to enjoy a few more."

"You will not ruin my birthday," Juliet said. "Why would you say that?"

"I have a message for the laird." His eyes widened until Juliet thought they would pop from their sockets.

"You will not be punished, Cowan," Juliet said softly. "Tell us."

Donnach cleared his throat. "Out with it, lad."

Cowan puffed up his chest as if he had an important message to relay. "Me brother, ye ken, he is always running off and playing in the woods instead of doing his chores. He is two years older, but does half the work I do. Mum says that play gets ye in trouble. 'Tis the devil's work." He shook his head. "But the lad sure do get to play."

Donnach threw his head back and laughed. "Aye, he does. 'Tis a good thing he has ye for a brother."

Juliet had learned Cowan's father died of the fever when the boy was five. His mother baked for the village and the MacLaren family. Donnach took a special liking to Cowan and made him his personal messenger, giving him a few shillings each time he brought a report.

"Sir, do ye want me to tell the news or wait?" Cowan had sat back on the bench and scooped a glob of honey onto his oatcake.

"We will enjoy our breakfast. 'Tis a special day." Donnach looked at Juliet and smiled, but it did not reach his eyes.

"Do not wait on account of me." Juliet's stomach tied in a knot. She could not eat now if she tried. Nessa placed a cup of tea in front of her. "Thank you," she said as she looked up at the maidservant. She poured a bit of cream and honey into the cup, hoping it would help calm her.

"Ye heard her, Da," Duncan said. "We might as well hear it."

Cowan stood at his seat. "Me brother saw three British soldiers riding this way. He heard them say they would deliver a message and be on their way to arrest more of those bloody bastard Highlanders."

Donnach lifted a brow. "So yer brother stayed this time and didna piss his pants?" He let out a low chuckle. "I hope they didna see him."

"No, sir. He stayed hidden, just like ye told him." Cowan smiled proud as could be. Honey smeared his lips and a bit of oatcake stuck to one cheek.

"Then they will soon be here." Donnach glanced over at Heather and Jamie, giving them a nod.

Without a word, they rose up and left the room. Juliet turned to Ross, brows crossed.

"I will tell ye later," he whispered.

They settled in and began to eat breakfast when a servant appeared in the doorway. "Laird MacLaren, we have visitors."

"Send them in." Donnach waved his hand.

Chapter Twenty-One

Juliet's heart pumped wildly. If one of them turned out to be John, she had no idea what Ross would do. She longed to hide behind him or run to their room, she did not know which. *I cannot bear to be taken again!*

Edward, her escort on her first trip to Scotland, was the first to enter, followed by two men Juliet did not recognize. She let out a sigh of relief.

"Please, gentlemen, join us." Donnach stood and motioned to a table.

"Your servant, sir." Edward bowed. "Thank you kindly. We are a bit parched. Some ale would suit us."

Donnach lifted his hand, and Nessa scurried to the table with three mugs and a pitcher. Andra placed a tray of breads and jelly in front of them.

"We cannot stay long. I have many messages to deliver." Edward stood in front of Donnach. "We are looking for men from the MacGregor clan. We believe one lives among you."

"Aye," Donnach said. "He was an apprentice to the blacksmith. Verra good lad."

"And did this apprentice leave his job last September?"

"Och, no, he stayed through the winter. Ye just missed him. He is on his way to the coast to start his own shop."

"That is very interesting. Your daughter went with him?"

Donnach gave him a troubled look. "My daughter?"

"I heard in the village your youngest daughter married the boy."

Edward turned to Juliet. “Am I correct, madam?”

No one in the village would tell him that. Is he trying to trick me into telling him? Her heart thudded against her chest. *Or Englishman to Englishwoman? Does he think I will choose to be loyal to him over my family?* “I have been away, Edward. I cannot speak for what happened in my absence.”

Edward bowed in her direction. “Very well then. We will refresh ourselves and be on our way. Know this, Laird MacLaren. Regiments of soldiers are scouring the countryside for traitors who fought against us. Anyone named MacGregor will be taken into custody whether they fought or not.”

“I understand.” Donnach’s eyes narrowed, and Juliet could not read his thoughts.

So that is why he sent Heather and Jamie away. He knew the soldiers were looking for MacGregors. Juliet’s hand trembled as she reached for her tea, remembering the story Ross told around the campfire about the MacGregors. She fought to steady it. “Cowan, it is nice of you to come for a visit. You will have to see the rocking horse we had made for Alec.”

“Can we go now?” Cowan slurped down his milk.

“I think that is a wonderful idea.” Fiona took Donnach’s hand. “Dinna ye agree?”

“Aye. Go.” He waved his hand at the boys, responding to the underlying meaning. The women wanted the children far away from the English soldiers.

“Eva will join ye,” Duncan said as he helped her from her seat.

“A word, if I may, Juliet? Before you go?” Edward stood and bowed. “If it is all right with your husband.”

Juliet looked at Edward then Ross. Ross folded his arms over his chest. “Why do ye need to speak with me wife?”

“A message from home.” Edward’s face showed no emotion as he locked eyes with Ross.

“Fine. Speak now,” Ross said.

“If I may speak to her in the hall … alone.”

“Ross, it is all right. I will just be out there.” She leaned closer. “If I need you, I will let out a very loud scream.”

A smile crossed his face, and he nodded his permission.

Juliet headed for the hallway and turned to see Edward on her heels. "What is it?" she hissed.

He took her by the elbow and walked farther down the hall. "John reported you were stolen away in the night by bandits. In reality, he was protecting his honor and knew it was the MacLaren clan that took you. He requested that I check on your safety and bring you back to England. He would have come himself, but his father has taken a turn for the worst."

"No! I won't go." She balled her hands into fists then relaxed them. "And I am sorry to hear his father is ailing," Juliet added as she looked into Edward's eyes. "You know my story. A year ago, I did not want to leave England. I thought I loved John and hated being torn from my life. But Ross is my husband, and I have grown to love him. John cannot accept that. He forced me to leave Glenhaven and took me to his estate. He was going to arrange a divorce and marry me on my birthday." *That could have already happened if Ross and Glynis had not rescued me.*

"He tells it differently."

"Does he? Did he mention he took me to Alder Estate and not my family home? He kept me as his prisoner. I was forbidden to leave the house."

The look on Edward's face said it all. "I am sorry to hear that. I did not know you were in England and was surprised to hear you were abducted from his home."

"John kept it very quiet, threatening his servants into silence. No one was to know I was there. Although I wish word would have gotten out. Gossip might have saved me." Juliet lifted her head.

"So, you came back to England under duress?"

Juliet thought of Donnach's threats then John's. "To put it mildly…yes."

Thank you for sharing your side." Edward bowed then relaxed his shoulders. "This is not over, Juliet. My friend has been acting strangely ever since you left. He cannot get over losing you twice. I feel he will do anything to win you back, and if his father was not ill…" He shook his head. "I had no idea."

Juliet's heart raced, and she fought to find her voice. "Edward, I am afraid of him."

"I will try my best to reason with him."

Juliet knew if the duke died, John would become a rich man with the means to make his threat come true. "Is his father close to—?"

"The old man is a fighter," Edward said with a smile. "He was up and around the last time I visited." The smile faded. "But not for long. He took to his bed the day I left."

Juliet had always liked the duke. "I am sorry to hear that. And Edward? Please send my best to my family and let them know I am well."

"I will. And I will make you a solemn promise. If I cannot keep John in England, I will join his entourage and come with him." Edward offered his arm. "I best get you inside before your husband comes for me. I have fought the best during the campaign, and I have a feeling he was one of them." He raised one eyebrow.

Juliet's stomach flipped. Was Edward sending her a message? Did he really fight Ross in battle? He could be the witness John needed to prove Ross was a traitor. "I am sure *you* would win any battle … and probably did." Juliet smiled to assure him she knew nothing as they went into the dining hall.

Eva gathered up Cowan and Alec when she saw Juliet and hurried them to the door. Juliet waited in the archway and followed the boys and Eva up the steps. They did not breathe a word until they were safe inside Juliet and Ross' chambers.

Eva waddled to a chair and sat down, and Juliet studied her carefully. She had seen many pregnant women, and Eva seemed close to birth instead of waiting two more months.

"Eva, are you counting the weeks until the little one arrives?" Juliet asked to test the waters.

"Counting the days," Eva said, and covered her mouth with a gasp.

"You slept with Duncan before you were married." Juliet did not ask it as a question.

"Aye." Eva hung her head. "I fell in love with the lad."

"And he with you." Juliet sat across from her. "Did everyone know but me?"

"Duncan knew but had already asked me to be his wife. Then he told his father and the word spread. Please do not think badly of me." Eva hung her head.

"I do not. I am happy for you. I just wish you would have told me sooner." Juliet let out a breath. "But I was preoccupied with my own life and sorry I was not there for you. I know what Duncan had to do to convince Donnach to let you wed. Glynis and I had many talks on our way here. Although she never told me you were this far along."

Eva blinked back tears. "I am sorry I kept it from ye. But ye did have yer own problems at the time and still do."

"I will be there for you, Eva." Juliet reached across the table and touched Eva's arm.

"Thank ye. I hoped she would be born on yer birthday, but it is not to be."

"Whenever the baby comes, the day will be a blessing," Juliet said.

"What happened with Edward?" Eva's eyes widened. "He looked so formal, not like the man who brought us here."

"Perhaps it was the war that made him that way. He said something strange, like he wanted me to know something."

Eva sat taller. "Do not keep me wondering."

Juliet leaned forward and whispered, "I think he encountered Ross in battle."

"What?" Eva covered her mouth.

"He did not say he did, but it was the way he said it. I am frightened, Eva. I always felt Edward was a friend, but he is John's friend also and more loyal to him."

"Did ye tell Edward ye are happy here?"

"Yes."

"Then if he is a good man, he should leave it be."

Juliet closed her eyes for a moment then opened them. "I hope you are right. Now, tell me about Heather and Jamie. What do you know?"

Eva lowered her voice. "A messenger from the MacGregor clan came to Glenhaven at the end of January. He was so cold when he arrived. He had been traveling for days. We never thought we would warm him up to hear the message. Fiona had Nessa find the best whiskey and set it down in front of him. He drank until he passed out, dead asleep on the table."

"Eva! Get on with it. You sound like a MacLaren now. They begin a story then tell another, taking forever to get to the end of the first one."

"Sorry." Eva giggled. "Do ye think I am a MacLaren?"

"Yes, as much as I am one. Now speak."

"That night the poor gentleman woke from a deep sleep, moaning and mumbling something over and over. After he was given some broth, he spoke with Donnach. He told him that Jamie could not go home, not even a visit. The soldiers were looking for MacGregors, every last one of them. They pulled men from their beds, never to be seen again. He advised Donnach to have Jamie change his last name, and if need be, go on the run."

"So that is why they ran off before the soldiers came. Where are they now?"

"They are in the cellar, but Donnach has a brother who lives on the coast. He always wanted to be a fisherman and has built up a good business there. When Donnach said Jamie headed for the coast, he dinna quite lie. He may have to eventually go there."

"What about Heather?"

"She will go with Jamie. Fiona begged her to stay here when the time comes, but Donnach disagrees. He feels she could be in as much danger as Jamie."

Juliet glanced at the boys playing together in the corner. Cowan found the sword she had made for Alec. He marched in front of the rocking horse Alec rode. "They are so innocent." She let out a breath. "I hope they never have to fight a war."

"May God Almighty hear yer words." Eva crossed herself. "Duncan said if a regiment comes to Glenhaven, they know Jamie is here and will arrest him. Jamie and Heather have to be ready to leave at a moment's notice."

"Let us hope it does not come to that." Juliet smiled at Eva. "We have a baby to bring into the world."

~ * ~

By mid-March Eva had still not given birth. Juliet laughed at Ross whenever he saw Eva coming his way. He pretended to have important business so he did not have to stop and listen to her complaints. Her back hurt. She could not walk down the stairs. She had no sleep that night. Ross would nod and agree in all the right places then make his excuses to slip away.

"I hope she gives birth soon, Juliet," Ross said on their morning walk. "I ken she has her womanly problems, but could she keep them to herself for just a day?"

Juliet giggled. "No, that is not Eva. She has always been like that."

Alec walked in front of them, skipping down the path to the stream. "Da!" He pointed to the water flowing freely over the falls. "No ice."

"A sure sign of spring, Alec. I will have to teach ye to fish."

The boy clapped his hands and ran up to the water's edge.

"And swim, too," Juliet said as she grabbed the boy's hand.

"Aye." Ross took Alec's other hand. "Ye ken not to go in the water. It will go over ye head. Ye canna breathe in water, Alec."

He looked up at Ross with wide eyes. "What if it does go over my head?"

"Ye swim, like yer mum said. I will teach ye how."

"Would you like that?" Juliet swept the boy's long locks back with her hand. "It will be fun." She looked at Ross. "He is growing too fast."

"We still have time with him. There is much to teach him."

"Ross! Juliet!" Duncan's voice called out to them. "I ken I would find ye here." He locked eyes with Juliet. "She needs ye."

"Eva?"

"Aye, I think today might be the day."

Juliet began to run. "Ross, make sure Alec does not go near that water!" she called over her shoulder. When she reached the castle, she bent over, hands on knees, to catch her breath. "I am coming, Eva." She continued on her way, and up to the second floor of the castle.

A loud scream greeted her as Juliet rushed down the hall. Nessa came out of the room, shaking her head.

"What is it?" Juliet grabbed her arms.

"It may be a while, milady. She has been asking for ye." Nessa did a quick curtsy and headed for the stairs.

"Eva, I am here." Juliet swept into the room, looking for something to do. "How can I help?"

Glynis rose from the chair next to Eva. "Let her squeeze yer hand for a while." She gave Juliet a sly grin. "I need to go for a walk."

"Go, I will stay with her." Juliet looked across the bed to see Fiona on the other side. She lifted her brows to ask how things were going.

"Eva is doing fine." Fiona patted the girl's arm.

Juliet stayed with Eva until the room grew dark, and candles were lit.

"Ye been here long enough, Juliet. Ye have yer own son to care for." Eva turned her head to look at Juliet. Sandy brown hair stuck to her face in a wet matted mess. Her cheeks had flushed red to match her rosebud mouth. Juliet thought she looked beautiful.

"I will stay. I have to see my namesake born."

The midwife from the village arrived after supper and began giving orders to Nessa and Andra. People visited on and off throughout the night. Juliet dozed in a corner, refusing to leave, when a chilling scream woke her. She covered her eyes from the sun streaming in the window.

Fiona had a leather strap in her hand, and after the screaming was finishing, put it into Eva's mouth. Juliet leapt from her chair to stop her, but as Eva bit down on it, she gave a look of thanks to her mother-in-law. Juliet stood motionless, fascinated by the procedure: screaming, pushing, and the return of the leather to Eva's mouth to ease the pain over and over again.

"'Tis coming," the midwife said. "Give one more good push."

Eva turned her head, sweat rolling down her face, and locked eyes with Juliet. Her face contorted into a twisted grimace, and she yelled out once more.

"You can do it, Eva. I have faith in you," Juliet said. Overwhelmed by all she had seen, Juliet still longed to be in her friend's position, to give birth to a baby.

"A girl!" Fiona cried.

Eva smiled at Juliet and reached out her hand. "And we will name her Juliet for her auntie."

Fiona clucked her tongue. "Donnach will surely love to hear that." Then she threw her head back and laughed loudly. "The old goat."

The room of women laughed with her. In that moment, Juliet hoped there had been a breakthrough for both she and Eva. Fiona's laugh sounded genuine for once. The midwife wrapped baby Juliet in a blanket and placed her in her mother's arms. Sunbeams bounced off the floor as the women welcomed the baby to the world.

"Juliet," Eva whispered as if she had a secret. "Come."

Juliet went to the side of the bed, and Eva raised her arms to give her the baby. She had dark hair like her father and Eva's rosebud mouth. "She is truly beautiful, Eva."

"She got me through the time ye were gone. I couldna have made it without her. I knew she was a girl. She just had to be."

Chapter Twenty-Two

Juliet chased Alec through the field dotted with spring wildflowers. She had been married a year on the second Saturday in May. Ross ran after her, placing pink and white blossoms in her hair. He spun her around, kissing her as he lifted her from the ground. "'Tis the best day of Da's life, Alec, besides ye becoming me son. Yer mum came from England to marry me."

"Is that bad man gonna take her away?" Alec circled around them, squinting in the sun.

Ross gently placed Juliet on the ground. "No, lad, I wouldna allow it."

"Donny did."

"Hey," Ross said as he ruffled the boy's hair, "he is yer granda. Ye call him the proper name."

Alec wrapped his arms around Juliet's legs and buried his head in her skirt. She petted the top of his head. "Da is not scolding you. He is…" She looked at Ross, and he shrugged. "Helping you."

"Donnach would say ye spoil the lad, Juliet. But I think ye are treating him just right." He kissed the side of her head. "I have errands in the village. Will ye be all right until I return?"

"I always am as long as you return." Juliet turned her face for another kiss. "Remember it is our wedding anniversary. Do not stay all day."

"I promise." He took her by the arms. "Ye should see yerself—flowers in yer hair, sun shining on those red brown locks and reflecting in yer blue eyes." He tucked a flower in her cleavage. "For later."

Juliet and Alec watched as he went to the barn. "Should we go inside and see if cook has baked something special for Mum and Da's anniversary?"

Alec nodded and pulled on her hand. As they walked along, a chill went through Juliet. *How long do we have before he comes?* She longed to know if John's father still lived or if Edward had convinced him to stay in England.

When they arrived at the kitchen, Eva and baby Juliet were at a table.

"Julie!" Alec squealed.

"I hope ye dinna mind we call her that now, Juliet. Alec has given her a new name," Eva said.

"No, Eva, not at all. I think Julie is a wonderful name for her."

At the sound of her name, Julie opened her eyes and stared at Juliet. Her hazel eyes had flecks of gray, a combination of the two families. She looked at Juliet, giving her a gummy smile.

"She likes ye, Juliet." Eva cooed at the baby. "Dinna ye, lass? Yer auntie is my friend. She will watch over ye too."

Tears welled in Juliet's eyes. "It is nice to have children in the family. We have a boy and now a girl."

"Soon to be more." A voice came from the doorway.

Juliet turned to see her sister-in-law leaning against the frame. "Oh, Heather! You are going to have baby?"

"Aye." She flushed and stared at the floor. "Mum agrees, so it must be so."

Juliet flung her arms around the girl. "I am so happy for you."

"Thank ye." Heather hugged her back. "Ye are not sad?"

"Heather!" Eva widened her eyes as she stared at the girl. "Ye are to keep that mouth shut. Lass, ye would tell a secret to the devil." She shook her head.

Juliet wrinkled her brow and looked at the women. "Something I should know?"

"Well," Heather said, "since I started it, I will finish. Eva told me how ye wish for a bairn, and it hurts yer heart when someone announces she is with child. She said to be gentle and here I go bursting out with the news."

"Heather," Juliet said as she took her hand. "That is kind of you but not necessary." She reached out her other hand to Eva. "I no longer have that pain. Alec has taken it away."

Eva squeezed her hand. "Ye are such a good mother to him, Juliet, but it willna stop me for praying to the good Lord to send ye one of yer own."

"Now that is settled, let us go to the dining hall," Juliet ended the discussion by changing the subject." I hear a celebration will be held there."

Alec clapped his hands then held them up. "Up, mummy, up."

Juliet felt the eyes of both women on her. She knew the family thought she coddled the three-year-old. As much as she longed to lift him into her arms, she said, "You can walk on your own today, Alec. I want to see how many steps you can count as we go down the stairs. Do you think you can do that for Mum?"

Excited, Alec tugged on her skirt. "Is Da home?"

"I hope so. Let us go and find out."

Alec counted to five and started over on the sixth step with the number one, making them all laugh. When they reached the bottom, he shouted in delight, "Four!"

"Verra good, wee one!" Glynis came down the hall to greet them, giving everyone a smile as she took the boy in her arms.

Juliet knew her quite well now and could tell she forced the smile. "Glynis? May I speak to you before we go in? Alec, go with your aunties." She waited for the others to go inside. "Is something wrong?"

"On yer anniversary?" Glynis shook her head.

"Have you been hunting today?" Juliet waited for an answer. "Glynis?" She crossed her arms. "You saw something. Tell me."

"A band of British soldiers is headed this way." Glynis shoved the toe of her boot into the floor.

"How far away?"

"They will be here by morning. I heard the commander say they would set up camp for the night and come for Jamie in the morning."

Juliet's heartbeat quickened. "You did not see John, did you?"

“No, he wasna with them.” Glynis shook her head.

“How long will it take them to get here?”

“I would say two hours after they break camp.”

“Glynis.” Juliet heard Ross’ voice. “Are ye telling her?”

“She asked, Ross. She deserves to ken.”

“I wanted to wait until after the anniversary supper.”

“We need to tell the family now, Ross. Heather is with child.” Glynis pushed him in the chest. “Think. We have to come up with a plan.”

“Go in. Let me speak with Juliet.” He waited until Glynis disappeared. “It may be the wrong time with all that just happened, but ’tis our anniversary.” Ross got down on one knee and looked up at Juliet with loving eyes. “I never got to do this properly. I love ye, Juliet. Will ye marry me?” He held up a gold band. “Yer wedding ring. Ye only have the family ring, and I want ye to have something I had made for ye.”

Juliet covered her mouth as tears formed in her eyes. She realized why Ross had been in a rush to get to the village. “Yes, Ross MacLaren, I will marry you. I would marry you every year on this day.” She gave him her hand to slip on the ring. “It fits perfectly.”

Ross rose from the ground and took her in his arms. “I have to go with them, make sure they arrive safely. Do ye understand?”

“Then I go with you,” Juliet said firmly as she pulled back and crossed her arms.

“No!”

“Why not?"

“Who will watch Alec?” Ross lifted his brow.

“He will go with us. We are a family. Wherever you go, we go.” Juliet pressed her lips together. “Decide now, Ross, before we go in. I do not want to argue in front of Donnach.”

Ross held up his hands. “Fine, ye stubborn lass! Ye may go.”

“And your anniversary gift from me will have to wait until we return,” Juliet said as she walked into the hall. She stopped and gave Ross a sly smile over her shoulder.

“I will hold ye to it,” he called after her.

Juliet worked her way around the dining hall, accepting congratulations from the family. By the look of Donnach’s expression, he knew British soldiers camped close by. “Good evening to ye.” He nodded at her. “Enjoy the supper we have prepared.”

Enjoy the supper? How am I going to do that? Her stomach clenched in a tight knot, unable to accept food. The aroma of meats on the table now made her sick.

“Wine?” Nessa held the pitcher, ready to pour.

“Whiskey, Nessa.” Juliet looked up at her. “Ross, too.”

“A toast to Ross and Juliet on their anniversary,” Duncan said and stood at his seat. “A year ago, we dinna ken this bonny lass. She was just a name on a piece of paper sent to us from the king. Today, she is a member of the family and the mother to my nephew, Alec. Eva and I have a new bairn, and I am delighted to announce Heather is with child. A new generation of MacLarens has begun.” He held up his mug, smiling at the people in the room.

Juliet picked up her whiskey glass and drank it to the bottom. Her eyes searched Ross’ face for clues of what would happen next. He rose up and hugged his brother then returned to his seat. “Let us eat!” he said and shoveled a large piece of venison into his mouth.

How can he eat at a time like this? Then it struck her, they needed strength to get through the coming weeks. Juliet forced a bite. She made sure Alec ate everything on his plate.

Once dinner had been cleared away and dessert served, Donnach took charge. “I have been given some disturbing news. Jamie,” he said to the boy, “’tis time for ye to take yer leave. The soldiers have arrived and will come for ye in the morning. We thought we could send ye to the coast for a bit, and all would be well. But I have been in contact with my brother, Gillanders. He feels ’tis no safer there. The British soldiers make monthly visits to Crail. They also stop travelers on the road for questioning on their journey to and from the village.”

Juliet’s mind raced. *Where is safe?*

Heather sat straighter in her chair, chin up. “Then where do we go, Da?”

“Let me finish, lass.” Donnach held up his hand. “Gill is a prosperous fisherman with his own business. He has connections.” He took a breath. “Ye will have to sail to the colonies if ye wish to be truly safe."

"No!" Fiona cried out and grabbed Donnach's arm. "Not another, Donnach. Please! Do something."

"I am, wife. This is how I save my bairn, the daughter who is most like me and looks as I did as a young lad. I have to send her away."

"We will never see her again!" Fiona wailed.

"Mum, ye can visit." Heather bit her bottom lip. "How do we get there, Da? To the colonies?"

"Yer uncle's arranged passage on a ship to France. It leaves in a week, and he will get ye safely on board. From there ye will be given a name to contact when ye arrive in Le Havre. He will get ye on a ship to Boston. Gill will give ye the names when the time is right. Best to keep everyone safe."

"She is with child, Donnach," Fiona said as she gained her composure. "She will be all alone."

"No, Mum, she willna be alone. I will be with her," Glynis said calmly. "I will travel to the colonies with them."

"What? I lose another? No!" Fiona pounded the table. "This bloody uprising did this to my family. Please, Glynis, think of yer mother."

"Mum, I have decided. Ye ken 'tis for best." Glynis stared at her mother.

Fiona's shoulder slumped. "Aye, ye are right. Heather is a babe in the woods and needs ye."

"Then 'tis settled," Donnach said. "Glynis travels to France and on to the colonies with Heather and Jamie." He turned to Ross. "Ye will escort them to Crail. Ye have been there before, many years ago, to visit yer Uncle Gill, if ye remember."

"I can take them, Da," Glynis said as she stood. "Ross needs to stay here with his family."

"Jamie and Heather may need to hide, Glynis," Ross answered. "A woman canna travel the roads alone. Ye ken that. A family will look less suspicious."

"Family?" Glynis tilted her head in question.

"Juliet and Alec will come."

"No!" Fiona pounded the table over and over. "No! No! No!"

"Ye dinna have a say, wife," Donnach said as he placed his hand over her fist. "Ross makes the decisions for his family. 'Tis a good one." He looked at Ross. "Ye leave tonight, after darkness sets in. All of ye best get ready."

Juliet rushed to Fiona's side. "I make you a promise, Mother. We will return. We will come home."

Fiona's hand shook as she reached out to touch Juliet's cheek. Tears glistened in her eyes, but she said nothing.

"What of me?" Duncan lifted his shoulders. "I stay here and do nothing?"

"Ye have yer bairn and yer wife to look after. Da needs ye here." Ross placed his hand on his brother's shoulder. "We will be back."

~ * ~

Spring travel appealed to Juliet much more than the winter journey she had to take. Still, she made sure they all had warm clothes for the nights on the road. She helped Ross pack the wagon with food and supplies. The back of the wagon had enough room for the women and Alec to sleep. Ross and Jamie would share a tent.

Glynis brought Lil' Horsie from the barn. "Alec may like to ride him on the trip. And when he sits up front with ye, I will walk the horse behind the wagon."

Without saying, Juliet suspected Glynis felt they may not return. She wanted Alec to have his horse. Juliet hoped that would not be the case. "Thank you, Glynis."

It had been dark for hours, and the time drew near for departure. Eva and Duncan stood in the courtyard to say their goodbyes.

"Be safe and come home." Eva's eyes shone with tears.

"We will. I will keep you in my heart." Juliet hugged her friend. "I feel like we are always saying goodbye. I hope this is the last time."

Fiona had Alec in her arms. "Bring him home to me, Juliet." She looked over at Ross. "Both of them." She handed the boy to Juliet. "Promise?"

"If you mean do not let Ross do anything stupid, I promise." She tried to smile and lighten the mood. Juliet hugged Fiona with her free arm. "I will miss you."

"I trust in ye, daughter-in-law. I ken ye will do the right thing to keep everyone safe."

Donnach spoke with Ross then turned to her. "I ken I have been a bloody bastard at times, but I do wish ye well. Come home, daughter."

Is that an apology? Or if I come home, so do Ross and Alec? "Thank you, Donnach." Juliet placed Alec in the back of the wagon. "You will ride with your aunt and uncle. Is that all right? We are going on a wonderful adventure."

Alec nodded and flung himself at Heather. She settled him in her lap and called out to her parents. "We are ready. I love ye, Mum! I love ye, Da! I will write when I can."

Ross helped Juliet climb in the seat next to him. The lantern between them was the only light that would guide them through the forest. Ross clucked his tongue at the horses. The wagon jerked, and they were on their way.

They rode until sun up and broke to make camp. Ross placed the wagon in the shade of a large group of trees. Jamie searched for sticks and dry grass to start a fire.

"Och! My bottom," Heather said as she rubbed her behind and stretched her neck from side to side. "Can I stand two more days of this?"

"We eat then sleep," Ross said. "I want to leave before sunset today."

"Well, he is the bossy one, eh?" Heather laughed and looked at Juliet. "Will we have any fun on this trip?"

"We will try," Juliet said. "But he is right. We need to eat and rest."

The first two days of the trip went smoothly. They rode through the night and rested in the day. On the last day, Ross gathered everyone together. "Tomorrow we will be in Crail. I was a boy of ten when I came with Da. Uncle Gill has a large home by the water and plenty of room for us," he said with a chuckle. "Trust me."

"I never met him." Heather shook her head.

"Aye, ye did. But ye were a wee bairn. Uncle came for yer baptism. That was the last trip he made to Glenhaven."

"Does he have children, Ross?" Juliet asked.

"Aye. Three." He held up his fingers. "All boys. But the youngest, Tyree, died a few months after his mum gave birth. Tavis and Geordie are his surviving sons."

"And your aunt? Is she a kind woman?"

Ross lowered his head and shook it slowly to one side then the other. "She died giving birth to Tyree."

"Oh. I am sorry." Juliet folded her hands in her lap, knowing that was the one of the consequences of childbirth. She said a quick prayer for Heather.

"Uncle Gill is verra kind to take us in," Heather said. "I canna wait to meet him."

"Ye will like him, sister. Da told me our oldest cousin Tavis has married. His wife is with child, too. So ye have someone to speak with about yer ails."

Juliet had to muffle a giggle. She remembered how Ross cringed every time he asked Eva how she fared. Heather had not complained on the trip, and she knew he was grateful.

"And after we discuss our womanly problems, brother, I will be sure to find ye. I ken ye have our best interests at heart." Heather tossed a stick at him.

"Ye ken me well, sister, or ye have been speaking with me wife." Ross flipped the stick back at her.

"I ken how to get to me big brother, that is all." Heather rested her head on Jamie's shoulder.

Juliet thought Jamie had been awfully quiet on the trip. He was not a talkative man, but had said little over the last two days. "Jamie, how are you faring?"

"I have been better, thank ye, Juliet. Once I get Heather to safety I will be fine." He picked a long piece of grass to chew on then looked into Juliet's eyes. "We are a bit afraid of the unknown."

"It is not easy to leave one's home," Juliet said. "It sounds like Uncle Gill knows many people. He may have connections in Boston, also. You will not be left on your own."

"His skills as a blacksmith should help, right?" Heather glanced around the group.

"Aye," Ross said. "Verra helpful."

"And we dinna have to stay in Boston." Glynis walked back from the wagon where Alec slept. "Many Scots are in the colonies of New Jersey and Carolina. Uncle Gill may ken some people that live there."

Jamie let out a breath. "That would be a blessing."

"Take one day at a time," Juliet said. "I think we should get some sleep for our last day of the journey."

~ * ~

When Juliet woke, she found Glynis preparing dinner over the fire. "Glynis, how can I help?"

"I can manage, Juliet. Sit." Glynis motioned to a flat rock by the fire. She looked at Juliet with a mix of fear and anticipation. "I never thought my dream would come true. I am going to cross the Atlantic Ocean!" Her voice went lower. "But the joy I feel is overshadowed by the thought of protecting my sister. I canna let anything happen to her, Juliet."

"You will not. I know you, Glynis. You are the strongest, bravest woman I know."

"Aye?" She smiled.

"Perhaps you will meet someone on the trip or in the colonies." Juliet cocked her head. "Will you allow me to wish that for you?"

"Ye can, but I willna be looking for a man. I will be too busy climbing the tallest mast of the ship."

"Oh my!" Juliet's stomach flipped. "Do not fall in the ocean."

Alec came running and threw himself in Juliet's lap. "Hungry," he said and pointed inside his mouth.

"Come here, ye little piggy," Glynis said as she held out her arms. "Glee-Glee will feed ye."

Ross slipped in next to Juliet. "I am teaching him to piss like a man." He smiled as Juliet rolled her eyes.

Heather and Jamie walked hand and hand to the fire pit. "We have something we would like to say. We may not get another chance." Heather looked at her husband.

"We want to thank ye for all ye have done. I am sorry the name MacGregor has caused these problems and made Heather leave her home. I am sorry to be taking her from ye. But she and I will always be grateful."

"If this is a boy," Heather said as she touched her stomach. "We are naming him Ross."

"Thank ye, Heather." Ross took Juliet's hand. "One day we hope to see the boy."

"Eat up," Glynis said as she handed the family plates of food. "We have to be on our way soon."

They packed up one last time, and Juliet's nerves tingled. She felt as if she could burst out of her skin. Once Heather and Jamie were safely in Uncle Gill's house she could finally relax.

Glynis placed Alec on Lil' Horsie, Heather and Jamie hopped in the back of the wagon, and Juliet joined Ross. Ross turned to give one more check then tapped the horses with the reins. They rode through the night, watching the sun rise over the horizon in the morning. As they grew closer to the fishing village, Juliet saw more people on the road. Ross would nod and say, "Good day," but kept moving.

A man on the side of the road waved his arms as he came toward them.

"I think he wants us to stop, Ross," Juliet said as she leaned into him.

"We stop for no one. We dinna ken who he is. He could be looking for a reward if he finds a traitor."

"Ross! How can you think that?"

"I have to—" He pulled back on the reins. "Whoa!" The man stood in the middle of the road blocking their way. "What in bloody hell?"

The old man's face was red and sweaty as if he had been walking all day. "Good morning to ye. A warning, sir." His smile showed brown and worn teeth. "If ye were part of the uprising, that is."

"We were loyal to the crown." Ross raised his eyebrows. "Bu if we were?"

"Soldiers," the man pointed over his shoulder. "A few miles back. They are on horses, so ye will come upon them any time." He closed one eye and looked up at Ross. "Could ye spare food for an old soldier looking out for his fellow countryman?"

"Aye." Ross turned in his seat. "Heather, give the man a loaf of bread and salted meat."

"I thank ye." The old man bowed.

Ross nodded and flicked the reins without a reaction to the news he just received. Once they were far enough away, he slowed the horses. "Heather and Jamie, get under the tent canvas and dinna move! Alec, can ye hear me lad?"

"Da!"

"Ye say nothing. If ye do, ye will get a whipping ye will never forget!"

Alec began to cry, and Juliet heard Glynis try to soothe him.

"Ross!" Juliet's eyes flew open, and she grabbed his arm.

"I have to threaten him," he whispered. "He is just a wee one. How else do I make him understand?"

Juliet sank her teeth into her lip and nodded. Off in the distance, she saw the distinctive red coats of two British soldiers. "Ross." She gasped and pointed down the road.

Chapter Twenty-Three

"Smile and remain calm."

"'Tis easy for ye to say." A voice came from the back of the wagon.

"Heather!" Ross hissed. "Silent."

As the soldiers approached, one held up his hand for Ross to stop the wagon. They removed their tri-corner hats and nodded toward Juliet. The one who held up his hand rode closer to them and said, "Good morning. What brings ye out on this fair day?"

"My family and I are traveling to Crail to visit my uncle," Ross replied.

"And what is your uncle's name?"

"Gillanders MacLaren."

"Gill is your uncle? He always serves us the best fish stew and the grandest whiskey money can buy." The soldier looked back at his companion and smiled.

The second soldier did not seem as impressed. "Did you fight in the uprising, Mr. MacLaren?" His face looked stern as he studied Ross.

"He was at home … with me," Juliet said.

The man lifted a brow. "An Englishwoman?"

"Aye," Ross said as he placed his hand on Juliet's back. "Can ye believe this bonny lass agreed to marry me?" He laughed, and the first soldier joined in.

That man asked with a bow of the head, "What was your name before marriage, if I may ask?"

Ross leaned toward him and said, "May I introduce Lady Juliet

Ki—"

"MacLaren," Juliet interrupted. "I like to be known by my husband's name." Her heart pounded, hoping they would accept her explanation. If they recognized her maiden name and knew John, they could be in deep trouble.

The soldier closest to them nodded at Glynis and Alec. "And who are they?"

"My sister and nephew."

"The boy has white hair, and your sister is dark. No way is he her son." The second soldier pulled up beside the first.

"Aye, 'tis true. His mother passed many months ago." Ross hung his head. "We thought the trip would distract the lad. He can learn how to fish from his uncle and play by the water."

"*Were* you loyal to the king?" The second soldier asked, ignoring Ross' story.

"With her for me wife?" Ross pointed at Juliet with his thumb.

The man finally gave them a slight smile. "I heard the MacLarens were loyal, although one of our commanders had his doubts. Be on your way. Tell Gill that David and Francis send their good wishes. We will be back next month for another visit. He insists on putting us up in his home."

"I will." Ross nodded. He flicked the reins, and the wagon jerked forward. He stared straight ahead. When Juliet tried to turn to look back, he stopped her. "Eyes ahead, love." He squeezed her hand. "Ye did well. I think being a Sassenach helped us out for once." He looked at her out of the corner of his eye then laughed.

"Ross!" Juliet nudged his arm and leaned her head on his shoulder. "Alec was so quiet we have to give him a reward."

"No, I dinna think so. The lad slept during the whole interrogation." He laughed again and sighed. "The worst is over I believe."

~ * ~

They rolled into town as the afternoon sun had begun to fade. Ross pulled the wagon up in front of a majestic house set back from the road. The land extended all the way to the waterfront, and memories of his visit started coming back to him. He nodded his head toward the home at the end of the walkway. "We are here."

The front door flew open and a carbon copy of Donnach came out to greet them. He still had his red hair but with streaks of gray, the only difference between the men.

Juliet gasped as she squeezed Ross' arm for an answer.

"Twins," he murmured under his breath. "He is the younger."

"Welcome!" Gill held out his arms. "I will have the servants get yer bags. Ye missed my good friends. They left this morning. 'Tis a shame. They would so have liked to meet ye." His smile said it all. The soldiers had left before their arrival, and he was delighted.

"Och, we met them, Uncle." Ross jumped from the wagon. "On the road."

Gill's smile changed to a frown. "Bloody hell! I tried to get them on their way, but they enjoyed their stay too much. They drank too much and ate too much, needing another night. I am sorry." He looked into the wagon. "Come, come. Let us get ye inside."

Heather and Jamie hopped from the wagon, and Gill ushered them toward the house "Come! Everyone."

Juliet took Alec's hand, following the group into the gray stone house, and let out a gasp as they stepped into the foyer. Ross smiled at her as she studied the home for the first time.

A grand ball could be held in the reception hallway painted bright blue. Its polished gray stone floor sparkled, and the white plaster ceiling had flowers carved into the wainscoting. A large crystal chandelier hung in the middle of the room with two smaller ones on either side. Each mounting on the ceiling was surrounded by a beautiful, rounded sculpture decorated with angels.

Little Alec stood with his mouth open. Ross knew it was like nothing the boy had ever seen. Glenhaven's walls were either stone or wood paneling.

Juliet took Alec's hand and pointed up at the ceiling. "Angels, Alec. They will watch over you."

Aye, as ye are my angel. Ross' heart filled with love for her and the lad as he watched them interact.

"I do a lot of entertaining so there was a need for the room," Gill said. "I commissioned William Bruce to build it to my specifications. The house has three floors and a cellar where I have a whiskey room." He winked at Ross. "We will visit later."

Ross bowed. "Thank ye, Uncle." He did not recall a whiskey room, but then he was just ten during his visit.

"This leads to the west hall," Gill said as he pointed to the left. "And the east hall." He nodded to the right. "Yer rooms will be in the west hall. Stairs are in there." He gestured to an opening. A set of dark oak steps went halfway up to a landing then continued on in another direction. "Me and the lads are in the east wing. The second floor is for family. The third for guests."

"How many bedrooms are there?" Heather's eyes widened.

"Eight on the second and six on the third, fourteen in all," Gill said with a look of pride. He pointed straight ahead. "Dining room." His arm continued to the left as he gave the verbal tour. "Then parlor and kitchen. And in the east hall, a lady's sitting room and a gentleman's parlor. There are staircases at the end of each hall also." He looked around. "Any questions?"

"Uncle Gill," Juliet said as she stepped forward. "You have been so gracious and kind to open your home to us. Before you grace us with any more of your hospitality, would you mind if we freshen up?"

"Forgive me!" He hit his forehead. "I dinna have a wife to remind me of those things. I was so excited ye were coming. Where are my manners?"

"Donny," Alec said and pointed at Gill.

"Och, the lad noticed. I look like yer granda," he said with a laugh as he lightly pinched the boy's cheek. "But I have a better sense of humor than the old goat."

That made everyone laugh. Ross lifted the boy into his arms. "Uncle Gill, we are a bit weary."

"Then let me show ye the way," Gill said as he headed for the grand staircase. "Ye can choose yer rooms, and I will get out of yer way. Cook has a late supper prepared for us. Tavis and his wife are at her parents for the evening, and Geordie is at one of the taverns with friends. Ye are stuck with me for company tonight."

"Dinna say that, Uncle. Ye are great company." Ross patted Gill's shoulder when they reached the top of the steps.

Gill stretched out his arm and bowed. "After ye, lassies."

Heather poked her head in the first room on the left. "Oh, Uncle, this is verra bonny. Jamie and I will be quite comfortable here."

Alec clung to Ross, and he felt the child shiver.

"Ross," Juliet slipped her arm through his, "Our boy is a little overwhelmed. Perhaps he should stay with us tonight."

"I have a better idea," Glynis said as she took Alec from Ross. "He will stay with me. Would ye like that, Alec?" The little boy nodded. "Then come with Glee-Glee." He slipped into her arms as she winked at Juliet. "We will be across the hall from yer mum and da. They will ken where to find ye."

~ * ~

Juliet and Ross stepped into the room across from Glynis'. "Oh, Ross, Heather was right. It is beautiful." She admired the rich blue and silver décor then turned to her husband. "And you might not have to wait for that anniversary present after all."

He lifted his MacLaren eyebrow. "Och, really, wife?" Ross slipped his arms around her waist. "I dinna want to wait, but Uncle Gill expects us for supper."

Juliet pulled her dress over her head. "We did say we needed to change out of our traveling clothes. How quick can you be?"

"How quick? Let me show ye."

Juliet bounced on the soft mattress, a relief after spending nights in the wagon. "This feels wonderful." She spread out her arms and rolled her head from side to side. "No stiff neck in the morning."

Ross dropped his clothes on the floor. "Ye are so bonny, Juliet." He looked down at her. "Ye have been a good wife and a kind mother on the journey."

"Thank you, husband." She crooked her finger. "Now come here."

Ross slid next to her on the bed. "Och, ye are right. This feels good. The servants may have to come and drag us to supper." He rolled to his side and placed his arm across Juliet's waist.

"Kiss me, Ross." Juliet closed her eyes and waited.

She felt his breath on her neck slowly move up to her cheek. His lips were so close she could tell even with her eyes shut. She quivered under his touch as he lifted her arms over her head, pinning her to the bed. She felt his body hover over hers, warmth radiating between them. He made slight skin contact and rose up, brushing against her over and over.

Juliet did not want him to stop. She wished they were home in their own bed, and the night was theirs. "Ross," she whispered.

His lips came down on hers preventing any more talking. He let go of her arms, and she wrapped them around him. They rolled to one side then the other, lips never parting. Juliet found herself on top of him. She lifted her head and stared into his eyes. "Happy anniversary."

~ * ~

The next morning Juliet headed down for breakfast. She heard giggling come from the dining room. Heather and an auburn-haired beauty had their heads together as if they were the best of friends.

"Juliet," Heather said when she saw her. "This is Tavis' wife, Kenna."

"Hello, it is very nice to meet you." Juliet rounded the table to greet her.

"Verra nice to finally meet ye." Kenna gestured to the sideboard behind the table. "Help yerself to breakfast. Heather and I have been so busy gossiping, we havena eaten yet."

"Anything you can share?" Juliet smiled, hoping to be included.

"Och, we are sharing stories of being with child." Kenna waved her hand. "Ye ken what it is like."

"No," Juliet said as she shook her head. "I do not."

Kenna looked confused. "Da Gillanders said ye had a bairn." She tilted her head. "Alec?"

Heather tugged on her arm. "Alec is my sister's child. Ye ken, the one who—"

"Died!" Kenna covered her mouth with her hand. "I am so sorry." She stood and took a plate with her. "Then ye have no idea what we are going through." She looked at Juliet with sad eyes.

Juliet felt her heart drop to her stomach. *No I do not, and I may never.* She fought to compose herself. *She did not mean anything by her comments. Do not show the hurt.* "No, you are right." Juliet turned to the sideboard and admired the food. "So much to choose from, I do not know where to start."

"Mum!" Alec ran into the room, straight to Juliet.

"How is my boy today?" Juliet petted the top of his head.

"Verra good." Alec placed his hands on his hips, which made everyone laugh.

"He is a fine lad," Kenna said. "Ye are lucky."

"Yes, I am." Juliet's fast-beating heart calmed. She gazed down at her child and smiled with pride.

Glynis followed Alec into the dining room with the men close behind, Gillanders leading the way.

"Juliet," Gill said. "I want ye to meet me sons. This strapping lad is Geordie, my youngest." He slapped his back. "And Tavis." He nodded to the other man heading to the sideboard.

Both had dark red hair like Heather's. The more Juliet looked at them, she felt Heather could be their sister. Tavis and Geordie had the hazel eyes and straight nose that flared out a bit at the end like hers and Donnach. Juliet thought they were good-looking, tall, and strong.

"Good morning to you. I am sorry, I have to put my plate down to formally greet you," Juliet said as she laughed.

"Not on my account," Tavis said. "Enjoy yer breakfast." He looked at Kenna. "Has me wife been entertaining ye?"

"We spoke only of bairns, nothing else," Heather said as she held a steady gaze on the men.

"Well, cousin, that would be a first!" Tavis threw his head back and laughed. Everyone joined in, even Kenna.

Earlier that morning, Ross told Juliet how he met up with his cousins in the whiskey room after supper. They stayed up late sharing stories and talked of the uprising. Tavis had joined the MacLaren clan during the fight, and they bonded during those months. Gillanders refused to let Geordie go off to battle. He insisted he needed help at the business.

After breakfast, Gill invited the family to visit the fishery for the afternoon and then dine in a tavern in town afterward. Until then, they were on their own.

"Lil' Horsie!" Alec clapped his hands.

"Can we walk him through town on the horse, Ross?" Juliet turned to him. "I do so want to visit the shops."

"Go in and out of shops?" Glynis asked as she lifted one side of her top lip. "Och, I would rather scale fish for the day."

Juliet smiled and shook her head. "Yes, you would. What do you prefer to do?"

"How about if I take this little piglet off ye hands for the day? We will meet ye at Uncle Gill's fishery later. I would like to explore the countryside."

"Dinna go too far, sister," Ross said. "Ye ken they are looking for Jamie. Friends may be spies."

"I ken how to be on me own, brother." Glynis gave him a push. "We will stay close to the water and the house."

"And Jamie," Ross said, "ye and Heather stay here until we go to the fishery. Ye can have a tour then return here."

"No tavern dinner?" Heather stuck out her lower lip.

"No." Ross shook his head. "That is not why ye are here, if ye remember, Heather. Ye have five more days before the ship sails and have to keep out of sight."

She hung her head. "I ken, and I am sorry."

"We will bring you something, fish stew perhaps?" Juliet said. "Would you like that?"

Heather lifted her head and smiled. "Aye, sister. I will look forward to whatever ye bring me."

Ross took Juliet's hand and led her to the front door. "I can barely remember my time here, but I do ken the town is a vibrant, bustling place. Ye will like it."

"Can we stroll by the water first?" Juliet had never spoken to Ross about Edward's last visit to Glenhaven and needed some questions answered.

As they stepped out into the sunshine, Juliet heard her name called.

"Juliet! Wait." Heather rushed after them. She grabbed Juliet's hands in both of hers. "I am sorry Kenna spoke to ye that way. I should have told her Alec's story, but there was no time. Then ye—"

"Heather." Juliet put up her hand. "It is quite all right. Thank you for thinking of me."

"Ye are me sister. I would never hurt ye." Heather dropped her hands and pulled Juliet into a hug. "I am gonna miss ye the most."

Juliet let out a small gasp. "Why?"

"Ye are a friend, even when I wasna. Ye went up against Da, the raging boar, when I forced ye to tell him I wanted to marry Jamie. When I get to the colonies, who will I have?"

"You will have Glynis. Confide in her, Heather. She is a fine woman."

"Ye mean the lass who wished to be a lad?" Heather giggled at her joke.

"There is more to her than that. Promise me you will listen to her and be there for her."

"I promise." Heather kissed Juliet's cheek. "I will let ye be on yer way."

Ross and Juliet followed the path that led to the back of the house and the view of the North Sea. The morning sun bounced off the calm seas as if diamonds danced on the water. A spring breeze swirled around them. Thistles stuck out of the craggy rocks along the coastline, leaning to one side then the other with the wind. Gill had installed benches by the shoreline path, and Ross headed for one.

"My sister loves ye, Juliet, I can tell." He squeezed her hand. "She is young and scared, though she would never admit it. Ye calmed her fears."

"I hope I did." Juliet met his eyes. "Now I need you to calm mine."

His eyebrows lifted in surprise. "Ye are afraid?"

"For Heather and Jamie? Of course I am. But there is something else. During the last soldiers' visit to Glenhaven, Edward asked to speak with me. Remember?"

"Is he the friend who escorted ye to Scotland?"

"Yes, I thought you knew him, but it does not matter." Juliet waved her hand in the air. “I need to know if you fought against him during the uprising. Does he look familiar?” She studied his face and noticed a slight twitch by his mouth. “Ross? Did you?”

“Why would ye ask that? Since ye think I didna ken him?” He wrinkled his brow. “I fought many men. Ye dinna want to hear of those fights.”

“No, I do not, just this one. Edward insinuated he met you in battle. Is he correct?” Juliet folded her hands in her lap and waited.

“I’d rather not think of that time,” Ross whispered. “But yes, I ken him. I could have killed him.”

“What?” Juliet’s eyes flew open wide. “So you did remember him?”

“Aye. How could I forget the man that brought me wife to me? I fought me way through a British regiment. Me sword met one sword after another.” Ross looked away in thought. “One soldier fought harder than the rest. We engaged in battle for quite a while. I had him backing away in retreat when he tripped over a rock. He fell at my feet. I lifted me sword to strike, and he looked up at me.”

“Edward?” Juliet brought her hand to her mouth.

“Aye, I recognized him. I couldna kill yer friend, Juliet. I let him go.”

“Thank you.” She rested her hand on his arm. “But because you did, he became the witness John needs to prove you took part in the rebellion…for the wrong side.”

“Wrong side? Depends who is doing the telling,” Ross said as he let out a sigh. “Edward didna say a word when he came to Glenhaven. He could have taken me prisoner then.”

“You saved his life, and he knows I love you.”

“Will that be enough to keep him from speaking to John?” Ross asked. “He is in possession of valuable information.”

“He comes from a rich family so he does not need money,” Juliet said. “John is his boyhood friend. They are loyal to each other. Loyalty may get the best of him.”

“And if not?”

“I cannot think of a reason he could want to tell him. You are safe.” Juliet stared out over the water. *Please, God, let me right.* She took Ross’ hand. “You promised to show me the town. I am ready.”

~ * ~

The family gathered at the fishery as the catch of the day came in later that afternoon. Silver fish glistened in the nets that swung from the boats.

“Fresh whitefish.” Gill’s step seemed to get lighter. “Nothing like it. We’ll make our deliveries then head to my favorite tavern for supper. They turn my fish into fine creations, fish pie, fish stew, or grilled over the hearth.” He winked at Juliet. “Best ever.”

“I cannot decide, Uncle Gill.” Juliet patted his arm. “You make it all sound so delicious.” It felt strange talking and laughing with someone who looked so much like Donnach. Her father-in-law would rather push her into the sea than have a conversation.

Gill offered his arm to Juliet as the family walked along the docks. “I have a fleet of eight ships, a crew of six men on each. They sail out at dawn and return at two p.m. The goal is to deliver the fish by three. Some will be scaled and deboned in our fishery for sale at our market. We caught some nice herring today. A treat for tomorrow’s breakfast!” He raised his arm in the air, and Juliet felt his excitement.

“He knows how to sell his product,” she whispered to Ross on her other side.

“Come,” Gill said as he waved his hand. “Let us go aboard.”

The group toured the ships, the wharf, and the fishery. Alec held his nose and made faces during that part of the trip. “Me no like, Mum.” He buried his head in her skirts.

“Och, lad, ye will learn to love it.” Gill lifted him high in the air. “Dinna smell the dead fish. Sniff the sea air. Take in the freshness of the creatures that gave their lives so we can eat. Rejoice in their sacrifice. Dh'iarr am muir a thadhal.”

“The sea wants to be visited,” Ross said as he took Alec from Gill. “That is what yer uncle is telling ye. Listen carefully to his words. He is a wise one.”

Gill strutted through the building, proudly showing off the process. They reached the front of the fishery where the market was located.

Workers bustled around tables, setting up for the crowd gathering outside.

"Everyone," Gill raised his arms. "If I could have a minute? Me brother's family is in town for a visit. I would like ye to greet Donnach MacLaren's son and daughters."

"Och!" One old woman, her faced weathered by the sun, pointed Jamie's way. "That one is not a MacLaren. I'd ken him anywhere."

Chapter Twenty-Four

Juliet felt as if the people around her froze in time. She studied the expressions on each face. Gill's wore a look of surprise and horror. Ross' jaw clenched, and his hand rested on his dagger. Heather's face took on a look of shock. Glynis appeared unmoved, but Juliet knew she was prepared for a fight. Jamie showed a sign of recognition then covered it by looking away. Her heart pounded against her chest, waiting for the outcome.

Gill held up his hand. "Aggie, if I may have a word with ye?" He motioned for her to come closer. "Now keep yer voice down, and tell us how ye ken the lad."

Jamie stepped forward. "She's a MacGregor, Uncle Gill. She lived in me village until I went to Glenhaven for the apprenticeship."

"Aye, young Jamie, ye remember me." Aggie wiped at her eyes.

"Ye made the best fish stew in the Highlands, Aggie," Jamie said. "How could I forget ye?"

"I thought ye were dead, killed in the war…or so I heard." Aggie looked as if she wanted to hug Jamie, but Gill put out his hand.

"Dinna act as if ye ken him any more than ye already have," he said through gritted teeth. "MacGregor men are wanted men or did ye forget so soon?"

Tears filled Aggie's eyes as the small woman looked up at Jamie. "They came to the village, Jamie. The soldiers took all the young men they could find. The Mr. and me packed up and fled in the middle of the night. Our daughters rushed from their homes to come with us. They live at our house here in Crail with their bairns, waiting on word of their husbands. Two never came home from the uprising, and one was taken by the soldiers." She nodded at Gill. "Mr. MacLaren was kind enough to give us jobs."

"Yer son, Angus?" Jamie's face had a look of hope. "What about him?"

"Killed in the war, I am afraid." Aggie hung her head.

Gill cleared his throat, reminding Juliet of Donnach, the signal that everyone needed to pay attention. "Now that ye had yer meeting, Aggie, ye will get back to work. Most ken yer name is MacGregor. So if ye are asked about Jamie, say ye were mistaken. As for now, tell us ye are sorry and ye dinna ken the lad. And say it verra loud."

Juliet glanced at Ross. "Is she a relative of Jamie's? Why treat her so poorly? She seemed so happy to see him."

"Some take on the name of the clan, Juliet. Their families go back in time and have lived on the land for generations. They may not be related except in name. From the sound of it, Jamie knew Angus. Perhaps they were friends." Ross took a breath. "Gill is not treating her poorly. He is saving a life. Look at Aggie's face. She kens."

"Och, dinna listen to the ramblings of an old woman," Aggie said as she raised her hand and waved toward the group. "Me eyesight is not what it used to be. The lad is quite handsome, but I dinna ken him. Good day to ye." She nodded and went back to work.

Ross pushed Heather and Jamie back inside the fishery warehouse. "We have to get ye home. Ye will stay in the house until the time comes for ye to leave. If anyone here is a British sympathizer, we will have soldiers upon us in days to check ye out."

"Aggie is a good woman," Gill said. "I saw the excitement in her eyes when she saw the lad. She dinna think." He slapped Jamie on the back. "Ye are right about her fish stew. 'Tis verra popular at the market." He led the family back through the fishery and out to the docks. "Jamie and Heather, get on that first boat. I will get someone to sail ye home." He gestured to the closest one at the dock. It was not a large ship but made for transportation and deliveries.

"I use it to travel home when I canna walk after a long day." Gill chuckled.

That made sense to Juliet. Gill could send items home and use the boat himself. They stood and watched until Heather and Jamie were safely aboard.

"Me!" Alec stretched his arms toward the boat.

Juliet looked at Ross and nodded.

Ross lifted the boy and carried him to the boat. "Looks like there will be one more passenger." He handed him to Jamie. "Hope ye dinna mind."

"Not at all." Jamie took Alec and placed him in Heather's lap.

"We will see ye after dinner." Ross raised his hand then turned to the group standing on the dock. "Uncle, lead the way."

~ * ~

The days went by slowly. Juliet's nerves felt so raw she jumped at the slightest noise. Every time someone came to the door, she expected British soldiers.

On their final night at Gillander's house, Juliet stood in the bedroom searching for items she might have missed while packing. The family would rise before dawn tomorrow and take Heather, Jamie, and Glynis to the ship bound for France.

"Ross? Did you give me everything you wanted packed?" Juliet called to him in the dressing room.

He stepped out, dressed for dinner. Splendid in his green and blue plaid with his best shirt underneath, he looked so handsome she gasped. "You are so fine-looking!"

His green eyes scanned her from head to toe. "And so are ye. Yer bonny in blue."

Juliet's cheeks warmed, and she placed her hand on her neck. "Thank you."

"My hair?" Ross pointed to the back of his head. "What do ye think? I havena time to think of my appearance and wanted to look good for our last dinner together."

Juliet walked around him, trailing her hand on his body as she went. He plaited his dark hair neatly and tied it with black ribbon. "You did a fine job, Ross." She ended up in front of him. "I cannot believe this will be the last time we will see them." Tears welled in her eyes.

"They may be able to come back some day." Ross placed his finger under her chin and lifted. "Would ye be willing to go there for a visit?"

"Cross the Atlantic?" Juliet pressed her lips together. "It would be an adventure."

"Aye, it would be that. Three months at sea."

Juliet wrung her hands. "I hope they make it safely."

"The month of May is a good time to leave. They should arrive mid-August." Ross crossed himself. "God willing."

"Ooh, Ross, do not say that. We will pray every day for them." She wrapped her arms around him and placed her cheek against his chest. "Your sisters are my sisters, but they are also my friends."

"I ken," Ross whispered in her hair. "They finally let ye into their hearts. I am sorry they are leaving ye." He took her hand. "Let us join the family."

Much talking and laughter ensued at the farewell dinner. Juliet had the feeling no one wanted to acknowledge the inevitable. Alec, the only child in the house, held everyone's attention. They showered him with love and applauded every antic. He was their best distraction. Since Gill wanted to have a final meeting after the meal, Juliet decided to let the child wear himself out so he would sleep well. It seemed like the rest of the family agreed.

After a rather rousing dance, Glynis scooped him up in her arms. "Time for bed, wee one." Alec struggled at first then rested his head on her shoulder.

"Mum." He reached his hand out to Juliet.

"I will come." She nodded and left the room with Glynis.

After they put Alec down to sleep, Juliet motioned for Glynis to join her in the hall. "Before we go downstairs, I want to speak with you. I may not have a chance in the morning."

"It will be a busy morning." Glynis nodded.

"I want to thank you for all you have done for me."

"Och, 'tis nothing."

"Nothing? You saved me from John twice! I will always be grateful to you. When you placed that dagger in my trunk, you will never know how much that meant. It saved me from a desperate situation. Then you came and rescued me. You did not have to."

Glynis shrugged. "That man was a pig. How could I sleep and ken ye were with him?"

"Oh, Glynis, that is what I love about you." Juliet pulled her into a hug. Glynis stood stiffly then placed her arms around Juliet.

Finally, Glynis let her body relax, and she gave Juliet a true hug. Warmth radiated from her body to Juliet's, and Juliet never wanted to forget the moment. Glynis let her go as suddenly as she had made the contact. She kissed Juliet on the cheek and left the room.

"I saw the tears!" Juliet called after her. "I know you love me and will miss me." She straightened her skirt and smiled. She hoped one day Glynis would be able to express her feelings and let someone see what an extraordinary woman she was.

Juliet rushed down the stairs and into the dining room. Gill was pouring whiskey for the men. He passed a glass down the table then filled another. When everyone had a drink, he held his in the air. "Jamie and Heather MacGregor, Glynis MacLaren. Beannachd Dia dhuit."

"Blessings of God be with ye," Ross whispered in Juliet's ear as the rest of the table repeated the words.

"Jamie, I will give ye the instructions one time. Ye have to remember the details in yer head. Tell no one what I say now. I have a friend, Bryson MacArthur, that will get ye on board the ship. He will sail with ye to France." He stared at the couple. "Ye have a new last name. Anyone asks, ye say Mercer." He closed one eye. "What is yer name, lad?"

"Jamie Mercer, sir."

Gill smiled in approval. "And ye, with the red hair and bonny face? What is yers?"

"Heather Mercer." Heather's glowing look of pregnancy had been replaced by sadness. She clung to Jamie's arm, and he gave her a look of reassurance.

"Good. Now, Bryson will sail with ye to Le Havre. He will leave ye in the hands of Phillip Edmonds. Phillip and I met a long while ago in France as young men. I saved his life. If he forgets, remind him." Gill chuckled. "He sails to the colonies on business every other year. He just so happens to be making a trip this May. He will buy yer passage and watch over ye until ye get to Boston. From there, he will give ye the next name, but not until then. That contact will help ye set up a blacksmith shop in Boston, Jamie."

"That takes money, Uncle Gill. I have none." Jamie hung his head.

"Ye will when ye arrive. Phillip will take care of it. Any questions?"

"No," Jamie said as he ran his hands through his hair. "Bryson MacArthur will sail with us to France. Phillip Edmonds takes us to the colonies."

"Good lad." Gill stared at him. "Ye will also provide for Glynis for as long as she lives in yer house."

"Uncle—" Glynis started to back up her chair.

Gill held up his hand to quiet her. "No. I promised Donnach ye would be taken care of and ye will." He gazed around the room, looking so like Donnach it made Juliet nervous. "Well then, it has been a pleasure having ye stay at MacLaren House. We hope ye will return some day." He walked over to Jamie and shook his hand.

Heather rose from her seat, weeping. "Thank ye, Uncle Gill. I dinna ken how we will ever repay ye."

"Ye dinna have to repay me, Heather. Ye are my family. Promise me to have a good life."

"I will." Heather nodded as she hugged him tightly.

"And Glynis," Gill said as he stood by her chair. "I ken ye will be strong." He extended his hand, and she shook it.

"Ye can count on me," Glynis said. She looked at Ross. "Tell mum I love her. I think I may have forgot."

"I will." Ross took Juliet's arm. "We all need to retire to our rooms. It will be a long day tomorrow."

"I have informed the servants to make sure ye are awake and ready before dawn." Uncle Gill headed out the door. "Good night."

~ * ~

"Juliet."

She felt a hand on her shoulder. "No," she murmured and pushed it away.

Juliet was having the most wonderful dream. She did not want to open her eyes. Eva and Ross' sisters were there, even Greer. Heather's baby lay on a blanket in the field behind the castle, and the women sat on blankets around the child, talking and laughing. Alec ran through the grass chasing a butterfly as Julie crawled after him.

"That is how it should be," Juliet said.

"What?" Ross' voice sounded louder.

Juliet opened one eye to see him staring down at her. "Nothing. It was just a dream."

"Ye have to get up."

"I know." She struggled to sit up and saw Ross had lit the candles in the room. "My, it is early." Juliet rubbed her face, trying to wake up. "This is so hard, Ross. I hate that they are leaving."

He pulled her to him and kissed her cheek. "I ken. I need ye to help me through it."

"Oh, Ross!" Juliet's hand flew to his face, and she caressed his cheek. "I am so sorry! I have been so worried about Heather and Glynis, I did not think of you. I dwelt on my own feelings, instead of yours. Please forgive me."

"Ye have been nothing but a help, Juliet. I love how ye treat my sisters. Ye got us through the week. But today, I need ye." He clung to her for a moment then released her. "I will let ye get ready." He headed for the door.

"Ross?" Juliet pulled her brows together. "Where are you going?"

"To get our son."

"Oh." Juliet nodded. "I like the sound of that."

"Today is the day, Juliet. We say he is our son with no explanations. He will ken his story, but he willna have to hear it every day. He needs to feel safe and wanted and loved by us."

Juliet bit her bottom lip to keep from crying. "That is a beautiful sentiment. You are a kind and loving father, one that thinks of their child before anything else. I love you for that."

"I will make sure to get all his things." Ross blew her a kiss and slipped out the door.

Juliet slipped out of bed and hurried to get ready. "I cannot believe today is the day!"

She went to the closet, found her traveling dress, and hugged it to her body. Her mind drifted to another time and place. She thought back to the glorious summer she spent with Ross and longed for those days. She recalled the breakthroughs she had with his sisters and the bonds they began to form. Maybe Donnach and Fiona would never accept her, but they had. She blinked a few times to focus, headed for the bed, and sank to the edge. Tears rolled down her cheeks. She wrapped her arms around her waist as a loud moan escaped. Her heart felt as if it was in a death grip and could be torn from her chest. Then she began to sob.

Juliet stuffed the dress into her mouth to muffle the sounds she made. She fell into the bed, screaming into the fabric. *This is not fair!* She lay on the quilt until the sobs quieted, hoping no one heard her. Nothing could be done. The reasonable part of her knew that. She could not erase the war as much as she wished she could. The uprising happened, the British won, and now they wanted revenge. They would hunt down every clan that took part in the war. Life would never be the same.

"Juliet?" Ross came through the door, holding Alec's hand. "Are ye ready?" His eyes opened wide when he saw her curled on the bed. "Ye need more time. I will take Alec downstairs and wait for ye there."

"I will just be a minute, Ross." Juliet tried to give him a smile. "Thank you."

Juliet hurried to get ready and found the family in the reception hall. Jamie paced back and forth while Heather stood with Glynis by the front door. Uncle Gill and Ross spoke in a corner. When Ross saw her, his eyes lit up for just a moment. "She is ready. Let us go."

The wagon had been loaded with their trunks and provisions for the trip home. Glynis hopped into the driver's seat as the rest of the family followed behind it. The wagon bumped along the cobblestone road, the only noise Juliet heard as she walked through the gray morning mist.

Heather came and took her hand. “Sister, I will miss ye.” She squeezed Juliet’s hand.

“And I will miss you, all of you.” Juliet squeezed back.

“I wish I could find the words to express how I feel, but there are none.” Heather glanced at Juliet. “How do ye describe a feeling ye dinna ken ye had? Is it hate for the British? Or am I longing for home? I love Jamie, no doubt. I will go anywhere with him. But sometimes I am empty with no feeling at all. What is the word for all of that?”

Juliet shook her head. “I do not know. But you have described it well. When you come up with the word, let me know.”

Heather tried to laugh, but it sounded more like a sob.

Gill led the family to the major seaport where a large ship was moored. A man approached him, and the two went off to speak in private. Juliet strolled along the boardwalk at the edge of the harbor. She admired the other ships anchored by the docks and tried to imagine boarding one to sail to parts unknown.

Glynis joined her on the walk. “I canna wait, Juliet. Is that awful of me? I can leave mum and da and even my country without regret.”

“No, you are following your heart, Glynis. Never feel guilty. We all just get one life.” Juliet stopped walking and looked out over the gray water. “Promise to write, to keep in touch.”

“Aye.” Glynis pointed to the east. “Look. The sun will make an appearance today.”

A pink glow hovered along the line where the water met the sky. “You leave when it rises above the water,” Juliet said. “We need to return.”

Uncle Gill spoke with Jamie and Ross as they neared the ship. Juliet assumed the man who stood silently by was Bryson MacArthur. She watched as he extended his hand to Jamie. The men shook hands, and Jamie motioned for Heather to join them.

“Glynis!” Gill waved her over.

Juliet searched the docks for Alec. Her heart raced when she did not see him. “Alec!” she called. “Ross, where is Alec!” *How could he not watch him!*

"He is on the ship with the captain," Ross said as he came to her. "Look at ye. Ye are shivering. Did ye think I wouldna watch the lad?" He lifted his MacLaren brow.

"No …I mean, yes, you would." Juliet let her shoulders drop.

"Mum!" Alec yelled to her from the bow of the ship. The captain stood behind him and waved. She lifted her hand in return.

"Feel better?" Ross pulled her close. "Juliet, my sweet lass, I love ye. I love yer heart and the concern ye have for others. But I am quite capable of taking care of me son. Aye?"

"Being a mother is new to me. I want to do a good job. Forgive me?" Juliet gazed into his emerald green eyes and saw nothing but love.

"There is nothing to forgive." Ross smiled. "Bring him down, Captain! We will let ye get back to yer duties." He turned to Juliet. "It pays to know the captain of the ship." He winked.

Alec disappeared from sight then marched down the gangway that connected the ship to the dock. The captain held his hand, seeming to enjoy the boy's questions. "Ye have a fine lad here, Lady MacLaren." He took Alec's hand and placed it in Juliet's.

"He is not—"

"Thank ye," Ross interrupted. "Is it time to board, Captain?"

"Aye. They can board when ready." The captain nodded, shook hands with Ross then Gill, and headed back to his ship.

"Juliet," Ross said as he took her arm. "I thought we spoke about Alec. No more explaining."

"You are right. It was just a reflex."

"Good." Ross nodded. "Then we have that settled. Time to say our goodbyes."

Juliet could not bear to say farewell one more time but forced herself to walk with her sister-in-laws to the dock. She hugged each one tightly, knowing they said their parting words earlier. "Stay safe," she whispered to each one. "And Jamie," Juliet pulled him into an embrace. "You are the man of the family now. Protect them."

Ross wiped under his eye then the other, fighting back tears. Juliet watched as he held each sister carefully in his arms, speaking softly to them. He petted their hair for a moment then let go. "God speed." He lifted his hand.

Heather sobbed as she hiked up the gangway, stopping every few moments to look down at them. Glynis followed her, patiently waiting each time she paused. Jamie carried the bags onto the ship. The trunks had already been loaded. Bryson MacArthur shook hands with Gill and sprinted toward the ship.

The scene was overwhelming, and Juliet had to remind herself to breathe. "I know it is the right thing, but why does it feel so wrong?" She turned to Ross and saw him shake his head. She remembered the conversation she had with Heather. "No words, are there?"

They stood in silence until the family was aboard. More and more people headed for the ship, trudging up the walkway. The crew began to untie the heavy ropes holding the ship against the dock. A few smaller sails unfurled, and the canvas snapped in the breeze.

Juliet watched the sun come out of the water and into the sky. It should have been a lovely sight, but it only brought her sorrow. The pink and orange horizon broke through the gray fog hovering over the water. Suddenly, the boat began to move, making Juliet's heart skip a beat.

"Ross, they are going. They are really going." She stared at the ship, praying it was all a dream.

"Aye, they are," Ross said as he lifted Alec into his arms. He took the boy's chin in his hand and turned him so they were face to face. "We start a new beginning this morning, lad. Today and from this day forward, ye shall be ken as Alec Kinkaid MacLaren." He dropped his hand and put his free arm around Juliet's waist as the three watched the ship sail into the morning mist.

Juliet placed her head on Ross' shoulder and lifted her eyes to meet his. "We are a family. I know that now. I told you once that you are my home. No matter what you do, no matter where you go, we will be with you—Alec and I. I love you, Ross MacLaren."

"And I love ye, and this wee one." Ross tickled Alec's belly to the boy's delight. "Today we shall start our journey home to Glenhaven." He kissed the top of Juliet's head. "Ye, Alec, and me—the MacLaren family."

“That sounds lovely.” Juliet’s eyes welled with tears, happy ones. She stared at the horizon, trying to keep track of the ship’s course as it sailed away. “Stay safe,” she whispered. “We will be here for you always.”

THE END

About the author

After a great career in teaching, Nancy found a second calling as a writer. Born and raised in Northeast Ohio, she currently resides in Mentor, OH. Ohio is her home, but she loves to travel the U.S. Now Scotland is on her bucket list as a place she'd like to visit. Nancy is married and has one son.

www.nancypennick.com
https://nancypennick.wordpress.com/
https://www.facebook.com/nancypennickauthor

Other Works by the Author

Waiting for Dusk Series
Waiting for Dusk, Book 1
Call of the Canyon, Book 2
Stealing Time, Book 3

Taking Chances
Broken Dreams
Second Chances
Frozen Moments, in Frozen, A Winter Anthology
The Perfect Beginning, Second Chance for Love Anthology